# All Downhill From Here

## Slippery Slopes

**Piper Sheldon**

Querque Press

*To J.R., always*

*And to those trying to make a big change*

# Chapter 1

Bee

"You would tell me if I were a ghost, right?" I asked Deckard before blowing out a hot breath on the café window. The tip of my finger made little snowflakes in the fog.

"Aren't you trying to clean that window?" he responded.

I spun to threaten my best friend with the bottle of glass cleaner. He flinched behind the safety of his laptop. He was a bit of a coward like that.

"You're avoiding the question," I said.

"Put the spray down." He held up his hands in surrender.

I spun back to the window I was, in fact, meant to be cleaning.

Grizabella's Café had been a pretty busy work day despite it being New Year's Eve. Lots of locals and tourists alike spent their new Christmas cash in the many eccentric shops of downtown Slippery Slopes, New Mexico. It had slowed down now and I wandered around, very ghostlike, attempting to straighten up the cat café.

Anticipatory adrenaline made me restless. Maybe because I

hadn't made plans for the night, or perhaps that magic that came with the end of one year and the hopes of a new one beginning.

Or the three mochas I'd consumed during my six-hour shift.

Upstairs, the owner, Mel, was warming up her vocals on her piano by singing a rendition of "Memory"—a little on the nose, to be honest. She did that for the tourists. Occasionally, she'd hit a high note that would cause all the cats in the café to meow in unison.

Except for Einstein, the fluffy ginger cat currently chasing a piece of paper stuck to his tail in circles—

"Oop." He fell off his wall perch. "He's okay." Sure enough, Einstein got back up with an annoyed sneeze and walked over to one of the beds lining the café floor.

All my homies at Grizabella's were fosters from the local no-kill animal shelter, Whisker Wonderland, and were available for adoption. Between Mel and I, somebody was almost always here to keep an eye on them and feed them. I usually took the opening shift and her the closing. Sometimes, Ellie from next door at Trailside Treats would come in and check on them too if need be. They stocked the pastries we offered.

Grizabella's was one of the two local cafés, in case you preferred your lattes sans cat hair. Just kidding, there was no hair in our coffee.

Usually.

"Deckard, I'm serious," I said, wiping away my breath snowflakes. Ghosts couldn't make breath drawings, right?

He turned from where he was perched on his stool, working on his laptop as always. He tilted his head with his classic half-smirk that drove the ladies wild and his brown flop of hair that fell into his eyes. He held my focus with his one green, one blue eye.

"I guess it depends on if I thought it would make you sad," he said.

I sighed and went to set the rag and cleaner on the counter. That's so typical. Trying to protect my feelings. But I was completely fine. This was why I didn't tell him about my parents leaving on their newest adventure on Christmas Day and being alone all week. He'd just give me that sad, pitying face when it wasn't even sad. My parents had me late in life, retired by my graduation, and have since lived their best life by cruising it up around the world most of the year.

Deckard looked at the half-cleaned, streaky window and back at me. "Aren't you going to finish—"

"If I'm a ghost, you should tell me. That's what friends do," I said.

"Okay, Bee, if you were a ghost and I was aware of that fact and also not a ghost, I would tell you. What's this really about? Does this have to do with your obsession with that statue?"

"I'm not obsessed." I shrugged, getting that prickly feeling when he tried to dig for information from me.

"You've asked everybody in town about it."

"You don't think it's weird that we have a giant statue in the middle of town, and nobody knows who she was or why we have it?"

"Everything about Slippery Slopes is weird."

"That's fair."

"So you're okay?"

I avoided his look.

"Of course," I said casually.

It wasn't about the statue, even though she was always on my mind lately. Not entirely. It was about the fact that all day long, I heard people discussing their exciting plans for the night, the new year bringing hope for the future and a new start. Not a single person asked me what I was doing or invited me, which I'd grown to accept, but for whatever reason, it wore me down today.

Deckard held my stare until I felt itchy. I carefully navigated my way through cats and back behind the counter.

"What are you doing on New Year's?" I asked.

He blew out a breath through pursed lips. "I haven't decided yet." He started counting on his fingers. "My mom has her annual New Year's Masquerade Party, but I don't know if I'm up for that this year." His mom was the mayor, and he had five, yes, *five*, older sisters. He switched to another finger. "Then there's always the big party at The Tipsy." The Tipsy Trekker was the bar the locals used, affectionately referred to as just The Tipsy. "I don't know. I can't decide. Why? Do you want to hang out? It could be like the old days, where we gorge ourselves on junk food and binge-watch *Terraformative*?"

I perked up hopefully. "Yeah? I'll bring the Pop-Tarts and marshmallow fluff."

(It would be difficult to believe that both Deckard and I were almost thirty based on this conversation.)

Deckard and I met in first grade, and by the time we were in fifth, we were inseparable. Much like most of the world, we became total *Terraformative* nerds and watched obsessively in high school. Even now, we returned to the old show as much as we could despite it having just celebrated its twentieth anniversary. One of the things we had in common was our ability to enjoy things that made us happy without concerning what others thought of us—him because he's beloved by all in town and me because nobody ever noticed me.

But even those traditions were fading as we got older, and the sentimentality I felt for those old days sometimes gripped me so hard I couldn't breathe.

"I'm getting dinner with Cass first, but then we could all meet up after your shift."

I had played third wheel to many of Deckard's "not real" dates over the years, and rarely did the women he went out with find it charming that he brought around his lovable, zany, perpetually single best friend. But at least I had plans now. I came around the counter to his table, feeling more excited. We could wear our old *Intrepid Trio* shirts, and maybe I could get him to be a model for my next knitting project—

"Crap." His eyebrows crashed back down as his shoulders slumped.

The flame of hope burning inside me guttered out. I knew that look. Deckard, bless his heart, always double-booked himself. A downside to being the best friend of one of the most popular guys in town. He was always helping a sister or his mom or any of the residents around town.

In addition to the absolute lack of attraction between us, this was one of the main reasons we would never work out. He's too busy. I needed at least three to four hours a day to sit and stare out the window in silence.

Thankfully, I had that in spades.

"I just remembered one of my sisters asked me if I would babysit after dinner." He tugged on his floppy hair. "You could join me?"

"Which sister?" I asked suspiciously.

"Dottie," he said, not meeting my eyes. I bore my glare into the side of his head until he looked at me. "Yeah, okay. Now, I remember why I didn't mention it before."

Dottie hadn't liked me since we were in the eighth grade and I accidentally set fire to her bedspread. It was an honest mistake, a science experiment gone wrong.

And then again at twenty-three. In my defense, the conditions were perfect for a re-trial.

She'd never forgiven me.

"She hardly brings up the peanut butter incident anymore," he said, but still wouldn't meet my eyes.

"Oh yeah, I forgot about that too," I mumbled.

Apparently, she didn't believe I was "fit to watch her children" when I had the attention span of a—

"Look! Mr. Sparkles is snuggling with Godzilla. That's adorable. Just last week, they wouldn't even be on the same side of the café," I said and crouched down to pet the two cats with their front paws wrapped in a hug. "Look at you cute wittle babies."

"What are you going to do then?" he asked me.

"I'm just gonna let them snuggle. I should take a picture, though. Good idea." I pulled out my phone.

"For New Year's, Bee," he said with another quirk of his lips before I looked back to add to my collection of cat photos for the adoption website.

I could be honest and say I had no plans, but Deckard would feel bad. Then I would get uncomfortable and probably do something stupid like knit little paw-puppets for the cats to perform a puppet show just to make him laugh. It would become a whole thing.

And I left my knitting supplies at home.

"Hard to say. I have so many options." Lies. I had one option: be a loner. Deckard's worry crinkled his brows. "I have big plans."

I waited for an invite all day to anything, but nothing ever came, and now even Deckard was busy. I rubbed my palms on my jeans. It was fine. I had work early tomorrow anyway. It was just another day ...

"Are you sure?" He was watching me intently again with his hypnotic heterochromia stare. He knew the power of that look. The door jingled with a new arrival. Saved by the bell.

In walked Cass, Deckard's current lady friend. She was a pretty brunette with a kind smile who worked at the hospital in the town over. She was a year older than us in school, and last year, I gave her a ride to work after her car broke down.

They greeted each other with that awkward hug thing people who weren't quite a couple did.

Then she noticed the third person standing there.

She extended her hand to me. "Hi, I don't think we've met yet."

We chatted three times last week. I shot Deckard a subtle look. Deckard refused to admit that the rest of the town could not see/remember me. He always told me that if I showed people who I was, they would love me. But I would have to be seen first.

I began to doubt his ability to even discern paranormal entities.

Deckard laughed. "Very funny. Imagine you just forgot she had lunch with us last week."

I waved at her with a flat smile. Even as she looked right at me, I could see her already Ctrl+Alt+D me from her brain to save room for more important things.

Cass laughed awkwardly. "Right. Of course. Nice seeing you again." She tucked her hair behind her ear and thumbed to the door. "Ready to eat?"

Deckard gathered his things and shrugged into his coat.

"Yeah. See ya, Bee. Happy New Year." We were too good of friends to hug, so we just waved.

"Happy New Year, Deckard."

He left without a glance backward. I stood at the door a moment too long, staring out the window past downtown. The setting sun cast a pinkish hue on the white peaks of the mountains surrounding our town. The one and only aerial tram slowly made its way up the side of The Slope, our only ski hill. I watched it creep its way up, a tiny dot, and wondered about the people in there now and their plans for the night.

"You can flip the sign to closed, Bee. I gotta start getting ready for the party," my boss said.

I startled and turned to see her all decked out in what looked to be a 1920s beaded flapper gown. Mel lived in New York most of her life, making a living as a chorus girl for a ton of Broadway shows. She retired to Slippery Slopes ten years ago to open a cat café after a "life-changing" trip to Japan. Mel always spoke like a news reporter and rocked a lot of boas. She pulled it off.

"Sure. Ready for what?" I asked and flipped the sign. "You look great."

"Thanks, Bee." She spun and then did a little Charleston kick. "The party tonight." My blank look led her to add, "'The Shake Your *Broadway* into the New Year' musical-themed costume party I'm having here tonight."

"Tonight?" I asked.

"Yes. It's why we're closed tomorrow."

"We're closed tomorrow?"

"Yes." She cocked a hip and rested her fist on it. "I swore I told you." She pursed her lips in concentration, the beads on her gown making an appealing clicking sound in the silence. "Remember that online vlogger lady from Cozy Creek, Colorado, is coming? I want the café to get a mention in whatever her next story is. It'll be a boon for the business."

My ears began to ring, and I felt like I needed to sit down. My own boss forgot to tell me about a party at my job? I'm her only full-time employee.

What was it about me that made me so forgettable to everyone in this town?

I plastered a smile on my face. "Oh. Is there any help you need or anything?" I looked around the café, still full of cats and no party decor. "I have a few minutes to spare."

"You're a doll, but no thanks. I have the gals coming over to help. You go party it up with the rest of the young ones," she said.

"Yep. Okay, cool. I have loads of things to do."

I crouched and said goodbye to all the cats, one by one, taking my time even as the others arrived to set up the party around me. I wasn't stalling in the hopes that they would invite me to stay. That would be pathetic, and I was *not* pathetic.

Eventually, though, I ran out of cats.

I collected my bag and jacket and made my way out to the town square to visit Jane Smith. The sun provided enough afternoon light, so I wasn't in the dark, but heavy black clouds rolled in fast on the horizon. The lingering snow from last week had all but melted except for the parts in the shade that never got hit with direct sun. It had been a mild winter so far, but supposedly, that would change soon. There were rumblings of a storm coming, but I'd only half listened.

Meteorologists weren't to be trusted.

I made my way to my favorite bench and sat down to share baby carrots with wild guinea pigs that roamed throughout the town. (That was a story for another time.)

There was a tight, painful squeezing in my chest. It was like this most days, but usually, it was easier to ignore. It felt worse this time of year—being a ghost in the town you grew up in.

I stared up at the statue I dubbed Jane Smith. She stood in her almost ten-foot (or thirty GPs, at least) glory just outside the roundabout in the center of town. (Important to note here that most people in Slippery Slopes measured height by guinea pigs or GPs. It was a fairly loose system and not really based on anything solid.)

Jane Smith was a bronze masterpiece of a woman who looked like she stepped out of the old-school computer game *Oregon Trail* with a baby clutched to her chest as she stared into the distance. I passed that statue on the way to work, long forgotten, covered in creeping vines and overgrown grass. Every day, I came here, ate my lunch, and looked up at her. I thought about the wind blowing her in perpetuity as the heavy strands of hair forever whipped along her face, the metal of her skirt tugged in the wind, and her ever-present maternal protection of the bundle in her arms. Was her baby okay? Who were they? Where were they going? And why did our goofy little tourist town have a statue of her? All my searching had led to dead-ends, and it was as though I was the only person who cared.

A group of passing tourists stopped to play on their phones in front of her, blocking my view. One of them almost sat on me.

"Sorry, I didn't see you," they said.

"You and the rest of the town, buddy," I said.

They shot me a confused look before the group scurried away.

I sighed.

"What am I supposed to do?" I asked Jane when I was alone again. "What would you do if you were me? If you lived in a place where nobody even knew you existed?"

I waited a beat, the cold air whipping through me, sending chills down my back.

"Probably not talk to inanimate objects," I answered myself.

Good thing I had Deckard, or it might seem sad that the second person I talked to the most was a statue.

I stared into her fierce bronze eyes. Something was shifting inside me. I was on a precipice. Maybe it was the rolling over into the new year, or the massive clouds on the horizon, or the still potent caffeine thrumming in my veins. Whatever it was, I had a choice. I could do things exactly the same and continue to feel like I was disappearing, or I could make a real change.

Jane Smith wouldn't put up with being forgotten. The weeds crept up her base, and dirt collected in her crevices. She used to be someone worth memorializing and now she was a Jane Smith. No plaque explained who she was. Another woman lost to history.

"No. I won't let that happen," I told her.

I stood and pushed off some of the dead leaves collected by her feet. "I'm not letting you be forgotten. And I won't be forgotten either," I said to her, my head tilted way back to meet her gaze focused on the horizon.

I couldn't go on like this. I couldn't roll in another year being forgotten about.

"If you wanna be noticed, then you have to do something noticeable."

Decker told me once or twice that I could be impulsive, but it was *hours* until midnight, and I was formulating a plan.

I shot another look to the tram and checked my watch. I had enough time to go home and pack a bag before the last one went up.

I would not start this new year the same. I would not go on as I had been. Bee Perkins will make an impression on this town one way or another. I could have a pity party. But I'm going to have my own party. I'm going to change everything this year.

New Year, New Bee, started tonight.

# Chapter 2

Owen

It really didn't feel like New Year's Eve, yet somehow, inexplicably, it was. I remained unchanged, neither nostalgic for the year ending nor excited for the new year ahead. It was just another day. No fireworks, no bustling crowds, and no parties. Instead, the Golden Sunset retirement community was as quiet as a graveyard this evening as Ivy and I sat side by side in her room—Okay, sorry, that was a *terrible* metaphor for the elderly home.

She sat in her overstuffed recliner, and I tested the strength of this collapsable plastic chair. We were reverse Goldilocks. Outside the hallway, two other residents fought over the last glass of champagne, but inside Ivy's room, things were as calm as we liked it, even if my ass went numb twenty minutes ago.

There were no big plans. No big hopes for the future. Just the quiet monotony of living day-to-day as the supposed town brute.

The TV played a soothing British game show starring comedians set to do different, seemingly simple tasks but then manage to boggle them terribly. It struggled to hold my attention as my brain was too busy calculating how many extra jobs I'd have to take on to make my own rent and Ivy's next month. Tomorrow was the first, and I only had a few days' leeway. It was tight before, but lately ...

"All the instructions are on the card!" Ivy jabbed her arthritic finger at the contestant running in circles on the screen. "Watching these bozos fail is rotting our brains, but God, I love it. Makes me feel superior."

I chuckled. "No worries there. Not much left to rot on this end."

She clicked her tongue and slapped me upside the head, which took some effort because I towered a solid four GPs—that was two feet, for non-locals—over her hunched form. "Owen Campbell, you know I hate when you talk like that."

"Sorry, ma'am." I apologized to my former teacher like I was back in school.

"I hated it back then, and I hate it now." She crossed her arms and lifted her chin defiantly.

"Yes, I know."

Ivy's silver-blue hair was shorn short and thin enough to see her scalp from this angle. As always, a blanket was laid across her lap and another around her shoulders despite it being a sweltering seventy-five in her room. I was tempted to stick my head out the window and into an old snowdrift to hear the steam come sizzling out.

Her watery eyes held mine, the pale gray searching me. "You better. You aren't some dumb, violent beast."

A familiar tug of gratitude had me smiling at her. Sometimes I wonder how I would have turned out if I didn't have at least one person believe that I was more than a thug. I envisioned the path I would have taken, but it always ended poorly.

A teenage intern who couldn't be out of high school

knocked on the doorjamb. "Hi, Miss Flores, just wanted to check to see if you needed anything before I left for the—" He spotted me when he stepped fully into the room, causing his voice to hitch and crack. His eyes widened momentarily as they flicked over me. Poor new kid probably heard all the rumors about me. "For-for the night," he stammered. With legs spread wide and arms crossed, my massive chest and biceps were even more exaggerated.

"I'm fine, doll. Happy New Year," Ivy said.

The teen mumbled a salutation in return before hightailing it.

I gave Ivy a pointed look.

"Yeah, yeah, you're big and scary looking. But only to those who don't know you." She rolled her eyes and snatched the remote from me. "And there's a reason you don't let anybody get to know you."

"You know me." I flashed her a smile.

"Dirty flirt."

And so she began another round of flipping through the only five channels this ancient TV set got through its antenna. I wished I could afford a few streaming services for her. The next channel showed crowds of drunk people huddled together in Times Square as an artist I hadn't heard of performed for the viewers at home. I couldn't imagine being in a crowd like that— the dirty looks I'd get for blocking people's views, the subtle pulling away of children, like I was a sewer troll sent up to disrupt their good time. But more likely than not, *if* I was in a crowd like that, I'd be hired as security anyway.

That was why I chose to spend the evening here. Most people wouldn't assume a thirty-year-old single man would choose to spend his last night of the year hanging out with his octogenarian best friend instead of hitting the town. (Not that my small town of Slippery Slopes had a swinging nightlife, but there were two bars, and both would be in high gear until after midnight.)

But those people could get over it.

I didn't want to be out in the cold, especially not with that winter storm front moving in.

In no version of this evening would Ivy make it until midnight, however, so I would have to head out eventually. After a few more rounds of *Change the Channel*, I'd be booted out so the evening staff could start the nighttime routine.

Usually, visitors weren't allowed to stay this late, but Head Nurse Laura tended to look the other way for me. More than once, I'd helped move some large furniture or shoved a broom into a spider's web in the ceiling corner. Plus, most people in this place didn't have many visitors. They weren't about to kick out one of the few regulars.

"Is it New Year's Eve?" Ivy asked.

"It is."

She had already asked me that. Half the time, I couldn't tell if she just did it to piss me off or mess with me. Her memory was fine, but she just loved playing up her age and being doted on. Mostly, she liked to give me shit whenever there was an opportunity.

"Why are you here hanging around an old lady?" she asked.

"I want to be."

"You are too young to be this old," she said.

We played this game a lot too. She told me I needed to get out. I pretended to consider it. In the hall, the on-duty nurse shot me a "time to head out" nod as he passed the doorway.

"I should leave before this snow gets any worse." I stood to stretch when my phone vibrated with a call. Tension immediately clenched my jaw, grinding my back teeth.

*Please, not tonight.*

The name on my screen showed Benny Gauner Jr. He was

my boss, most of the town's boss, really, because he owned half of it. And while most people around Slippery Slopes were welcoming and quirky, Benny had fully taken on the Mr. Potter qualities that came with the ownership of a town when his father, Ben Gauner Sr., passed. He was a grumpy little shit who took pleasure in bossing people around. Not only was he the man who paid me for security around his properties, but he also hired me for miscellaneous odd jobs. I was always flush with work, so no matter how much I disliked the slimy guy, I needed to keep my temper in check if I wanted to make money.

"You been drinking, Soupman?" Benny said by way of greeting. I winced at the horrible nickname he managed to get most of the town calling me.

"No," I said, looking left and right. I assumed he didn't mean the cup of tea sitting next to Ivy's.

"That's right, you aren't a drinker. Not like you can afford to lose any more brain cells," he said.

"Happy New Year to you." My back teeth were close to shattering.

"Not yet, it ain't." The background noise of his call made it hard to hear him until the sound of a door shutting muffled the crowd. "You wanna take a job?"

"Tonight? It's a holiday."

"Since when does that matter?"

I thought of my nice, warm bed and maybe picking up some chimichangas from The Quickie on the way home. The last thing I wanted was anything involving my boss, especially if it involved going out in this weather. Big guys get cold just like the rest of the world. Plus, slipping and falling on ice was a lot scarier from this height.

"What is it?" I said dryly, still not fully committing. I couldn't be the only person for this job, but Slippery Slopes was a small town, and I was the resident muscle for hire.

"The security camera is offline up at the shop, and I need somebody to go make sure there wasn't a break-in."

I closed my eyes. I had a feeling I knew which shop based on the context, but of all the properties in town Benny owned, that was my least favorite to visit. My stomach roiled at the thought of being that high up off the ground.

"Which one?"

"Peaked Interests, you goon. Use your brain for once, would you?"

Ivy had her head turned listening to the conversation, nostrils flared.

"You really want to send somebody up there?" I asked, ignoring his insults. It wasn't any different from most of what I heard every day.

"Yeah, and every second you waste asking asinine questions is another minute wasted."

"Aren't you able to go?"

Peaked Interests was a gift shop located at the exit of the tram. Tourists stepped off the aerial tram into an explosion of overpriced goodies stamped with "Slippery Slopes." The alarm was probably set off by one of the wild guinea pigs. They'd managed to make their way up the mountain in their search for dominance. There were so many details about Slippery Slopes that nobody outside this town would believe. But despite all our quirks, I doubted anybody would break into a kitschy thirty-year-old tourist trap on New Year's Eve.

Benny snorted. "Can't. Been drinking. Some of us celebrate holidays. Also, the road up is closed, so you gotta take the tram. Faster anyway, but just letting you know you can't drive up."

"I didn't say I would do it." I was absolutely not doing it now. Fuck that mountain, and screw that tram. No, thank you. I was too big for the tiny metal box the employees called The Can. I hated that my body weight made it groan and swing. I got motion sickness just thinking about the twenty-minute trip up The Slope.

"Oh yeah? Hot date with the old teacher?" He mumbled something else I couldn't hear.

I wouldn't expect Benny Jr. to understand the concept of found family.

"I can't," I said.

There was a beat of silence, followed by an exacerbated sigh.

"I'll pay you twice your going rate. Just go up there. It's probably some punk kids. Bring 'em down so I can beat their asses. Then you collect your money, and Happy Freaking New Year."

I scratched at my eyebrow. Ivy shook her head emphatically. Ivy's room was in desperate need of wall art or flowers, anything to give it more life, but the fees alone took every one of my extra jobs. She spent her life helping generations of Slippery Slopes students and deserved more than this.

I sighed, avoiding her gaze.

"Triple. Holiday pay," I said.

After yet another long beat accompanied by an even more dramatic sigh, he said, "Fine. But only because I feel festive. But you better bring down whoever is up there. I'll make them pay for ruining my holiday. They'll find out who they're messing with. They wouldn't pull this shit with my dad—"

"I'll call you when I find out what it is."

I ended the call before he could dive into the injustices of his inherited properties. Poor, poor rich guy.

I pulled on my heavy winter coat and hat.

"I know you aren't still working for that bonehead," Ivy said. "At least his daddy ran these shops honestly. That man only cares about get-rich-quick schemes and taking advantage of tourists."

She wasn't wrong. But Benny Jr. was my boss, and my résumé wasn't fit for anything else.

"It's that or sell my body, Ivy," I said as I wound the scarf she knit me around my neck. The dread of going out in the cold already made me cranky.

"Like you wouldn't make a killing," she said.

"Now, who's the dirty flirt? You shouldn't objectify your students."

"Former student. I think that statute was lifted with my retirement party two decades ago."

"Dirty old woman."

"You should be so lucky," she said.

We both broke our glares. I bent to kiss her forehead. "Happy New Year."

She held my gaze a beat too long, and I felt her gearing up to ask me something personal. "You need to take a finance management class," she said.

I frowned at her with narrow eyes.

"You have to be making good money with all these side hustles you do. Where does it all go? You have a secret gambling addiction?" she asked with a teasing tone, but I could see the worry that laced her words.

I forced a casual half grin. "I told you just a few more hands of online poker, and I'm really gonna turn my luck around and hit it big."

She rolled her eyes but patted my cheek, not yet letting me pull away. "I have money, doll. You're welcome to it. You know that."

My knees went watery as they did any time she mentioned her money. My stomach tightened worse than the thought of the death trap that was the tram. Ivy didn't have a penny to her name. Her asshole son made sure of that when he took off with what was in her accounts and stopped paying her bills last year.

Until I was able to square things up, there was no use in letting her know how her only family royally screwed her over.

"One day, I'll take you up on that. You can take me on a cruise around the world," I said.

"Pfft. Like either one of us would like that shit. Nah, we'll go out in style. Buy a bunch of fireworks and make them blow up that damn tram."

"Now you're talking. Don't stay up too late. I'm going to go freeze my balls off."

"There's no better way to ring in the new year!" she called after me as I closed the door on my way out.

I still wasn't convinced it was more than bad weather that had knocked out the camera, but life-threatening storms aside, it would be easy money. Nobody was ridiculous enough to go up the mountain in the middle of the night.

# Chapter 3

<br>

Bee

IF EVER MY GIG AT GRIZABELLA'S CAFÉ DIDN'T WORK OUT, I could totally make it as a *cat* burglar.

I was stealthy. I was agile. I was the night!

I killed it at making it up the mountain unnoticed. For once, my not-so-super power worked out in my favor.

I went through the mental checklist.

Peaked Interests Gift Shop employees gone? *Check.*

The single ancient security camera dealt with? *Check.*

Bikini on and ready to go? *Double-check.*

Okay. Well, that was the entire list. Now, I waited.

New Year, New Bee (NYNB for short) was officially in action. Sure, I was currently dressed only in my bikini under this trench coat and regretted not wearing thicker socks, but I wouldn't be going outside, so I would be fine. Normally, I'd rock one of the colorful sweaters I knitted and some matching thick leggings or jeans, but I'd been in a hurry. Over the years, I grew to dress more for myself and less for others. Since I wouldn't be noticed anyway, I might as well make myself happy.

Not all the logistics were worked out yet, but things were already lining up in my favor. Mel's mention of the vlogger gave me an idea, and I sent her a message. She'd already responded, and she would be there for my grand reveal tomorrow. (More on that later.) For now, I took things one step at a time.

There was an upside to breaking into an establishment older than the Internet, not a lot of security protocol. The old gift shop consisted of one large room, one corner filled with a snack bar and eating area, and another for tee shirts, souvenirs, and miscellaneous ski/snowboard supplies. A few bathrooms were located at the other end of the room, and that was it. I'd probably be too excited to sleep, but if I needed to rest, I could always use one of those orange booths near that old popcorn machine that filled the air with the smell of stale popcorn and greasy butter.

I wouldn't sleep.

A sneaky thrill tickled down my back as I stealthily crossed the snack bar and toward my final destination—the women's room. Maybe not usually a place for changing one's life, but it was today. The *Mission Impossible* theme song trilled through my brain as I hummed along out loud. I wasn't stealing important information or dodging alarm-activating lasers, but the mission was every bit as important.

I was changing my entire life.

No more being overlooked or ignored. I would sashay down Main Street of Slippery Slopes, and people would *see* me. They would whisper behind hands, *isn't that Bee Perkins? No! Couldn't be.* And I would strut by with my chin held high. *She used to be such a nobody. I never even noticed her.* And I would pause, looking over my shoulder to serve my best face to which they would gasp. *She's so cool.*

*She's unforgettable.*

I stopped in front of a rack of ancient ski clothes that had been "on sale" since I was a kid. I flicked through the neon colors, cringing at the embarrassing nineties fashion. I won't be needing one of these.

The saddest part was that I didn't even have to try to avoid the notice of the closing shift member, Azi. He looked right at me, eyes never stopping like I was no more remarkable than the ancient wainscoting lining the walls. In fact, he knew a person came up on the last tram run, and by the time he left, he had no recollection of me nor the giant overnight bag that I'd lugged up with me. I could be preparing to rob the place, and nobody would be the wiser.

And maybe I would! Was that what it would take to finally get noticed? Maybe if not for the fact that the gift shop was an ancient tourist trap that didn't make any money since Benny Jr. started running it. There was likely more change in my parents' couch cushions than in the register's till. I'd still have to live in Slippery Slopes. Getting arrested would make a lasting impression, but maybe not the vibes I was going for? That'd be plan B.

Also, stealing was wrong. Obviously.

Tomorrow, I would be unforgettable. It shouldn't be so hard to stand out in a town of less than ten thousand people, yet there was no doubt that the collection of oddballs here in Slippery Slopes was the highest in the country per capita.

And I was aware of Florida.

I was just in the middle of grand *Sound-of-Music*-esque spins in the middle of the gift shop—the hills were alive with the sound of subterfuge—when I heard the old gears of The Tram coming to life.

I stopped and spun in the direction of the metallic clanking, my body rigid and ears piqued. The sounds came from the doors that dumped tourists into the gift shop before they could go out to the lookout and spend more money to use the binoculars.

The tram was coming up? But I made sure that there were no more rides scheduled for tonight.

This was so not the plan. Who would be coming up here now? Unless …

My heart dropped. What if there was a robber, and I just happened to pick the one night they were going to do it? It was New Year's Eve, for crying out loud! What was wrong with people?

I hid around the corner, swallowing a lump in my throat as I waited to see who was coming. It took years for the ancient box to make its way to the dock. Another decade for the single occupant to come out with an icy breeze.

A massive looming shape appeared, as tall as a Sasquatch and as wide as a refrigerator. The lights backlit him, so I couldn't make out who it was, but I wasn't going to stick around to find out.

This situation was not ideal.

"Did you shut down the lights when you closed up?" a deep voice asked into a walkie-talkie. The radio on the other end cracked something I couldn't make out. "Well, everything is still on up here." He sighed, annoyance rigid in the set of his shoulders. I tucked myself further back into the darkness.

The giant went to the camera I had skillfully disengaged with my new cat burglar prowess and tech-wit.

"And somebody unplugged the camera." More static and indecipherable talk. "Yeah. Yup. I'll sweep the perimeter."

Oh, that sounded fancy. I would be stealing that—*sweep the perimeter*.

Benny Jr. must be on to me. Maybe I wasn't as stealthy as I thought in this last-minute strategy to change my life. An urge to quit this all had me almost stepping forward and giving myself up. I'd been caught.

But then I thought of Jane Smith.

I recalled how my boss had forgotten about me and how my best friend was moving on in his life. (Not that it was Deckard's job to keep track of me.) Or how my parents rarely checked in with me. All the tiny little microaggressions of a town I'd grown up in.

I wouldn't be a ghost in my own life.

I stepped back into the darkness. I re-engaged stealth mode as I crept silently on creaking floors to the back hallway with the bathrooms. If he was looking for an intruder, I'd just lay low until he got bored and left. Hopefully, whoever was here would have the decency to assume that the women's room was off-limits.

And if anybody did go in there? Well, I'd just have to attack him and hide the body.

Just kidding, just kidding. I'd figure out a way to get him out of my hair.

Speaking of ...

I had a plan to stick to. And phase one of that plan involved a haircut. Aside from the colorful outfits nobody noticed, I often wore my long chestnut hair in fancy braids or twists. It flowed down to my lower back at this point when not done up. And what was the most dramatic thing a lady experiencing a life change could do?

Give herself bangs.

Yes, that was right—a haircut up here at the top of the mountain. If I was going to change everybody's perception of me, I had to start with the physical traits.

I set down my overnight bag and nodded at my reflection in the mirror. My brown eyes gleamed with excitement. I pulled out the small black kit from my bag, spread out a towel around my shoulders, and pulled out my tools.

Big moves started with big actions.

I snapped the scissors twice to test the metal tongs just pulled from the utensils' drawer.

I'd seen a video where a girl cut her own bangs, so I was fairly certain I could figure it out. I sectioned my hair in half vertically, the opposite of pigtails, so that my long hair stuck straight out of the top of my head. I bobbled my head back and forth so the ponytail spilled like a fountain around me.

"Here we go." I let out a breath and brought the scissors to my head. "New Year, New Bee: Act One."

# Chapter 4

Owen

My hopes that this would be a quick in-and-out job were dashed before I even got up the mountain.

Azi, the operator at the base, shot me a weary look before opening the doors.

"Benny Jr. called me. Pissed I had to come in but sucks worse for you, Soupy," he said, slightly slurry and bleary-eyed. A red flag that he'd been called in from whatever festivities he'd been partaking in.

Soupy was another charming take on my nickname. Any sympathy I had for him being hauled into this shit show went out the window. And anyway, he wasn't the one who had to be hauled up the side of a mountain in a growing storm in an oversized tin can held on by a string.

My face must have done something scary because he shrank back. I couldn't help it. It was an ingrained defense mechanism. The twentysomething went to the panel, avoiding my gaze.

"Radio on?" I asked, looking down at him.

"Yeah. As soon as it's cleared, I'll bring you back down. Don't take too long. I don't like the look of this storm."

Another red flag. I sighed out my flared nostrils.

"I-I told Benny I wasn't sure this was a good call, but you know how he is." Azi scratched at the back of his neck.

Not much to be argued when the person signed your checks.

"I'm sure it'll be quick," I said, completely unsure.

I should have turned around and skipped the paycheck. But I wouldn't, not even when my guts were screaming to turn tail, not when the money would go straight to Ivy.

I nodded and gritted my teeth before stepping into the tram. It dipped with my weight, and I fought to hide the sinking feeling in my gut. Nobody liked it when the tough guy got scared.

Inside, The Can was roughly the size of a small home bathroom. Six people could sit comfortably, maybe ten standing if things got personal. The Slope wasn't a super popular skiing range with several more well-known ski cities so close to Slippery Slopes, but tourists were aplenty because of the long history and legends surrounding the town. Between them and the eccentric locals, business was always ensured.

There were two bench seats, one on either side, that were that hard plastic orange of the seventies. A buttery yellow light came from built-in lighting in the floors and ceiling, the plastic casings so scratched up after these years that the light was muted and soft, adding to that creepy liminal space feeling.

I stayed standing and gripped one of the three bars in the center.

"Here we go," Azi said through the radio.

The tram lurched out of the bay, and as soon as it wasn't protected by the enclosure at the base, a massive wind hit the side, swinging it roughly. My insides roiled, saliva collecting in my mouth as the back of my neck burned.

Azi gave a very unconvincing thumbs-up when I glanced back to the operator window. I faced away, the side of the mountain looming like a dark tsunami in the night. The howling wind and fat flakes falling fast against the clear enclosure were too much to witness. I closed my eyes and breathed in and out. After the longest twenty minutes of my life, I felt the familiar crunch as it slid into the dock.

The doors opened, and I got off that thing as fast as I could. If I wasn't aware that I had to continue the pretense of "big tough security guard," I would have fallen to the ground and kissed the earth. I clawed off my hat, scarf, and gloves, stacking them near the door, and then took a deep, slow breath in.

I radioed down to Azi, noting that it looked like things hadn't been closed up, and he confirmed that he had. Maybe it was just the ever-constant dread of not wanting to be there, but I had the eerie feeling of being watched. I turned in a slow circle, eyes darting around the shop, not finding anything out of the ordinary that I could tell.

Racks and shelves of useless trinkets and tee shirts were stamped with Slippery Slopes or The Slope, as well as shot glasses, handblown glass hot air balloons, key chains, and refrigerator magnets. Aside from the absurd history of Slippery Slopes, the red and green chile that put us on the map was incorporated into everything. Need green chile jelly? We've got you. Toothpaste and pistachios? Even that. The Red Or Green Fest of early September was one of the biggest events in the state after the International Balloon Fiesta down in Albuquerque.

I radioed that I would check out the place and tensed my shoulders. I didn't have a weapon—aside from my size—I didn't like them. It was too easy for someone to get hurt as it was.

Violence was the tool of the thoughtless, and I may not be smart, but I wasn't cruel.

From the out-of-date skiwear to the snack bar, there was no sign of a break-in or theft. Who needed an ancient pair of neon green snow pants anyway?

"I'm not seeing anybody," I said to Azi.

"All right. Head on down before you get stuck up there. That would be a shitty way to ring in the new year."

"No kidding—" There was movement in my periphery. A shadow shifted under the door of the women's bathroom. I hadn't even thought to look in there.

An instant rush of adrenaline prickled my scalp.

My hopes of being in and out quickly were dashed. Somebody was definitely up here.

I hated this job. Please don't let it be anything weird. Weirder than normal Slippery Slopes.

"What is it?" Azi asked at my abrupt silence.

"Standby." I turned off the radio so as not to warn the intruder.

I took five slow steps in the direction of the restroom, breathing deep and slow. My palms grew damp as the distance closed. I tried to move stealthily, but the old wooden floor creaked under me.

The light in the bathroom went dark.

"Shit," I muttered under my breath. I'd be going in blind.

Would it be better to yell a warning or go in proverbial guns blazing?

Or maybe it was best to have the element of surprise on my side. I had an image of my fumbling into somebody, accidentally breaking one of their bones, or hurting them in any way, and felt my stomach turn. I couldn't handle it.

Better not to surprise them.

I slowly pushed open the door. I held one hand up, palm out

in protection, and the other reached for the light switch I hoped would be near the door.

"Is somebody in here? I was sent by—"

The room illuminated, and I had just enough time to register a crazed maniac lunging at me, hair sticking up wildly around their face, a heavy trench coat belted up to their neck, and, most notably, a gleaming weapon in their hand.

I stepped aside in plenty of time, flipped behind the attacker, and grabbed their wrists easily with one hand as the weapon clanged to the floor. In the same easy motion, I scooped the hapless criminal into a massive bear hug from behind, surprised to lift them a good foot off the ground effortlessly.

My hand cupped soft, round flesh where only a flat plane of chest was expected. The shock of the attacker being a woman caused my grip to slip and my steps to falter back.

"Let go of me, you big brute!" a woman shrieked. Hands, now released, flailed wildly, smacking me on various body parts. "I will cut you!"

Even though her smacks were about as effective as mosquitos on a windshield, they were annoying and at risk of poking me in the eye.

"Ouch." There it was. "Would you—" I grunted, one injured eye shut, as I pinned her arms down to her side, this time careful not to accidentally brush a breast. "Stop squirming."

"Get off me!"

"Stop attacking me, and I will," I said. She was strong for a little thing. Her body wiggled and gyrated all around, making a good grip impossible.

"You attacked me."

"You're trespassing," I gritted out.

"I have rights. I won't let you manhandle me, you oaf!"

Something about her voice and size helped me put the pieces together. "Bee Perkins?" I asked in surprise.

She stilled. "Owen Campbell?" She wiggled to turn awkwardly in my arms and look at me. I swallowed as her big brown eyes moved over my face, squinting in confusion. "How are your folks?"

"They're well, thank you. And how about yours?" I said, too stunned to do anything but speak on autopilot.

"On a cruise."

"Wow. Where to?"

"Around Africa." She jabbed an elbow. I grunted. "Can you loosen your grip? You're giving me a wedgie."

I loosened slightly but didn't let her go.

"What are you doing here?" she asked.

Like everybody in this town, Bee and I had known each other most of our lives, especially as we were around the same age. I never knew what to feel about Bee. She was beautiful with gorgeous dark hair, often twisted up or braided in fancy styles. She had wide brown eyes and a sense of style that paired different loud patterns and were completely all her own.

I'd always been drawn to her in the way you're drawn to watch a violent monsoon pass across the valley. She had been cute since school but closed off and shy. A few times, I almost worked up the nerve to go to the cat café, but ninety percent of me was intimidated by her and the quiet confidence she carried with her. She was smart, and I was an idiot who wouldn't know the first thing to say to her.

The other nine percent feared her. Which was ironic since she, like most of this town, probably saw me as a violent bully.

The last one percent was because I was allergic to cats.

But she seemed edgy and unpredictable, just like those monsoons that swept through the sandy desert, quickly destructive and wild. She dressed like she was auditioning for a children's show, but there was so much intense tenacity behind her eyes.

As evidenced by the way she launched herself at me, she didn't seem afraid of much.

It took me a moment to realize I had been studying her face and wild hair without answering for a few beats too long.

"Benny Jr. sent me up to investigate a break-in." I let her out of my arms, but she didn't move all the way away.

"I knew it! A criminal! Where?" Her head whipped side to side.

"You, Bee. You are the criminal."

"No, I'm not. I'm on a mission," she said, her features going carefully blank as she lifted her chin.

"What happened to your head?" I asked. The "weapon" that fell was confirmed to be a pair of sharp silver scissors. "Are-are you cutting your hair?"

"I was until you interrupted me." Her nostrils flared.

"What the hell are you doing up here? Benny Jr. is pissed."

"I'm not doing anything." She scooted back and tried to look innocent.

The effect was ruined by half her hair sticking out wildly around her and the trench coat, making her look like a bad guy in a movie. I was even more confused with every passing second. Why was Bee cutting her hair in a trench coat on the top of the mountain on New Year's Eve? Why was she acting like this was a totally normal thing? Why did it seem like I was the one out of line when she was very clearly going through something? If I hadn't been so anxious to get the hell out of there, I might have had more time for this.

"Right." Whatever this crisis was, it certainly wasn't my problem. "We gotta go. There's a bad storm and—"

"I'm not going."

"You can't stay."

"Just call Benny Jr. and tell him I'm not going to steal his crappy dollar-store imports with a four hundred percent inflation price tag. I ... just need to stay the night. He'll be fine with it. Now get out of here."

With that final thought, I allowed myself to be shoved out the door, leaving nothing but stunned silence in the aftermath.

I did what any grown man would do in this situation. I called my boss to tell on her.

"Did you find the bastard?" Benny answered right away, slurring into the phone. "Robber? Huh? Shit out of luck. I haven't had money up there in years unless you count the penny press machine." His voice was edged with a vehemence I didn't like.

"No robber—"

"Hooligans, then. Some of those high school shits trying to start trouble."

"No. No, it's, uh, Bee."

"Who?"

"Bee Perkins."

"I don't know who that is. Sounds like a family-friendly chain of breakfast restaurants."

How could he not know who Bee was? She was a staple of the community.

"She works at the cat café."

"Sure. Right," he said, but I wasn't convinced he actually knew.

I remained shocked into silence.

"What the hell is she doing? What a little weirdo," he said.

I strongly disliked how he spoke about Bee. He had a tone. I didn't know Bee well, but at least she wasn't a shady businessman who sent people up a deadly mountain on a holiday.

I ground my jaw before I shared the worst of the information. "She says she wants to stay the night. She said she isn't going to mess with any of your stuff."

"In that case, sure, tell her to put her feet up and make herself at home," he said in a cloyingly saccharine tone. Then, before I could get a word in edgewise, he added in sharp sarcasm, "I don't give a crap, Soupman. This isn't Maybel's B and B. Get her the hell out."

"She isn't doing any harm." I thought of her scissors, over-sized trench coat, and shifty gaze. I didn't think she was doing *well*, but I didn't think she had any intention of trouble, outside of attacking me. And I didn't begrudge her for that. I was big and scary. At least she tried.

"Get her out. Why are we still talking about this? I'm paying you to bring her down the mountain."

"She says she won't go."

Something crashed on his side of the line, followed by a series of whoops. "Then drag her out. She's what, five GPs shorter than you and a hundred pounds wet?"

This was another reason I hated being a big guy. Everybody assumed you were comfortable throwing your weight around.

"Look, I won't be sued for some shit if she gets hurt by staying there unchaperoned," Benny Jr. said. "I don't know what she's trying to pull, but get her out by any means. Then I can press charges."

"Against Bee Perkins?"

I imagined Bee in her colorful tights, patterned dresses, and sweaters, rolling around the cat café, giggling with a pile of kittens in her long brown hair that flowed down her back. Or at least it had. She didn't scream criminal.

"I think she—"

"You aren't paid to think, Soupman. For fuck's sake. You are paid to use those meat cleaver hands to get shit done."

My throat grew tight. I wouldn't scare her or hurt her. I didn't care what he said. "I won't —"

"If you end that sentence with anything other than 'let you down,' I swear to God. If you want to have any sort of job in this town, you better just do what you're told."

He ended the call.

I could get her out. If it was for her own safety, it was better for me to do it than the police. On the other side of the door, Bee hummed a tune. This was going to suck.

# Chapter 5

Bee

So, THE BANGS SITUATION GOT OUT OF HAND QUICKLY.

The intention had been long, wispy bangs to frame my face. But every time I checked my progress, they were uneven. Then, with each adjustment, I was forced to go shorter and shorter. Then I started pulling hair from the top and sides to try to even it out.

Everything happened so quickly.

Now I had half a bowl cut and half long—a blender-made mullet. I could fix this. I had to fix this. I continued to cut at the stubborn mass sticking out of my head, tongue peeking out of my mouth in concentration. There was a soft knock on the bathroom door.

And there was still *that* whole complication. I thought he would have forgotten about me by now.

He knocked again.

"Who is it?" I yelled.

There was a brief pause. "Still me." Then another pause. "Owen."

I frowned at my reflection. "Boo. I thought you left."

Of course, the *one time* somebody actually seemed to notice me ...

"Nope. Still here," he said.

"I wasn't talking to you."

"Well, I heard you. I have to bring you down. Benny Jr. says so," he added, like a sibling telling their mom.

I sawed at my hair with the scissors I found in my mom's travel souvenir room, aka my former bedroom. They were rather frail decorative things with "Tijeras, New Mexico" on the side. They weren't ideal for cutting through my thick brown locks, but needs must and all that.

I didn't respond to Owen. Maybe if I stopped talking, he would give up. Another chunk fell into the sink. This was going from bad to worse. At least half a GP more needed to be cut. I wasn't sure when I decided to just chop it all short, but that was the new plan. I knew I had a ton of hair. It was a whole thing every few days to wash and deep condition it—a routine I'd been doing for years. The silver lining in my accidental hack job was that I'd have less hair to maintain, which would free up so much time for activities.

"Bee. We need to go." It was cute how he tried to put authority behind his voice.

Owen wasn't the big, tough guy the town thought him to be. He scared me less than Slippery Slopes's resident guinea pig gangs that loitered in town and chattered when you got too close.

Once, about two years ago, Owen was passing by Grizabella's when one of the new foster kittens bolted out the shop door. I shouted after her, unable to leave the café unattended. Without hesitation, he stopped what he was doing and went after her. For over an hour, I watched as he patiently chased her around the gazebo in the center of town, cooing softly, half hunched with large hands cupped. When he eventually returned to the café, covered in scratches and sneezing, she slept soundly on the torn shoulder of his shirt.

A regular ruffian would never.

While I appreciated his stern voice, I didn't feel threatened at all.

"No, thank you," I called back to his demand.

"Bee," he groaned. I was fairly certain the soft thump was his forehead hitting the door. "We have to get out of here. The weather is dangerous. The road back is already closed. We need to get in the tram before that closes too."

When he said my name, little hairs prickled on the back of my neck. Owen was the definition of the strong, silent type. Handsome too. Always had been. With his big muscles and kind blue eyes. He didn't have the short, neatly trimmed beard back in high school and wasn't quite as chiseled, but he had always been large. He was a grade older and hung with the jocks. Of course, being the nerdy girl who somehow talked too much yet not enough to make any impact, I was ignored by his ilk. But I'd always liked how his eyes crinkled when he smiled. He didn't seem to smile much anymore, though, when I spotted him around town.

His deep, rich cadence now had a surprisingly tingly effect on me.

More surprising than that, though, were the tingly sensations when he scooped me into his arms. Maybe it was the adrenaline of self-defense, immediately followed by the relief of hearing his voice and not that of a violent attacker, but being held in his steel-banded embrace had made all the tiny little cells of my body vibrate. His large hand splayed almost all the way across my upper ribs and chest. He held my boob for half a second, and if it wasn't for his instant regret and the blush that spread over his ears and cheeks, I might have assumed he wanted a little taste of Perkins. But sadly, he had been equally shook by the accidental boob squeeze. It hadn't bothered me as much as it probably should have.

Lord, I was starved for attention when light, accidental manhandling revved my engine.

If ever there was a reminder that NYNB all went for the greater good, it was that whole exchange with Owen and his capable hands. The plan was in place, and Mother Nature herself wouldn't stop me.

"I promise I'm not going to steal anything. I mean, what sort of criminal would that make me if I stayed after I cased the joint?" I narrowed my eyes. That wasn't the right expression.

"Do you mean robbed?"

"No," I snapped. I *had* meant that.

"Cased means to scope out the target before a heist," he explained.

Gah! What did he know anyway? "You can go now, Owen. Bye."

"I wish that was true. But I can't leave until you do. And you can't spend the night here. It's an insurance liability," he explained.

Another jagged chunk of hair dropped from my fingers. The left half of my hair was meant to match the right, but the dark length was a little longer.

I tilted my head to the right.

*Perfect.*

"Pfft." I called to Owen, "Like Benny Jr. pays for insurance."

Owen pushed open the door slowly.

"I'm decent," I said as he gave me plenty of time to stop him.

I wasn't actually decent under this coat, but he didn't need to know that.

I met his gaze in the mirror, and his eyebrows just about jumped off his forehead when he took in my hair despite his best effort to quickly lower them. With the trench coat, the half-chopped hair, and the weapon-wielding, this looked like the prologue of a thriller.

"It's not that bad," I said.

"I didn't say anything."

"You winced."

"I didn't wince." He wasn't able to meet my eyes.

"There was a definite wince. Plus, this is just temporary until I can see Tess at Slippery Snips. She'll even it out. Also, it's just occurring to me that is a terrible name for a salon."

"It really is."

"I'm just getting a head start." I snorted. "*Head* start. Feel free to get out of my *hair*. I'm on fire."

His mouth opened, and a question started to form. Thinking better of it, he shook his head. He repeated this two more times.

"We have to go," he finally said, holding my gaze in the mirror so intensely I had to look away. "This weather is serious."

"So go. Save yourself." I lined up the next bit of hair. It took some sawing to cut through. A tiny twinge of guilt lanced me as I acknowledged that this was a predicament for Owen. I could go back without a fight, but it wasn't just me. It was the statue too. We deserved better than this. He didn't have a life of unending anonymity sprawling in front of him.

Also, he had really nice hair.

"I feel you wincing again," I said.

"You're just ... are those scissors meant for hair?" His face was contorted in pain.

"It's fine." It wasn't.

"Bug bomb," he said, snapping his fingers as he paced the short spaces in front of the stalls. The floor shook with every step, jostling my unsteady fingers.

"What?" I sighed, setting down the crap scissors to turn to him, hand cocked on my hip. "Stop pacing."

He stopped.

"A scheduled bug guy is coming. The whole building is getting fumigated. We gotta go."

Gosh, he was precious when he was full of shit. "It's the dead of winter. Find me a single bug."

"There are bugs in the winter," he said flatly.

"It's the holiday, and I can promise you Hank at Bug Busters is not working. Nice try, though. Much better name for a business."

"We really love alliteration in this town."

"I'm not leaving, Owen." My legs widened, and I set my stance. "There's nothing you can do."

He scrubbed at his face, mumbling something about jobs and women and Benny Jr. When his hand dropped again, his handsome features were twisted up with worry. Was he that bothered by a bad haircut? His gaze moved over me, flicked to the bag, and then back to me. Assessing. He was calculating how much energy it would take to heft me up and throw me over his shoulder. But he wouldn't do that.

He wouldn't throw his weight around like he was all muscle and brute masculine strength—like I was just a rag doll to be put in whatever position he needed.

When did it get so hot in here?

"Just know that I don't want to do this." He took a steadying breath.

I took a step back. "Well, then don't. Benny Jr. isn't the boss of you." I pinched my lips. "I mean, I guess he *literally* is, but you have free will."

The determined set of his shoulders and the frown pulling at his mouth told me he wasn't listening, or at least didn't think the free will part to be true.

I wasn't going down there without changing my life. I would not go back to being set furniture in somebody else's movie.

I picked up the scissors again, gripping them with all my might as I thrust the rounded down edges in his direction. He plucked them like a dandelion and tossed them into the overnight bag.

"Sorry, Bee. A job is a job."

He stepped closer until I was backed up against the bathroom sink, cold ceramic digging into my lower spine. He loomed over me, smelling like cold air and manly shampoo that probably had an anchor on the bottle or at least a topless mermaid. His heat seared up my front as he overtook my entire vision until it was just his stupid, handsome face. He kept his hair short so the sandy brown hairs weren't more than a centimeter long, and I wondered if it would tickle to run my palms over it. His full lips were usually set in a firm line and now was no different as his blue eyes moved over me. His darker beard was trimmed and tidy but only added to his attempted aura of intimidation. My hands gripped the sink basin, and I leaned back so that he wasn't the only thing in my field of vision.

"Last chance to walk out of here with me." His deep voice curled through me like wisps of perfumed smoke, intoxicating and heady.

I lifted my chin and held his stare. "Not. A. Chance."

His gaze moved over my features and lingered a moment on my lips. Awareness passed through my body. Was it my imagination, or was he totally checking me out? I didn't have a ton of experience with these things, but there was a vibe here. Maybe this was part of my transformation? Maybe this newfound confidence made me infinitely more alluring. I'd been waiting patiently since high school to have my glow-up. Perhaps all it took was a hack job of a haircut and a total personality overhaul.

At some point in my internal musings, he'd moved even closer. The arch of my spine smoothed out as my shoulders relaxed, and I stopped pulling away. There was hardly half a GP between us now. His heat was palpable, his blue eyes narrow rings around blown-out pupils. Were we about to kiss? Should we kiss? For the story?

I could make room for this on the agenda.

He swallowed audibly in the whispered space between us. The hum of the heater went away, along with the whistling howls of the snow through the tired, creaking vents. Only a low-level buzz of electricity vibrated between us. I felt powerful. Fearless. His gaze moved to my hairline before coming back to meet my eyes. Sure, I wished my hair wasn't currently half cut, causing a mullet effect, but other than that ...

"You really aren't afraid of me at all, are you?" he said, head dipping ever closer like this mere GP between us kept him from understanding me.

This time, my gulp filled the quiet space. I shook my head slowly once, watching closely as he pulled in his lips to bite at them briefly. "Nope."

My nipples hardened along the fabric of my bikini, making me hyperaware that only a few *very* thin layers separated us.

"Hmm." He stepped back. "You probably should be."

I let out a breath from my stinging chest and had no warning for what happened next.

In one fell swoop, I was scooped up and thrown over his shoulder. (I was right about that.)

I yelped and kicked my feet wildly.

I hated being manhandled like this.

At least ninety percent of me hated being manhandled like this.

Seventy-thirty max, definitely, sort of hated it.

"Put me down!" I yelled.

"Sorry, Bee." Without any effort, still while bracing me on one shoulder, he bent and grabbed my overnight bag and carried me out of the bathroom. "I did warn you."

"But my hair ..." I whimpered.

# Chapter 6

Owen

Bee fought and kicked, thrashing around as I carried her through the building, past the tourist knickknacks, around the deep red of the scratched vinyl booths of the snack bar, and back toward the launching dock.

I hefted her up higher, repositioning her unexpectedly heavy overnight bag so that I could radio down to Azi. "Hey. Can you call Benny and tell him I got Bee, and we're headed down? I got my hands full at the moment."

The entire time I coordinated with Azi, Bee hollered nonstop. "This is kidnapping! I won't go down without a fight! You aren't the boss of me. Oh, how much are those chile socks? No. Not the time. Unhand me!"

"I can hear that." Azi laughed. "Who was it?"

"Bee."

"Are you saying 'bee' like a bumblebee?"

This was not happening again.

"Bee Perkins," I ground out. "Works at Grizabella's."

It was hard enough to manage her, let alone trying to explain things to Azi. How could he not know who she was? What was wrong with this town?

"I don't know who that is," Azi said.

"Typical," she grumbled. Bee groaned and relaxed her muscles so she was somehow both harder and easier to handle.

Unexpected protectiveness surged in me. It was one thing for me to be enchanted and annoyed by her, but it was another thing entirely for Azi to have never noticed her. As far as I was concerned, this was mostly his fault. I mean, aside from it being very obviously *her* fault. Where had she been when he closed up shop earlier? Had he not seen her? I was close to snapping at him, the anxiety of the upcoming trip down the tram making me irritated.

"Are you ready to get us down?" I asked instead of scolding him.

"Ready when you are. I was starting to sweat it, Soupman. It's rough out there and getting worse every minute," Azi said, not helping my churning worry.

"I can't believe you're actually doing this." Bee slapped at my back and smacked my ass in the process. "Sorry," she squeaked in a high voice. "I didn't mean to—hey!"

I patted her ass lightly in retaliation. I hadn't meant to. It was a reflex. We both stilled, neither acknowledging the weirdness before I kept walking again.

"Ah! Stop! Do my needs mean nothing?" she continued. "Can't you just pretend I'm not here like the rest of the town? Why, of all the times, does somebody actually care about where I am?"

I had no idea what she was talking about, and I was too absorbed in my growing trepidation to focus on her ranting. I set her down just inside the tram doors, blocking her from any chance of escape. It was at least twenty degrees colder outside the shop on the loading dock. She huddled her arms tight around herself despite the fury that made her cheeks rosy. The cheeks on her face. Though there was a chance that now her ass ...

I cleared my throat, determined to stay attentive. I scanned her from head to toe, then dropped her bag on the bench in the tram behind her. We had to get going, but that weird excuse of an outfit wouldn't cut it.

"You're going to freeze out there. Get your heavy coat on. And any other layers you have." I jutted my chin in the direction of her duffel, which should have clothes along with the bricks that had to be in there.

"I came from work. I didn't have time to change," she said, not meeting my gaze.

"Is this all you have to wear?" I reached out to feel the material of the long coat she wore, which was hardly warm enough for a mild spring storm.

"No touchy." She smacked my hand away.

I narrowed my eyes at her but lowered my hand. She huffed with annoyance. "I hadn't planned to go outside."

"Ever?"

She crossed her arms and glared.

"It's winter. On the mountain," I added.

"Thanks. I didn't see that," she said dryly.

I gestured to her high collar, and she flinched back again, turning away. "What have you got on under there?" My curiosity was piqued.

"Absolutely none of your business."

I pinched the area between my eyes where a growing headache named Bee formed.

"Anything warm at all in that bag? The tram has a heater, but the wind cuts through."

"I'll just stay here where it's nice and warm then. As planned." Her face was scrunched up in a stubborn scowl.

"Hang on, Azi. Five more minutes," I said through the radio as she glared at me.

"Really gotta move out, Soups," he said.

"I'm trying," I ground out. To Bee, I said, "Stay. Here. Or there will be consequences."

She eyed behind me.

"Don't even think about it," I said.

"You can't control what I think. I'll think whatever I want." She held my gaze, dark with fury. "I'm thinking about things *so* hard right now." She was defiant even as her teeth chattered just from standing near the threshold.

I didn't like how my body reacted to her words. Even at the worst, most annoying moment of my life, a part of me still crushed on her and liked her defiance, her lack of fear. What would she trust me with? What would she let me do to her?

"Fine." I scooped her back up, not even breaking a sweat, as she yelped. There was less resistance this time as I carried her over to the dusty old nylon snowsuits.

"Pick your size." I set her down, holding her shoulders in place while facing the rack.

"I'm not buying these. Aside from being grossly overpriced, they're very out of fashion," she said with a curl of her lip.

I took a deep breath in and out, calming myself. "Benny Jr. will pay. Work expense. Now pick something, and let's get going."

With every second that ticked by, my anxiety grew. If even Azi, the most mellow dude, was getting anxious about the snow, then we didn't have time for this.

She hemmed and hawed between two different suits. Pulling one out, she held it to her waist with a thoughtful *hmm* before doing the same with the other.

"You pick, or I will," I said.

She blew out a breath, making her lips raspberry. "Fine." She grabbed one off the rack. "At least the style matches my hair. If we happen to travel thirty years into the past, I'll fit right in."

I glanced back at the waiting tram. "Come on, put them on."

"Right here?" she asked.

"We don't have time. Let's go." Anger made my tone sharp, and she flinched.

Shame lanced me. Up until that point, she'd not seem to fear me even a little. My anxiety made my temper short.

Her gaze shifted from side to side. "Turn around."

"Nice try. Not letting you out of my sight," I said.

"Well, I'm not getting dressed in front of you."

I sighed. "I'm not asking you to get naked; just take off that pointless coat and throw those on over your clothes ..."

As I spoke, her hand crept to the high collar and gripped it tighter.

"Tell me you're not naked under there." The headache pulsed along with a flash of heat down my neck.

"I am not naked under here," she said robotically.

What sort of weird, kinky shit had she been up to up here? Why was my heart hammering suddenly? Why was I desperate to see what was hidden under that coat?

"I don't want to know." I scrubbed at my head. "Look, we really don't—Just. Fine. I'll turn around, but you better keep a hand on me at all times"—she opened her mouth to argue—"or foot or whatever. Something better be touching me, or I'll turn around, finished or not."

She made another petulant sound but nodded.

I turned around before I could blush. Ridiculous. She was just a woman. I'd seen plenty of women. But whatever it took to get her out of there and not make her flinch away from me again.

There was a soft sound of fabric brushing before the coat fell down the back of my legs to pool on the floor at my feet. I was keenly aware of her at my back, *not* naked but wearing something indecent. My mind was having a field day, imagining what she was up to.

I cleared my throat. "Hurry it along."

"It's not easy with one hand," she said as the loud material shuffled.

"I can reach out a hand and hold you if that's easier." I hadn't meant for my voice to come out so deep.

"No. This is ... I'll just." The flat, dainty expanse of her back pressed against mine as she leaned into me. Her heat and round edges rubbed against me with every movement as she shifted and wiggled. She smelled so sweet and clean, and her half-cut hair brushed my shoulder. My head moved ever so slightly to the side, and her shampoo's sweet smell had my eyes falling closed.

I jolted, head up and eyes open. I counted the spots in the ancient popcorn ceiling, teeth clenched.

"Okay. Done," she announced.

I turned around to find her swimming in the too-big snow-suit. The bright pinks, purples, and oranges of a neon sunset striped across a faded, yellowing white. "Good enough," I said.

"I am much warmer." She shrugged.

"Funny how that works." Some of my tension released to finally be moving forward.

I frowned to find her feet hardly covered in thin canvas tennis shoes that provided no protection.

I grabbed a pair of thick socks.

"Yay! Chile socks," she said, snatching them from me.

I held her material by the sleeve and dragged her back to the dock, gathering the outerwear I'd set down earlier. I shut and locked the door to the gift shop behind us.

"Loaded and ready," I said to Azi as we gathered into The Can.

Bee gazed pitifully at the building we'd just left behind, but I couldn't move fast enough.

"Okay. Let's go," he said. After a beat, the familiar whirring of the engine kicked to life. "Hang on tight."

I shot one last look at the storm before the tram engaged. She sucked in a breath when we lurched into motion. As soon as we left the half-housed safety of the dock, a massive gust rocked us to the side. My palms were damp in the thick gloves as my stomach roiled and attempted to spin out and up my throat. I clamped onto the pole, breathing through clenched teeth.

The mission was almost over. Bee and I would be down this mountain in twenty long minutes. Benny would pay me, and I would ring in the new year in peace, just like I wanted. I just had to get through twenty minutes. One thousand two hundred seconds. Easy.

Bee went to one of the bench seats, threw her bag on the floor, and slumped into the chair. The smooth texture of the chair combined with the suit's fabric meant she kept slipping down and then had to push herself back up every so often.

Her antics distracted me for a while, but the motion sickness returned. Or maybe the fear of plummeting to our death.

This was the longest tram ride of my life. Every minute passed like an hour. I tried desperately not to look out the windows because there was only darkness and wind and unimaginable horrors.

I held on to the rail in the middle, not letting my anxiety show. The last thing I wanted was for Bee to get scared and have to worry about soothing her too. She kept glancing at me to check for safety, the way the passengers of a plane looked at the flight attendants when turbulence got bad.

I put on my most placid, stoic face, pretending not to notice her glances.

For once, my strength and size might provide comfort.

# Chapter 7

Bee

Owen looked one more gust away from hurling.

Poor dude was not doing well.

Maybe I should go over and give him a little pat on the head so he didn't pass out. Some people just weren't cut out for heights. Every time I looked in his direction, his pallor grew a tinge more green. He was bundled up in all the layers he brought, but the exposed skin of his forehead was pale and speckled with sweat. He gripped the pole like it was the only thing keeping us from crashing into the side of the mountain.

I wasn't thrilled about this turn of events myself. This wasn't a part of the NYNB plan, and the second I could get myself back to the top of the mountain, I would. Benny Jr. didn't scare me. Being constantly overlooked meant that people gossiped *aplenty* in the cat café, never noticing as I filled up their cups or straightened the menus to their left.

I wasn't saying I would blackmail Benny, but I wouldn't let him bully me either. I hadn't broken a single law.

Except for probably trespassing.

Semantics.

Actually, I wasn't clear on the laws, but I would bet money that Benny Jr. wasn't either, and what he was up to was probably worse. I wasn't stopping until I got back up that mountain, come hell or high water. I appreciated that Owen had a job to do, but so did I.

A massive wind blew the tram, whistling through the cracks as we rocked with gusto.

Owen made a soft, pained sound, but his face was emotionless when I looked at him again.

He was awfully pitiful. I couldn't feel bad for him when I was on a life-changing mission. I didn't even have any hand puppets to distract him with.

"That was a doozy," I said.

He blinked at me, swallowing audibly.

"Look, the good news is, we're almost to the halfway mark," I said. "I've gone up and down the tram many times in my life. I have almost every peak and valley memorized. Once we go over the central tower, that's halfway. It's all downhill from there."

"I'm fine," he said through clenched teeth.

"Sure you are, big guy. You know what's funny?"

He closed his eyes and mumbled something unintelligible but obviously disgruntled.

"All downhill from here. It can mean things are easier from here on out because now you can coast. But it can also mean things are only going to get worse. Let's hope it's the former," I said helpfully, but his eyes squeezed tighter.

"An autoantonym or a contronym," he said.

"Say what now?"

"That's what that's called. When one word or expression can have opposing meanings. A contronym," he explained slowly as though choosing his words carefully.

"Cool. I had no idea that was a thing." Could a person be a

contronym? Because the more wild I acted, the more eccentric I dressed, the less I seemed to be noticed. I didn't want to ponder this right now. Instead, I studied Owen carefully, an idea forming to help distract him.

"What's another example?" I asked him.

He shuffled on his feet, but when he shot me a quick look, he had to have seen my sincerity.

Again, he chose his words slowly. "I think a common example is probably 'bound.' It means to be restrained but also to go forward."

"That's just a failure in the English language."

"Oh or, uh, overlook," he added with a little more pep.

"Because you can overlook something right in front of you—"

"Or 'overlook' to watch over. Exactly."

I wondered if he'd intentionally chosen that last example because of who I was or … it didn't matter. I'd distracted him. Go me.

"Well, you taught me something new today. I appreciate that." He held my gaze for a beat, and for a fraction of a second, I thought I might get to see his smile again. I pretended to look out the surrounding windows with almost no visibility. "Almost to halfway. Looks like it's all downhill from here."

He huffed out a shuddered half-laugh.

As if on cue, the tram rumbled as it went over the center support tower that marked the midway point. The ground was at the closest point for the trip, with a pretty ridge to the left. If it wasn't nighttime and whiteout snow conditions, the emergency cabin, aka the Hookup Hut, would be visible where it was tucked not a half mile away into the trees. It was meant for hunters or hikers in an extreme emergency but was mostly known as a sexy-time spot for tram employees/ski instructors who kept it well stocked with booze and food (and probably condoms). Not that I had personal experience, but I was aware of these things.

"And as soon as we get over this bump, we are ..." I started.

The Can came to a slow creaking crawl, then stopped so abruptly we both slipped sideways.

"Huh," I said.

"What was that?" Owen asked, eyes wide and bouncing around the space.

"It appears we have stopped."

"That's not normal. Is that normal?"

"That is not *typical*." I stood, went to the window, and tried to crane my neck to see the top of the tram where it dangled from the cable thingy. Not that I could see anything. Not that I knew what to look for, even if I could.

Silver lining: Being stuck at this point on the tower meant we were locked more firmly in place, so the swaying lessened. The bad news was we definitely weren't supposed to be stuck here. I'd heard stories of this happening before. Probably more than any sort of federal regulation would allow. But that was Benny Jr. and his shoddy business practices for ya.

This was not the plan. This was getting further from the plan. Why did the universe smite me? *Why, universe, why?* All I wanted was to prove I wasn't the dorky little wallflower this town made me out to be, and it wouldn't even let me do that.

My anger instantly spilled up and out of me, needing a place to land like lightning from the sky onto the nearest tall pine.

I spun to Owen. "This is your fault!" It wasn't really.

He still gripped the pole, but his head flinched back. "My fault?"

"Yes," I snapped, working myself into a truly Bee Perkins tither—a bee in my bonnet, if you would—all my frustrations and worries came spewing out toward him. "This wouldn't have happened if not for you! I wanted to stay up there, and you took me against the wall." His face blanched, and I realized what I'd said. "I mean, you took me *against my will*! I did not mean to say that other thing. Ignore that." I frowned. That took me too close to embarrassment, so I yelled louder. "If we die of exposure, I'm suing you!"

His dazed expression cleared, making way for his own anger. "Yeah, go for it. If we die from exposure, I'm telling everyone that you were cutting your hair and possibly planning to be a professional flasher!" he roared back.

I snorted a laugh. Was that what he construed from my trench coat? What a funny guy. He wasn't that far off.

"Like anybody would believe you. They wouldn't even know who you were talking about."

"You were breaking and entering!" He said it like *I* was the one missing the point.

"I broke nothing and was already entered. It's not my fault that literally nobody ever sees me!" I threw my arms out to the side. "Azi was meant to close up and check to make sure everyone was down, wasn't he? He looked right at me and didn't even see me. How is that my fault? So, for once in the history of my sad life of always being *overlooked,* I played it to my advantage. So sue me." More came pouring out than I meant, and a wave of itchy embarrassment followed. I wanted to do something ridiculous to distract him from my truths, but there was nowhere to hide, and again, still no hand puppets. "Don't actually sue me," I said softer, losing steam. "That would suck."

I didn't appreciate the pitying look that passed over Owen's features. He let out a rush of breath before pushing up his winter hat to scratch at his scalp. "Let's just take a breath and calm down. Okay?"

I dropped my chin to glare at him.

"We don't even know the situation yet. Maybe it isn't that bad. Maybe we'll get moving here in a moment," Owen said.

Poor, sweet, naive man.

"Yo, big guy?" The radio crackled through the thick material of his jacket.

Owen fumbled in his layers to grab the walkie-talkie. "What's going on?" he asked.

"The tram stopped," Azi said.

"Yes, we noticed that too." Owen met my gaze as we shared a look of *no, duh*.

"I was afraid of this happening. This isn't the first time the line has frozen. Benny Jr. was an idiot to send you up to begin with."

All color drained from Owen's face.

"Are either of you injured?" Azi asked.

Owen scanned me from head to toe as I shook my head. "No. We're both okay," he said.

"Just freezing," I grumbled.

"That's the good news. The bad news is, we can't send anybody up right now," Azi explained. "Whiteout conditions, my man. So long as you guys are okay with waiting it out, we can't risk anybody else going out in this."

I opened my mouth to argue that we were so not fine, but seeming to understand that Azi was about to get a verbal onslaught, Owen held up a gloved hand, finger up to preemptively stop me. I mimed biting it.

The side of his mouth twitched.

"Right," he said to Azi.

"Sorry, man. It's a crappy way to ring in the new year. But just hunker down, and as soon as it's safe, we will send someone —" There was a brief silence after somebody shouted something to him in the background. "If not me, somebody." Everybody was already celebrating the new year and wouldn't be able to operate machinery—snowmobile or otherwise—for quite some time.

"Yep. Gotcha," Owen said shortly.

"If things get too dicey up there, there's the Hook—the emergency cabin less than a quarter mile away. If you can get down the tower, then you can wait it out there. It has a wood-burning oven, plenty of supplies, and food reserves we just restocked. But if it were me, I'd just hang out until this storm passes over. No sense in leaving the heat of the tram."

"Yeah," Owen said.

"Hunker down. We'll de-ice the line as soon as possible. I'll make sure someone is here if you need anything," Azi said.

They wrapped up, and Owen put the radio away with a long sigh. "Well, I guess that's that."

"Eff that noise," I said. With a growl of determination, I grabbed my food-laden bag, slung it over my shoulder, and then went to the doors.

# Chapter 8


Bee


I WEDGED MY FINGERTIPS BETWEEN THE HEAVY METAL auto-closing doors, attempting to claw them apart. I was instantly blown back by a gust of wind before they snapped shut again. Owen lunged at me, causing the tram to rock in one direction. With his arms around my waist—the man was far too tactile—he hauled me back to the opposite side. The Can rocked back in the other direction. We tumbled against the wall, but he never loosened his grip.

"What are you doing? Are you crazy?!" His hold was like a vise, but his voice shook.

"I'm not staying here, and I am not crazy! That's terribly offensive." I hit at his hands, but he didn't so much as flinch.

"That's a twenty-foot drop or more. You would break every bone in your body!"

Why did he care about my safety so much? Why was he so determined to bring me down this mountain? It didn't make any sense. Even if everybody else thought I was ridiculous—if they thought of me at all—at least I knew who I was and what I wanted. I just really wanted NYNB to work. I wasn't ready to give up.

"I don't think it's that high. And there's a little ladder on the pole thing. I wasn't going to jump down. Look, I'll show you," I explained, trying to get up.

He didn't let me move an inch.

"You probably couldn't see it anyway, but trust me," I mumbled.

"Yes, you've instilled nothing but trust in me since we met," he grumbled in my ear, not letting me go.

I suppressed a shiver as his breath tickled down my collar.

"If I climb down the ladder, it's only a few feet drop into all that fresh powdery snow. Like jumping onto a bed," I explained. He was too clouded by his own fears to see the situation clearly. Not like me. Thankfully, one of us was being rational.

"You cannot be serious," he said.

"I am."

"Then what? It's horrible out there," he asked, his breath hot against my ear, his voice rumbling against my back.

I straightened, and the muscles in his arms flexed.

Fine, I'll stay contained within your rock-hard flesh prison where it's warm and yummy smelling.

"We only rode ten minutes," I explained. "This thing can't be going faster than a couple of miles per hour. So that's what, two miles tops? It's just a straight shot back up to the mountain."

"None of that math sounds right."

"Give it up. You're not getting me back down this mountain tonight. At least let me go back up." I struggled futilely against him. Not that I was keeping track, but Owen and I had embraced a lot tonight already.

"As the crow flies," he said, low and menacing.

"What? Nobody is even talking about birds right now. Now, who's the insane one?" I grumbled under my breath. His body was still pressed hard against mine. It didn't matter that there were all the layers between us. I was too aware of him.

"That calculation might be right as the crow flies, but you're talking about climbing through wild, unmarked forest in a whiteout at night. That's a recipe for death for anybody. Think about how many peaks and valleys there are. Isn't this thing a thousand feet off the ground at one point?"

I didn't want to speak because I wasn't ready to admit he was right. Sometimes, my body launched into a plan without fact-checking with the brain. It would certainly be memorable if I died trying to climb my way back to the top, but not the sort of impression I was going for. The fight died out of me, and I slumped back against him.

"It's warmer and safer in here. Walking back to the top is not an option," he said with finality.

The plan would still happen. This was just a hiccup. NYNB didn't have to be thrown out the window; it would only be put on hold until survival was no longer the top priority.

"Okay," I said. He relaxed enough that I could finally move out of his arms. I probably should.

Eventually, I did.

We would ride out the night here in this freezing box of death. There was still time.

"Bee? Are you okay?" His gaze searched mine, and I could only begin to guess what he thought of me. We hadn't met in stellar circumstances, and now we were about to become trauma-bonded.

"This is stupid," I said.

He huffed out an amused breath at my verbal eloquence. "There's no reception in this dead zone. But we still have the radio if there is an emergency," he said, delivering more fun news.

I groaned and dropped my head into my hands, my half-cropped hair swinging past my ears. "Damn this weather. Damn this town," I said. "For getting us stuck here."

He stood. "We have heat. We have supplies. We're going to be okay. It might be a long night, but as soon as the sun rises and the storm passes, help will come." He sounded optimistic. Delusional but optimistic. Very much on-brand for me. I begrudgingly respected that.

I sighed and settled into the hard plastic bench. He sat in the one across from me. The cold was noticeable through the snow pants. I would be miserable if he hadn't gotten me these clothes. It would be polite to thank him, but I wasn't ready to. I had to keep my guard up around him. Not because I was scared, but because ... well, I didn't want to think about why. I just wanted to mourn the failure of this night so far. I pulled my hands into my sleeves.

"Azi said there are extra blankets and pocket hand warmers around here somewhere. We can break into the emergency stash any time we need to. I don't have food or water—"

"I have food." I perked up.

Bee for the win.

I dug into my bag and pulled out a water bottle and a plethora of assorted snacks. I also had several pairs of panties. It was only meant to be one night, but you could never be too careful. He saw none of this except the food I fanned out between us.

"Were you planning to be up there a while?" he asked.

"No," I answered too quickly. "That would be weird." I focused intently on tucking away the panties deep into the bag to hide the guilt written all over my face.

I had been planning on at least the night. I wouldn't feel comfortable stealing goodies from the snack bar.

"You didn't have a winter coat, but you packed"—he turned

over the treasures in his hand—"cookies, fruit snacks, and not one, but two different types of trail mix."

"Sometimes you want more savory than sweet." I shrugged.

He studied the assorted snacks. "Did a toddler pack your bag?"

I quickly shoved everything back into my bag, chin lifted haughtily.

"I get low blood sugar," I said with a sniff. Thank God, the Pop-Tarts didn't fall out, or I'd never hear the end of it.

One didn't pack health food and protein bars when having a life-changing adventure.

"Oh no," he said, his tone suddenly serious. "You're diabetic?"

I narrowed my eyes. "No. But I get really hangry."

He let out a breath. "Not really something to joke about."

I looked at him blank-faced. "I'm not joking. I turn into a different person. Just ask Deckard. You think I'm short-tempered and impulsive now ..."

His eyes widened fearfully. "Let's hope it won't come to that."

We both looked out the window. The tram didn't shake as much, which was a miracle with how close he'd come to hurling just a few minutes ago. With snacks returned for now, I rummaged around until I found the chile socks.

I looked up from where I tugged off my canvas shoes and slid on the extra chile socks he snagged for me. He watched me thoughtfully, worrying his big, pouty bottom lip. He was considerate. Aside from the abduction thing. I still didn't understand why, though. Was it just for his job? Was he looking to be employee of the month? He didn't have to make me feel comfortable too. I didn't know how to handle this sudden attention and likely wasn't handling it well. I would thank him when this was all over.

Not yet, though.

After that, we fell into silence. I checked my phone. No reception, as he warned. I looked out the window, not sure what I expected to see. It was called a whiteout for a reason. In the dark of the night, the streaming white flakes by the lights gave the effect of flying through space.

A chill wracked a shiver through me, but people making grand plans to change their lives weren't put off by a little snow.

"Are you okay? Need the extra blankets?" he asked.

I really did, but I figured I should wait as long as possible before adding the extra heat because, after that, it was over. Again with the worry. I wasn't used to this much notice. Even Deckard was a typically oblivious guy most of the time.

"No. I'm okay. I'm tricking my brain into thinking my body isn't cold," I said.

"How's that going?"

"Splendidly."

Not true. It was going terribly, and I couldn't think about anything but the biting cold of the seat on my butt or the way my nose felt like it was minutes from falling off my face.

What we needed was a distraction. I reached for topics of conversation with Owen, but it felt like every single word had been blown out of my brain with this windstorm. What were words? What were icebreakers? Heh. Icebreakers. Relevant.

How did we kill time when we were trying not to freeze to death?

But more frightening was that I wanted to understand more about him. I felt intrigued by his gentleness and depth. I wanted to learn how he knew what a contronym was and to hear more examples. Were there any other cool words he could teach me? I found myself just basking in his general worry for me. This wouldn't do. I was meant to be changing my life, not developing a crush on the guy who was supposed to stop me.

I had to stay focused.

For every fidget of my hands or tap of my heels, bouncing my head, he was as still as though in meditation. How could he be so serene? What sort of worries occupied his thoughts?

He just kept looking at me, checking on me. *Seeing me.*

I couldn't stand this. If I had to stay looking at him, cataloging his attractive features and thinking of all the ways he'd cared for me already, these confusing, muddled feelings I was developing would only get worse. I wouldn't make it another ten minutes if something didn't change. My mind raced, and my body refused to stay still. It had only been ten minutes, yet a hundred years had surely passed.

I had to do something.

"Play a game!" He jumped when I shouted out of nowhere. I lowered and smoothed my voice. "To pass the time, we could play a game."

# Chapter 9

Owen

THE LONGER I STUDIED BEE, THE MORE CONTRADICTORY she became to me. She wore bright patterned clothes (usually), yet nobody seemed to know who she was. She was impulsive and hotheaded but listened to rational explanations and seemed naturally curious. She was stubborn in her mysterious pursuit but then thanked me for teaching her something new.

To think that I could be capable of teaching anybody anything was a laugh.

And based on her inability to sit still under my assessing gaze, she didn't appear to like that I was studying her. But I liked looking at her. Even with her new hair and her ridiculous snowsuit. I liked the playful gleam in her dark eyes and how expressive her features were. I swore every thought that passed through her mind played out on the pout of her full lips or the scrunch of her pert nose.

Within five minutes, her foot began to tap. Not long after, she looked around, eyes never settling on me, desperate for something to comment on. Her body was never still, like a kid in the waiting room of a doctor's office. It was as though words were bubbling from her gut up into her mouth, and the longer we sat there, the more I expected a verbal onslaught would come exploding out.

Sure enough, the words came.

"A game?" I repeated.

Bee nodded, rubbing her hands gleefully. The good news was there wasn't a chance that Bee was afraid of me. The bad news was I hadn't had a full conversation with a person outside Ivy in ... a really long time.

I had nothing against it, but most people assumed I was not the chatting type. They assumed stringing more than two words together was a challenge for me. Then, when I did speak, the pressure not to sound like a moron usually manifested in exactly that. I stumbled over words that I read often and knew well but somehow sounded wrong when said out loud. Sentences I'd rehearsed in my head only to fumble, firming the perception of me as a big dumb idiot who only communicated through violence.

But I had taught Bee a new word.

I blinked at Bee, face placid. If we played a game, would she see me trip over my sentences? Would she mock me if I struggled to say the five-dollar words I could say perfectly in my head but only to stumble in execution? I didn't think she would, but I wasn't ready to find out.

"No," I said. Her mouth snapped shut into a tight line. "Thank you," I added when that line of her mouth turned into a pout.

"Fine. I'll just play with myself. And I will have the best time." She crossed her arms and lifted her pointed chin. After a second, a frown formed, and her eyes widened comically. "I said that wrong. I'll play a game *by* myself. I won't play *with—*"

"Go for it." I interrupted before she could dig herself any deeper.

Maybe I shouldn't have picked the seat right across from her, but it was that or sit right next to her, and the situation wasn't so dire for that. Not when she *just* talked about playing with herself.

I eyed her wearily, trying to get a grip.

She bit her lip and tucked her hands under her legs—or where I thought her legs most likely were. At this point, she was more of a brightly colored amorphous blob with a face. Amorphous was a perfect example of a word I knew, but when I tried to verbalize it, it would inevitably come out completely wrong— like amphibious or something.

"This game is called 'Name all the cats from the cat café.'" She cleared her throat, still not looking at me.

"What?" I tried so hard not to smile.

"Shh. I'm not talking to you." She leaned back and closed her eyes in thought. "There's sweet Simon, who's probably older than me and yells for food all day. There's Slider, who randomly attacks me. It's how he expresses his love. Then Maverick, the strong silent type." She opened her eyes just long enough to shoot me a pointed look. "You'd get along. Then we have Binx and Callie, who are total opposites but madly in love. There's Bear, who manages to shove all fifteen pounds of himself in places he has no business being. There's Zeus, who thinks she's a dog. And François, who actually is a dog that thinks he's a cat. Don't tell him otherwise."

On and on she went. Listing names until they were swirling around my head like birds in a cartoon. Dachs and Socks, Pepper and Pudge, Tommy and Zombie ... I didn't think the café was that big, but when she was on her twentieth cat, I was ready to be done.

"Lena and Dallas—"

"What type of game would we even be able to play?" I asked, interrupting her.

Her eyes brightened, hopeful. "Oh, we've got lots of options. We could play twenty questions or two truths and a lie. We could list notable historical figures in alphabetical order. Or we could try to name every country. Really, the options are endless," she said with pep.

"Truth or dare?" I asked.

"Sure," she said right away, happy I'd contributed to the ideas. "I feel like the dare options would be somewhat limited since you wouldn't even let me open the door. But I'm sure we could think of something," she added and then suddenly blushed furiously red at whatever thought just flashed into her mind and tried too late to hide it. Just what sort of things would she want to do if we played together? "We don't have to play a game. It was a stupid idea." Her mouth tugged at the paracord, tightening the hood around her head.

"A distraction is a good idea." I swallowed.

"Right." Her blush faded away, but I still fixated on where her thoughts had gone.

We settled on a game where one of us would name a celebrity, and whatever letter their name ended with, the other person would have to think of a different celebrity starting with that letter. The problem with that game was that we quickly learned how many names end with *s* and *n*.

"I met that actress once," I said when she started throwing out random names.

Bee gasped. "No way! Did she visit here?"

"Nah. I went to LA to visit my cousin, who is a bodyguard there. Or was. He quit, I think. I'm not sure exactly."

"So cool. So big, tough guy energy runs in the family?"

I shrugged.

"Was she nice?"

"No comment. But my cousin did say Emma Flynn is as amazing as she seems."

"I believe it. I wish a celebrity would come to Slippery Slopes. I would be so chill, like fame was no big deal." She sat back, blowing out a breath. "Should we try twenty questions?"

We played twenty questions next but found it even less challenging. For being almost strangers, we guessed each other's answers within a few questions. After the fifth round, we gave up.

"Damn, these psychic abilities," she said.

"Seriously, get out of my head." I relaxed and leaned back, feeling peace I hadn't had since Benny Jr. called.

It was like being with Ivy. I wasn't overthinking every sentence. I didn't have time. Bee verbally bounced around topics like a Ping-Pong ball, and there was no time to overthink or feel judged.

It was unexpected.

The only thing that took my attention now was how my mouth had grown tacky with dehydration. I regretted all the times I didn't drink when water was right in front of me, the way I missed being able to breathe out of my nose when I was sick. I promised I'd never take it for granted again. I leaned my head back and let out a long sigh. "Tell me that took at least three hours."

The *shoosh-shoosh* of her nylon snowsuit was audible as she checked her phone. "Not quite. Forty minutes," she said with a groan.

"How?" I asked, genuinely shocked.

"Time is relative, and apparently, it goes at a fraction of its normal speed in this box."

"I'm so thirsty." My voice sounded even raspier than normal.

"Here." She thrust me a water bottle from her bag.

"Thanks." I smiled at her, and she lowered her head to dig through the bag. "How many more do you have?"

"Hmm ..." She disappeared into the Mary Poppins' bag, counting to herself. "Six, including that one." That explained some of the weight, along with all the sugary snacks.

"Okay. We'll pace ourselves, just in case. Just a few sips here and there."

She chugged half her bottle before my words sank in. She stopped with a sheepish look and wiped her mouth with a nod. "Good idea. Starting now."

She noticed me holding out my bottle, waiting for her.

"Cheers," I said.

"To a better next year," she said.

It could only get better.

Another contradiction about Bee that had been nagging at me just clicked into place. She was here on New Year's Eve alone. She mentioned her parents were out of town. Deckard Sparks was *something* to her, wasn't he? Why wasn't he here? Where was her family? How could anybody so interesting and pretty and full of life be alone?

Alone like me.

I wanted to ask her about her wild plans or her family, but instead, I just said, "Cheers to that," and tapped against her bottle.

She took a little sip this time, licking her lips and humming slightly in contentment as she did. I cleared my throat and looked away. I guess I hadn't noticed what a nice mouth she had earlier. She used it so much that the full curve of her lips was lost in chatter, but it was such a pretty little mouth.

Her eyes suddenly widened, and I worried she really could read my thoughts. I flashed with guilt over ogling her.

"What's wrong?" I asked.

She shook her head, a few strands of the shorter tufts of hair coming out to frame her face.

I waited patiently for the silence to get the truth out of her.

"I might need to pee!" She looked around wildly. "I shouldn't have drunk that. There aren't any, uh, you know, facilities."

"Do you have to go?" I asked.

"Not right now." She gnawed at her bottom lip before stopping herself. "I went before you kidnapped me"—I frowned in confusion—"but it's gonna become an issue. I can't just whip it out and go off the edge like you."

I felt the world spin around me at the thought of opening that door. It occurred to me then that I hadn't thought about being this high off the ground in a while. Maybe the monotony of hearing about all the cats numbed the fear center in my brain.

"I wouldn't do that." I looked around, feeling anxious again.

"Oh my God. Oh my God. Oh my God," she said, rocking back and forth. "I can't pee on this tram."

"That's true. You cannot," I said. She moaned. "Don't think about it," I tried to reassure her.

"Oh, sure. That always works."

"Maybe help will come before it's Situation Critical," I said. Her worry nestled into my own mind, though. "Damn. Now, I cannot stop thinking about it."

"At least you have more options. Ugh. Men get everything," she said.

"Listen." I reached for anything to distract. "Let's just not think about it. Tell me a story. Uh, tell me ..." I frantically looked around for a topic as if it would be written on the walls. *Why were you cutting your hair? Why are you so determined to get back to the top of the mountain? Why do you have an overnight bag filled with panties and candy?*

"Do you like working at the cat café?" I settled on.

Her expressive brows shot up. "Yeah. I love the cats." I made a mental note that she hadn't said the people. She frowned a bit and asked, "How come I've never seen you in there?"

I had tried a few times. I'd wanted to get to know her better, but my conversation skills always held me back. That and my cat allergy. I shrugged. "I've thought about trying some coffee, but I'm allergic to cats."

"Oh." Her gaze went hazy as her mind processed something behind the scenes. "Well. If you ever want to come by, I can make you a cup with zero steps inside the building. Just come to the to-go window."

"There's a to-go window?"

"There is *a* window that opens, and I can put coffee through it." She smiled so fully that my heart lurched as if the tram shook again.

"Thanks," I said, feeling a warmth spread into my chest. I didn't get a lot of offers for unplanned visits around town. Usually, when people saw me, they assumed there was a debt to be collected. I suddenly hoped that we would see each other after tonight. *When* we got through the night. "That'd be great."

"I won't even charge for the cat hair," she said so flatly I almost missed the joke.

We shared a quick smile. She was funny. Weird. But funny.

"You didn't really come from work, did you?" I asked.

"Why?" she asked defensively.

"No cat hair on you."

"I don't lay on the floor with them in a big furball pile." She waited a beat. "Not all the time," she mumbled. "I have a question for you."

There were a thousand things I didn't want to think or talk about. I would see what her question was before committing either way.

"Why Soupy?" she asked, taking my silence as permission.

I laughed once without humor. "I imagine breaking down the evolution of my nickname would be like trying to break down a really bad joke, but here goes."

She leaned forward eagerly; the nylon singing the song of its people.

"I was never Owen. I don't know why. People have never called me by my name." She watched me with wide eyes, rapt in attention. "I was always Big Guy or Gigantor or BFG. Ever since I was a kid, I was always given a nickname because of my size. It was worse when there was more fat than muscle and before I joined the football team."

She frowned, her eyes going hazy with memory. "Kids can be so cruel."

I nodded. "I decided that I didn't want that anymore, so when I joined football in high school, I convinced them to call me by my last name. So it was Campbell at first. Then Campbell's Chicken Soup. Then just Chick Soup. That was very short-lived. Then The Soupman to Soupy, because I guess it rolls off the tongue better? Sometimes it's Cam Cam the Soup Man if they feel particularly feisty."

"So, you're not like, really into soup?"

"I am the normal amount into soup."

"I thought maybe it was that, or you liquefied people's insides."

I frowned but pressed on. "Ironically, the longer people know me, the longer the nickname gets. Counterintuitive. Better than Big Guy," I'd admitted without thinking.

"You don't like that?" Her eyebrows furrowed.

"My size will always be the most defining thing about me."

Her face twisted in thought. "It is strange, now that I think about it. If I had a birthmark on my face, people wouldn't feel comfortable using something like 'Spot' as a nickname." When I nodded in agreement, she added, "Sorry I called you Big Guy earlier."

I shrugged. "Sorry if I scared you." I held her gaze.

She snorted. "No offense, but you haven't scared me once."

My head shot up. "No?"

"I'm more scared of the guinea pig gangs around town."

"That makes sense. They're terrifying." I thought of the time I came across five of them in the alley behind The Tipsy. They stopped and looked at me like I'd interrupted an important business meeting. "They just stare at you with those little beady eyes," I said.

"And make those chittering sounds."

We both shuddered.

"I remember you in high school," she said quietly, not meeting my gaze.

All at once, I felt sick again. "Oh?"

"Yeah. It was a big deal when you made the team."

I swallowed with effort. "Yeah."

"Not a lot of sophomores made varsity." She nodded.

"Those guys I hung out with at the time weren't the best. Sorry if there was ever any bullying," I said, meeting her eyes.

I hated high school. I hated the reminder that I hadn't felt comfortable in this body in decades. I needed to turn this conversation around. Nausea crept back up my throat.

"No." She blinked and then toyed with her hands in her lap. "You'd have to be noticed to get teased." Again, I wondered where were the people who cared for her and looked out for her? "I shouldn't have called you a big dumb brute," she added.

"You didn't."

"Not out loud." Her brown eyes flicked to the side.

"I didn't have the best crowd in high school, so I wouldn't have blamed you for thinking the worst of me. At least until I quit the team."

"Why did you quit? It was quite the drama around town."

We weren't talking about this. No matter how long we were here.

"Ah, you know," I answered noncommittedly, scrambling for a distraction when a shiver wracked her body. "Are you okay?" I asked, changing the subject.

Her teeth chattered. "The heater sucks."

"Yeah, it's pretty old." I tugged off my gloves and hat and leaned across the aisle to hand them too her. "Here, take these."

"Are you sure you don't mind?" She already had her hands in them when she asked. She sighed, eyelids almost closing. "So warm."

"Go ahead." I felt a rush of relief to watch her pleasure.

"I really wouldn't want to impose," she said, tucking the beanie on next. Her shoulders did a dramatic shimmy as she tugged it down over her ears. "God, that's amazing."

I chuckled. "I don't mind." I rubbed my quickly cooling hands together before tucking them under my arms.

She frowned at me, looked at the gloves, and then back at me in confusion. A question formed on her lips, but she closed her mouth again. She looked up from her lap and finally said, "We'll take turns."

I cleared my throat with a nod. "We could, uh, also sit closer if you want."

# Chapter 10

Bee

Now we're talking!

For once, I caught myself before shouting out the first thing to come to mind, which in this case was, "Hell yeah!"

And actually, aside from a huge part of me that really loved the offer, there was a loud, nagging worry that wondered why he was concerned about my comfort at all. Was he genuinely that nice, or was he just doing his job? Was I that used to my lot in life that I couldn't take basic human concern at face value?

His hat had been so warm that I wished I could shrink myself down and curl up inside it like literally any of the cats did with every single empty shipping box. His gloves too; when I slid my hands in, a part of me wondered if this was what holding his hands might be like.

I wouldn't let myself fall into whatever trap this had to be. Surely, no man this good-looking could also be this thoughtful and protective.

It sent alarm bells off all over the place. *Be careful, Bee, he's using you as a means to an end, and he'll forget about you when this was all over.*

That being said, I really, *really* wanted him to come over.

I must have waited too long to answer, lost in the never-ending corridors of my mind, because he shifted and spoke up.

"Listen. I'm not trying to, uh ... I'm not being ... forward," he said.

I bit my lip to keep from guffawing with laughter. Seriously, how could so many people in this town be afraid of him?

"For warmth?" I asked.

"For warmth," he said at the same time.

I was still focused on the NYNB plan, but do you know what else new me would totally do? Snuggle the hell out of Owen Campbell. At least while I had him.

Owen didn't look at me like that. Most men didn't. It was a relief most of the time, this sort of "invisibility privilege" I had. It protected me from the worst. I was aware of how awful men treated women they found attractive—like those women owed them something. But this felt different and nice.

I would not make the situation weird like I always did.

I would keep my cool.

"Okay dokey, artichokey." I patted the seat next to me with enthusiasm. Shivers wracked me, but these felt more anticipatory than cold-based.

He chuckled and didn't curl his lip in disgust, so that was something.

"Right. So I will just go scooch on over to you then," he said but didn't move. He swallowed and eyed the booth where my hand patted again.

"Did you say 'scooch'?" I looked up with my chin pointed down so he hopefully couldn't see me fighting back a smile.

"No. It was something much more masculine and commanding." He cleared his throat as he stood and stretched. He rubbed his hands together and tucked them in his armpits.

Was he nervous? Because of me? It wasn't like I bit. Except for that one time earlier when I tried to bite him.

Owen went to the front of the tram, every step shaking us, and reached into a box built into the side. He pulled out a silver rectangle and flicked it out with a flourish.

"This is an emergency thermal blanket. It will help keep our body heat trapped," he said, delaying the inevitable.

I was aware of how thermal blankets worked, but men like to feel useful, and I was too cold to point out his patriarchal shortcomings. Plus, I didn't want to screw this up before it started.

Probably best if I didn't talk at all.

A second later, his whole right side was pressed up against my left as his large arm encompassed me in the blanket. I grabbed one end to help wrap us up like a burrito. The thin material worked quickly except for my poor nose, but my teeth stopped chattering almost immediately.

"Better?" he asked.

I nodded. "I feel like a package of Pop-Tarts."

Well, the not talking lasted roughly twenty seconds.

In my defense, being enveloped together like this, every sense was on high alert. There wasn't much room left for critical thinking. His voice rumbled through me, causing a wave of much-needed heat. There was no way to inhale without smelling him. (I wouldn't want to anyway. He smelled like a cozy pile of fresh-dried laundry.) His large body expelled so much heat that it felt like standing next to a space heater. He was so good-looking that even his profile made me blush. I couldn't taste him, not without making it really weird, but I bet he would be delicious.

"Are you okay? Is this weird," he said.

My head snapped to him. Had I been talking out loud? But his look was only that of cautious concern. I had to get my act together.

"Weird? No, not at all. I do this all the time." It was best to let him think I was as experienced with touching as he was.

"You cuddle with men you don't know to stay warm?" he asked.

"Oh yeah, like weekly. If not biweekly." I never knew if that meant twice a week or every other week. "I am a total snuggle ho, fo' sho. Don't you?"

I was handling this so well, considering. Otherwise, he might think I was a total dweeb.

His chuckle was so deep it wasn't audible. It just rolled through me like a silent tremor.

"Okay, good. Just checking," he said.

Did that mean he was a snuggle ho?

"You're probably used to this too," I said, fishing for details on his life. I didn't know much about him other than a few surface details, but I didn't think he was dating someone. "I mean. Not in a sexy way. I'm not gonna say sexy. I just mean, you're a bachelor in a town filled with many single people, and with all the tourists coming through, you probably have your fair share of dates. Deckard says they're 'thirsty.' The tourists. Which I don't really understand because we literally have water bottle filling stations all over town, but he knows more about that sort of stuff than I do. Unless he means because of the supposed healing power of the hot springs."

Slippery Slopes was a town long before New Mexico was a state, and it has a long and weird history that draws a lot of the woo-woo crowds who swear that this is a place for the mystical and spiritual. Some even claim to see mysterious sightings, but they're probably just rogue guinea pigs. Slippery Slopes was less cowboy boots and "hello, ma'am" small town and more "your aura seems off today, swing by my shop so we can charge your crystals."

"It feels like I'm talking a lot. Am I talking a lot?" I asked.

"I'm not seeing anybody." There was a curious flatness to Owen's tone. I hadn't specifically asked, but I was flooded with relief, nonetheless.

"Good. Cool. Not that this is a date. If it were a date, it would be the worst date ever, am I right?"

He shifted slightly next to me. Was that to put distance between us? Or to get closer? Maybe his butt was going numb from the cold too. "Are you seeing somebody?" he asked.

I was so glad we sat side by side so that my face was mostly pointed away. I couldn't bear it if he was making fun of me. He had to know how alone I was.

"Oh, you know. I like to date casually. I'm not really steady with anybody right now."

It wasn't *not* true. Did people say "steady"? There was a beat of silence, and I waited to see if he would call me out.

"Not even Deckard Sparks?" he asked nonchalantly.

"Ha!" I cackled. I hadn't been expecting that at all. "Deckard? No. He's a great guy, but he's just a friend. We've been friends for forever."

"Gotcha. I think a lot of people assume you're together."

"People would have to know I exist to think that," I said with a dry laugh. When Owen frowned with what might be concern, I quickly added, "No, I just mean that he's always got some new lady friend."

He frowned.

"You're together a lot, and he's sort of the town's biggest catch." He watched me carefully as he spoke.

"Biggest catch." I rolled my eyes. For being such a *catch*, he had a heck of a time being caught. "Nah. Deckard and I don't fit like that. There's no *spark*." I snorted. "See what I did there?"

Owen's face had moved close enough that when I looked to meet his gaze, he was right there, a breath away. His focus bounced between my eyes, a soft smile on his mouth as he nodded.

How did we get here? Two single people smooshed up close, talking about their single-ness. What a predicament.

"That's good," he said with a swallow.

What was good? What had I said? Something about sparks? I felt them now, shooting off like sparklers in the air around us. The plan had changed again. The bones were still there. I was getting to the top of that mountain, but this detour could involve some kissing. That might be okay.

My brain misfired. Abilities like speech and breathing short-circuited so that I could only stare up at Owen, mouth slightly parted. The comfort of him was unexpected. His hard edges pressing against me settled my agitation. My body naturally leaned into his like seeking warmth from the sun. Every nerve of my body lit up as his eyes moved over me.

His gaze moved over my face before drifting up and behind me. *No, come back to staring at my lips.* His gaze tracked something along the ceiling before it settled on my shoulder.

"I wasn't totally wrong. There are bugs in the winter," he said.

I was so confused by the random subject change. Weren't we talking about being single and sparks and not how he tried to trick me onto this tram? "Okay." It took me a second to catch up. "As long as it's not spiders. Perk of a cat café. Nary a spider to be seen."

His smile melted away as he sat back, and a growing trepidation simmered in me.

"You don't like spiders?" he asked cautiously.

"Does anybody *like* them? With their hairy little legs and creepy bodies." I shuddered.

"Okay, don't freak out," he said.

"Has saying that to somebody ever worked?" I ground out through clenched teeth. My body was coiled as a cat, ready to pounce.

"It's just a little baby spider."

My heart sank into my butt.

"Where?" My voice was a breathy whisper—my whole body was pumping with adrenaline already. Was it here this whole time? Was it watching us through its numerous eyes, waiting for the perfect time to attack?

"I'm going to get it. Just be still," he said.

"Where?" I repeated, growling.

"It's on your shoulder, but don't move—"

I jumped up with a shrill scream. My whole body convulsed as I shook off anything that might be able to stay on me. I could feel a hundred legs crawl up my neck and down my arms. Everything touching me was a potential spider body part. I clawed at the zipper at my neck. I couldn't strip off this snowsuit fast enough. I threw off his gloves for dexterity and finally ripped off the jacket.

"Stop! Bee, you're rattling the whole—"

Owen was worried about a little shake of the tram while I was being eaten alive?

I didn't listen. I just unzipped, unsnapped, and unbuttoned everything all at once. I shucked off my clothes faster than our resident world record-holder, Quentin Rex, shucked corn. (One of several of his world record titles.)

"Is it on me? Is it still on me?" I spun in a circle like Einstein, the fluffy ginger cat, had earlier today, only this was a matter of life and death.

I didn't feel the cold. I wouldn't worry about anything but the million little legs crawling down my spine. I groaned another loud sound of horror. His arms reached for me, but I couldn't sit still until I was sure nothing was on me.

"I can't see ... you won't hold ... still ..."

I stopped moving as Owen's voice trailed off, his eyes widening. Whatever he'd been about to say melted from his mouth as he backed up with an audible swallow.

This was it. It was the end for me.

Like in a scary movie, the spider must be right behind me, growing larger, rising on its back legs, ready to attack, fangs dripping with venom. I spun around, arms wide, ready to defend myself, but there was nothing.

"What—Where did it go?" I spun in a full circle, arms bent at right angles and poised to karate chop.

When I turned back to Owen—hyperaware of every brush of air against my skin—it wasn't fear evident in his gaze. It was pure heat. His pupils were blown out, his mouth slightly parted. His breaths came in little pants as his gaze moved slowly up and down my body. I could almost feel it—a tangible relief compared to the phantom spider tingles. As his gaze skidded and stalled on my breasts, my nipples chose that moment to remember the freezing space and poked hard against the thin material ... so thin I almost didn't feel it.

He blinked and seemed to come back to his body to meet my gaze.

Just then, I spotted a little fuzzy dot in the corner of the tram. I froze, ready to scream again, but the spider wasn't having it. It crawled up the wall and out the tiny crack at the top of the door. I had no way to prove it, but I swear it lifted one of its little arms to flip me the bird before it squeezed out. The damage was done. The havoc wreaked.

"The little bastard just went outside." I let out a long breath and shivered all over once again, but this time, the tension melted out of me. "That was close."

Owen still wasn't talking. Had I overreacted? Not even a little. His mouth opened and closed. His eyes spun up to study the ceiling. His focus was so intense he could be trying to burn holes through the roof.

"Owen? Man, my heart is racing." I put my hand on my chest to find only bare skin.

"Your, uh, clothes," he said.

Now it made sense. I was pulling a peep show in my bathing suit. "Yeesh. You act like you've never seen a woman in a bikini before."

Owen's jaw was clenched, the muscles in his neck tense, eyes still trained on the roof, as he lifted a finger and pointed in my general direction. "I think, uh, in the jumping around the, uh, string got caught. You're ..." His face contorted in a wince.

I looked down to discover that, yes, in fact, in the chaos of my jumping around, the tie holding my top together must have come undone. Hanging out for all to see was my left boob. The headlight was on full display, and the right one was seconds from the same fate.

At least it was the better-looking boob.

# Chapter 11

Owen

I spun around, facing the opposite wall. I bent over and grabbed her outerwear and the hat and gloves, tossing it all back in her direction.

"Get dressed," I said.

"I sort of want to burn these, but okay." There were more shuffling sounds, and she added, "Sorry about the nip slip."

I cleared my throat aggressively. "We don't need to talk about it."

I had seen women in bikinis before. I had seen breasts, of course. But not Bee's. Her breasts were full. Her hips flared out. Her smooth skin begged for a hand to run all over it. I would never shake the image of her standing there with that perfectly delectable breast on display, except for the neon green pieces of fabric that barely covered her. Or in fact, didn't cover her at all.

Those breasts, so soft yet heavy and begging to be pushed together and played with.

I balled my fists, trying to take control of my mind that wanted to go down that path further. I tried not to think about kissing and touching her. I wanted to make our own heat in this little box until the windows steamed. Until nothing else but her pleasure was on my mind. My attraction to her had always been there as a low-level simmer in the background, but now, it boiled over. I was never bold enough to act on my crush. I never felt good enough for her company, never worthy enough to talk with her.

But this night, chatting with her, laughing with (and at) her unique way of seeing things, the attraction roiled out of control, demanding more of my attention, more than the fear or anything else that might be on my mind.

I swallowed and shifted. These feelings for her were too strong, too fast. It didn't make any sense. I had to get a grip. I needed to get it together. She might not be afraid of me, but that in no way gave consent for all the dirty images in my mind.

*I could lift her onto me so easily …*

I was here for a job.

"Are you decent?" I asked, an edge to my voice.

"As if I ever stopped." There were more shuffling sounds as the tram shook with her movements. "But yeah, I'm dressed."

When I cautiously spun around, she was back on the bench, shivers wracking her small frame again. I sat next to her but gave her space.

Time to get my head on straight. It wasn't smart to think of her as anything other than the package to be delivered to Benny. I was here to get paid, not drool over Bee. I tilted my head from side to side, finding relief in the cracking.

There had to be an explanation for all of her actions leading to this moment, and it was time she delivered.

"Now," I said. "I think it's time you explained what the hell you're doing in a bikini and why you are so desperate to get back up that mountain."

"You don't even want to know." She sighed and looked away.

"I guess if you're too chicken, you don't have to." I had a feeling that might be a more fruitful approach to take with Bee.

Bee's mouth dropped open before it snapped shut, pinching as tight as her narrowed eyes. "I am *not* a chicken."

That much was obvious. There were many words to describe Bee in our short acquaintance—rambunctious, precocious, life-threatening—but *chicken* was not even close. If she was so eager to talk, let her talk. I'd finally crack this mysterious little nut yet.

Seeing her in that bikini unlocked a new neural pathway. Bee and her neon green bikini were now linked in my mind like peanut butter and jelly, but sexy.

I'd noticed her figure before today. Of course, I had. Those vibrant outfits she wore always drew my attention her way. The fact that she kept herself buttoned up in thick fabrics and chunky layers made me wonder what was concealed underneath.

There had been this one time as I passed her café. She was up on a step stool, a brown corduroy skirt lifting over bright purple tights, and reached up to a top shelf to grab what appeared to be a troublesome cat. I watched a moment too long before I realized what I was doing. When I glanced up from her legs, our eyes met through the glass. A slow smile began to light up her features, but I tucked my head and walked away before I could see it at full wattage. I had no idea what to even say to her. That night, I had a very inappropriate dream about her, where she was my librarian, and I had to be quiet.

She shifted.

"It's a long story," she mumbled, anger staining her cheeks and ears red.

I leaned back, crossing one leg over the other.

"Lucky for us, we have nothing but time." I opened my arm to welcome her back into the cocoon of warmth we had created.

She shimmied herself back up next to me so I could wrap us in the foil heat blanket. I took a long, deep breath of cold air to distract from focusing on how her soft curves fit perfectly against mine.

"You know that statue in town? Outside the plaza, between the yoga studio and the newer weed shop, High Altitudes?" she asked.

It took me a second to locate the statue in my mind because that had been so far from what I expected her to say.

"Laura Ingalls Wilder?"

Bee gasped and turned toward me. "That's her name?" Hope shone from her big brown eyes.

"No." I chuckled. "That's just what I call her. Because of the author of those *Little House on the Prairie* books."

"Damn. I thought that name sounded familiar." She sat back, deflated, and let out a long sigh that pursed her lips. "Do you know her actual name? Or anything about her?"

I shook my head slowly, still waiting to understand the connection to the bikini. And not just because I enjoyed contemplating the bikini.

"Dangit. You're not alone." She fidgeted with a Velcro pocket, not meeting my gaze. "I walk past that statue every day." Here, she hesitated, and her shoulders rolled forward as though she were protecting herself. "I sort of became obsessed with her, my Jane Smith. There is no information on the statue. She's terribly overgrown and neglected, and nobody in this town can give me a single answer about who she was or why she's been memorialized. Here is this larger-than-life memorial for a woman who has now been lost to time."

Her eyes crinkled with a frustrated sort of disbelief as she spoke with more genuine sincerity than I'd seen from her yet.

"My fixation began slowly enough. I asked Mel, my boss, first. She hasn't lived in Slippery Slopes her whole life, but as the owner of the cat café, she knows a lot of the town lore. She didn't know anything about the statue. Neither did the town manager, Jean Sparks, Deckard's mom. Neither did Samuel Clemens—"

"You were really desperate. Talk about a *Twain* in the ass." I cut in, trying to break the tension, and she huffed a soft laugh.

If that was even his real name, Samuel Clemens touted to know everything about everything and dressed suspiciously like Mark Twain. He was a wealth of knowledge but had a hard time stopping once he got going.

"I know. I lost an hour of my life talking about the history of the printing press." She shrugged. "Actually, it was pretty interesting, but he didn't know about Jane. I also asked the oldest man in town, Ned Fled. He said he might have an idea, and we were supposed to meet again to talk more about it, but he forgot about me or rather our plans." She flicked a look at me and laughed, but I didn't think it was funny. How could anyone miss a chance to talk to her more? She hedged on before I could say something.

"Anyway, I even asked the head librarian, Connor Finkle. My questions began here and there at first, and then I became more focused. I looked online. I studied old newspaper clippings. But nobody knows who she was or why we have her in our town. And nobody seems to care or notice besides me. An important fixture diluted to a PokéStop for those still playing and nothing more." She let out a long sigh.

"Nobody knows anything about her," Bee went on. Her pale hands twisted in her lap. "I don't understand it. There isn't a single document. It's a big statue! At least twenty GPs tall. Shouldn't there be some sort of registry for that stuff? It feels so reprehensible that somebody with such an important role in life —worthy of being immortalized—can still be forgotten."

As she spoke, her eyebrows twisted with worry. For all her fiery, impassioned persona, she was a deep well of vulnerability that only became more apparent in time. I was starting to understand why she might feel an affinity for the statue, but I didn't want to jump to conclusions. Sharing this story of her Jane Smith statue felt like a confession she wouldn't share with just anybody. I wanted to support her and say the right thing.

"I think that's the nature of life. We're all eventually destined to fade into oblivion," I said, then winced internally.

"Wow. So comforting." She poked the back of my hand with her gloved finger playfully.

I ground my molars. Why did I think I could be her confidant when I never said the right thing? Why did I think I could make her feel better and not worse? She didn't want to talk to me about important things.

She groaned in discontent. "But doesn't that scare you?"

"It doesn't matter when I think," I said, feeling ashamed, knowing she wouldn't want to talk philosophy with me.

"Of course it does," she said. I sat still, looking forward until her hand moved to gently touch my chin. I let my head be turned in her direction until I looked down into her curious, dark eyes filled with sincerity. "I wouldn't ask if I didn't want to know," she said. "I want to know more about you."

I studied her features, feeling a sensation like looking over the edge of the tram. Something was shifting in me too quickly to track.

She wanted to know more about me. I wanted to share. I took my time to form my thoughts. I felt pressure to get it right, but for once, not because I thought she would judge me, but because I wanted to be understood by her more than anybody else.

"I guess if I think about our lives, our relevance in the grand scheme of things, it can be scary." I put an arm around her when she shuddered. I wasn't sure if it was because of the cold or the vast, unending nihilism of our existence, but I held her just the same. Our faces were just inches apart as I spoke softly, watching her expressive eyes take in my words. "I also think that there's a sort of freedom there. That if we are from stars to the stars, there's really no reason to let things hang over us so much. We are less than a blink in the cosmic grand scheme. So who cares about the little stuff?"

I did think that, on some level, I tried to live that way, but was that true? Or was I hiding just as much as anybody else from monsters in my closet I didn't want to acknowledge?

She leaned into me. "From the stars to the stars ..." she whispered softly. "I like that, Owen."

"I didn't come up with that," I mumbled, flushing under her heavy gaze.

We stared at each other as that feeling of tripping over the edge intensified. My palms sweat despite the cold. My heart thumped wildly against my chest. Was she leaning forward? Was I?

Another heavy wind whistled, causing the track lighting to flick on and off. It was enough to break whatever connection had been pulling our mouths closer together. We both turned to look in the opposite direction, but she shuddered and moved closer when there was already almost no space between us.

"Wait." I shook my head. "We're talking about you and that bikini."

"Ah, damn."

"Nice try, Nietzsche." I pulled her closer, her head tucked

under my chin. The scent of her shampoo tickled my nose, closing my eyes ...

"I'm going to ski down The Slope tomorrow in that bikini. In only that bikini."

My eyes widened. I could feel my brows creep closer to my hairline. I waited. Any second now, that sentence would make sense.

"There's this journalist with a cute blog and video channel where she travels all over the country and interviews big characters in small towns. I'm going to be one of them. Though, to be fair, she has plenty of fodder to choose from here in Slippery Slopes. She's coming tomorrow with her boyfriend. They drove down from Cozy Creek, Colorado. I got in contact with her and told her my plan, and she agreed to interview me. So I have to get back up there. That's the only time they'll be there." Her head tilted in the direction of the peak.

"You're skiing down the slope in a bikini because you want to be in an online blog?"

"Yes. Well, no. Kind of. That's just extra."

"That's why you were hiding out with an overnight bag?"

"Yes. I planned to hide until tomorrow and ski down in the morning, hopefully with a big New Year's crowd. Until you caught me." She flicked a worried glance up at me. "And now I don't know if I'll get back up there in time."

It was a reflex to promise to help her get back to the top, but I wasn't about to get involved. I couldn't get involved. Not if I want to help Ivy. *Not my circus.* "Wait. What does the statue have to do with this?"

"Isn't it obvious?" she asked with the lift and drop of her shoulder. "If I can get some attention to Jane Smith, then maybe somebody will know something. Clearly, my going around asking isn't getting me anywhere. People forget me the second I walk away. This will get some real eyes on her. Her life won't have been wasted. She won't just fade into nothing."

There was more to this that she wasn't sharing, but this confession already cost her so much that I wouldn't push.

"I want to make a difference. I want to be somebody who makes an impact," she said, her brow pinched with ferocity.

"And that's what you want to be remembered for?" She glared, and I was quick to add, "It's an interesting idea. Memorable for sure. I just mean, why *that*?" My eyes flicked to her chest and back up.

She chewed on her lip. "I thought it was a little sexy and provocative. It just popped into my head, and I thought it was a good idea. I just went with it. I'm not one to overthink."

"I got that." I softened my tease with a smile.

Her gaze flicked to my mouth, and her eyes widened. "There it is."

"What?"

"Your smile. I haven't seen it in a while."

"Oh." I guessed that was true. I didn't know she'd been paying attention. Bee was up here to try to change her life, and I was doing everything in my power not to change.

"And I won't be talked out of it. I will find a way to get back up there," she said determinedly.

"Your new year, your choice," I said. But even as I said it, I wondered how true that would be. Even if we could get out of here, Benny wanted me to bring her to him. Was I still on contract with him at this point, or did the whole getting stuck thing negate all that? I needed to get paid and make sure that Ivy had a home for another month. But I also ...

She huffed with a nod.

"Is that your New Year's resolution?" I asked.

"I guess so. I didn't put it like that in my head, but sure. New Year, New Bee. But it's not about attention," she explained after a moment. "Well, I guess that's exactly what it is. But attention defined my way."

"You'll never be able to control how people see you," I said more fiercely than I meant. I could tell because her gaze faltered on me for a fraction of a second.

"But I can control that they *do* see me," she said.

I let her words sink in. This was really important to her. This lovely woman, so determined, so funny and strange in the best way. I never could have imagined this was her plan when I found her cutting her hair tonight, but she continued to impress me. She had a plan to change.

At least she wasn't content to hide who she was.

There was a freedom being stuck up here. I liked talking to Bee. I hadn't liked talking to anybody in a long time. But I liked it here. With her. I felt free to be heard and was actually listened to. She didn't see me as a big dumb lug.

"I'm not sure what it says about me that this is the most fun I've had in a long time," I said without thinking.

She tensed and turned toward me, slow and menacing.

"Is it surprising that you're having fun with me? Did you know I existed before tonight?" I opened my mouth to defend my comments, but she wouldn't let me speak. "Why would anybody think somebody dressed like a kindergarten teacher could be a good time?" She sat up straighter, her brow furrowing as she found fuel for her speech. "And tell me, why is that the epitome of an insult? That I dress like a stereotypical kindergarten teacher? Teachers are patient and kind and put up with more crap than most people. So what if pretty colors make me happy? So do clothes that are comfortable while stylish. I like rainbows and sparkly things. Do I have the temper of a toddler on a good day? Yes, I do. But that doesn't make me unintelligent. I feel things quickly and deeply and move on. It's better than repressing everything like most people. Just because I like simple things or pretty things doesn't mean I'm not complicated. It doesn't mean I don't feel hurt when I'm looked over or brushed aside. I like who I am and how I dress."

"Bee." I couldn't take any more. I wanted to grab her shoulders and shake her just to stop the defensive rant.

"Society hates a contented woman." She shook her head. "No. Worse than that. They don't even see her."

"Bee!" I yelled to be heard.

I was equal parts terrified and turned on.

"What?" she yelled back.

"I see you," I said, setting my hands on her shoulders slowly. She had been breathing heavily, but when I said that, her whole body froze. She went statue-still. I lowered my voice and rubbed my thumbs in soothing circles on her shoulders. "I like you. I'm having a nice time with you. That's what I was trying to say. I meant even though we are trapped in a tram, verging on turning into human popsicles, I'm enjoying myself with you. That's why I said that."

"Oh." She licked her lips. "Sorry. I think I need a snack." She took a deep breath in and relaxed again. "I like talking to you too."

"Good. I don't talk to people much." I pushed some hair back that got stuck to her lashes when she went off on her rant. She watched my action with wide, hesitant eyes.

"Really?" Surprise was written on her features. "I don't either, truthfully. Outside of work." She gauged my reaction as she spoke.

This was the first time I felt myself wanting to *talk*. The first time I felt like there weren't enough hours in the day for everything I wanted to say to her and hear her talk about in return. There couldn't be enough time, not when I was also desperate to occupy her lips.

But what did she feel? What did she want?

"All things considered, I'm having a nice time."

"Me too," she said. She rubbed her lips together, straightening so our faces were close again. It would be so easy to lean in and test the softness of her mouth.

With each passing second, I forgot why I shouldn't be kissing her.

# Chapter 12

Bee

AFTER A NIGHT FILLED WITH ONE EMBARRASSING MOMENT after another—getting caught cutting my hair, having to be tossed around like a tantrumming toddler, accidentally flashing my whole boob—it made very little sense to me why sharing my plans to ski down The Slope was the thing that made me go hot with shame. I had done my Bee thing and got defensive because I'd been on edge, waiting to be mocked. But why? Owen had been nothing but gentle and understanding, but that scared part of me could not let go of the feeling that it wasn't real. It was all a setup to let me down.

*Don't get attached. Don't hold on to hope.*

Yet, here and now, with our gazes locked and our mouths hovering a few inches apart, those worries were shoved way to the back of my lizard brain. There were more important matters.

As I wasn't one to normally overthink anything, I lived purely in the moment because that's all there was, but going through a hypothetical checklist of interest, Owen checked boxes left and right.

Did he want to spend time with me? Yup. Okay, so maybe he didn't have a whole lot of choice in that arena, but he was sitting under the wrapper with me when there was a whole other bench, and it wasn't *that* cold.

Did he keep finding excuses to touch me? Indeedy. The fact that half our bodies were smooshed together cemented that point.

He asked me questions and listened when I responded. Check-a-roonie.

What magic was this tingling through my body, to be *seen?*

And the way he looked at me right now, with those gooey eyes that roamed over my features. It really seemed like the man was going to kiss me.

Was that too soon? Was that what I wanted? Was this *real* or just a reaction to the first bit of attention I've received?

A heightened awareness passed through my entire body of the growing heaviness of my breasts and rapid heartbeat. His eyes were molten when he'd seen me in my bikini. That had to mean something. His warm, spicy-clean scent encompassed me and clouded my senses like stepping into a hot spring. His strong body occupied my entire focus, and I wanted the freedom to touch his body, so unfamiliar and different from my own. I wanted him to touch me, too, and study his face as he discovered the bits he liked the best.

What would happen if we kissed? Would it change things? What about my plans? My needs? Would he return me to Benny the second this tram got moving?

Because when I shared with him, he hadn't mocked me. He was surprisingly profound and paid attention to me.

Maybe I didn't always live in the moment because suddenly, I envisioned a future where we got off this mountain, and Owen never wanted to see me again. A future where I was no longer the subject of his questions and long glances, and I found I didn't like to think about that.

How long had we been sitting here in silence, staring at each other's mouths?

Easily five years.

I checked my phone and gasped when I registered the time.

"It's almost midnight," I said. He blinked and sat back so his face no longer hovered a breath away. I regretted speaking immediately—a common affliction. "We should celebrate," I added.

After a second, he swallowed with a rough nod.

"I'll break out the water bottles," I said and reached under the seat to grab the bag.

I dug through and handed him a bottle.

"I'll grab the Pop-Tarts too," I said. "You've earned it."

"So generous," he said with a soft, almost grin.

If you put together all those half smiles and smirks, that easily equated to a handful of full smiles. Not that I was count-ing, but he'd smiled more tonight than I'd seen around town in years. It made me feel like I had a sort of magic.

Soon, we were situated with our treats—I guess he was worthy of sharing with after all.

"Now that I told you my New Year, New Bee resolution. What about you?" I asked him.

He watched me curiously as I nibbled the corner of the pseudo-pastry.

"What are you doing?" he asked.

"Building a kayak."

"Sugary foods make you snarky."

"It's the lack of them more accurately."

"You only eat the edges first?" he asked.

"There is no other way to eat them. Get the healthy part out of the way," I explained, even though it's obvious. How else would they even be eaten?

"Healthy part?"

"The *not* pure sugary goodness. Normally, if they were toasted, I'd eat the edges, then slide the two halves apart and save the frosting side for last." I'd probably also burn the shit out of my mouth in my impatience, but he didn't need to know that part. The more I spoke, the more he fought a smile. "Is that *not* how everybody eats them?" I flicked a look to the side.

He took a bite, and half the treat was gone.

"Monster." I shuddered.

Alluring muscles in his jaw moved and flexed as he chewed. After he finally swallowed, he started speaking. "To answer your question, no resolutions."

"Tell me you aren't one of those people too cool for school and think they're a joke."

I cringed as he ate the rest *in one bite*. I wouldn't be sharing these again.

"I don't think they're a joke. I just didn't really think about it," he said.

"What better time than now!" I clapped three quick bursts. "Think of one." I glanced at my phone. "Now. You have two whole minutes until midnight. No pressure." I sucked on the frosted bit in my mouth. As his gaze moved to my lips again, I came up with about five solid suggestions for his resolutions, all of which involved his tongue or mouth region.

"I guess ... I'd like to get some more decorations for my friend Ivy's room. Make it more comfortable."

The more he shared, the more questions I had. Was Ivy the woman he visited at Golden Sunsets? The fact that that was the first idea that popped into his head made my heart tighten in a curious way. I was too close to developing a crush.

"That's sweet, but more like a to-do list than a resolution.

Any big changes? Any major life upheavals? Any swimwear you're dying to wear in public?"

He chuckled and shook his head. "I'll think about it. I think my two minutes are up."

I tossed my hand out with a sigh of exacerbation. "Now, time is flying."

I held my phone between us so we could see the screen.

It didn't take long until we neared the final, final countdown (insert eighties guitar rift here).

"Three ..." I said.

"Two ..." He joined in, our bodies leaning closer.

A kiss at midnight hadn't been on my list, but I'd been adapting so well, so far, I might as well—

"One ..." he whispered, head lowering.

My racing heart had to be audible. Every part of me was on edge and sensitive and an exposed nerve.

"Happy New Year," we said in whispered unison.

In my periphery, my phone screen exploded in colorful fireworks before rolling over to the new year.

Owen bent and brushed his lips against my cheek. Before I even knew what was happening, he straightened away.

My mouth, which had been parted slightly, closed as a disappointment ached through me.

I couldn't read men at all, it turned out.

We toasted our bottles and grabbed a second brown sugar Pop-Tart. At least I'd always have carbs.

"Living our best life," I said, hating that my voice sounded breathy and shaky with loss.

"I really am," he said as if he was just as surprised as I was.

His gaze moved over my face. His soft smile locked in place, and there was a hazy expression I couldn't translate.

"Good," I said with a forced pep.

New year, same me, same unkissed lips.

"Are you okay?" he asked.

"Yeah. Totally. I'm having fun." I couldn't quite meet his eyes.

"Okay. Good. Me too," he said.

When I flicked a look at him, his brows were pinched with thoughtfulness. Maybe he was trying to work out just how much longer we'd be stuck together.

"And I didn't even finish telling you about all the cats," I said.

He chuckled, and I really liked how it felt. Even if I wasn't joking.

I understood now that he wasn't laughing at me.

"You're pretty remarkable, Bee," he said.

My head turned back in his direction, treat forgotten. He watched me carefully.

"Me?" I asked. That was literally the first time I'd ever heard that. I was as markable as a dry-erase marker, let alone remarkable ...

An internal feminine alarm blared back to life. Had I shut down the offices too soon? Was court back in session? Because Owen held a tension in his shoulders and swallowed audibly. He leaned closer yet again.

"Maybe this will be the year where everything changes," he said, holding my gaze.

"Yes," I whispered. "I really hope so."

My heart thumped hard in my chest. The tingling in my body was back, up and down my front and back all the way to the tips of my fingers. Inside, I was running around in a circle, arms flailing in the air. Outside, I kept as still as possible, afraid I'd do something to mess this up. How did I show I was interested in return?

His head lowered toward mine. My chin lifted in response.

Oh, so it was instinctual. My body knew what to do. I just had to listen.

Owen's large, calloused, and surprisingly warm hand cupped my face delicately. He drew me in with his own sort of magic, and I went willingly. His thumb swept across the apple of my cheek, sending a full-body thrill through me. His nose glided alongside mine, his mouth meeting mine so gently, in a barely there whisper-soft pressing of his lips.

This was it. Time for a kiss to measure all future kisses against.

His was so warm and soft, and I immediately needed more. I moaned and pushed harder into him, eager and impatient. He smiled against my lips; his other hand rumbled slightly as it grasped the back of my neck.

He held me like I was precious.

The awareness of our bodies meeting was explosive. It was a tangible source of power thrumming between us. Energy sparked off me and between us.

Metaphorically.

Which was ironic because that was exactly when the power went out.

Quite literally.

# Chapter 13

Owen


Bee sat back with a gasp. "Did I do that?"

I had been about to tilt my head and deepen the kiss when she broke away. I reluctantly opened my eyes to the noticeable absence of her mouth. I had been so lost in her sweet, soft touch, her charming eagerness, that I still wasn't caught up on what happened. I wasn't sure what drove me to kiss her, except that it was a new year, and our discussion about plans had inspired me to take action. Or at least that was what I told myself.

Probably, more simply, I wanted to kiss her. I liked her, and it felt like the right move at the moment. So much for not mixing business with pleasure. But this night was so weird; this woman was such a pleasant surprise.

"What?" I asked, confused with my limited mental faculties. I couldn't see her. It was pitch-black. Bee was still close enough that I could feel her quick pants against my cheek but couldn't make out the shape of her.

"Nothing," she said quickly. "What happened? Why are the

lights off? Are they motion-activated?" I felt the air shift as she rocked back and forth, likely flailing her arms.

My suspicions were confirmed a second later when one of her flails caught the side of my head.

"Ow." I reached for her in the darkness and stilled her.

"Sorry."

"Not motion-activated," I said, worry growing.

That was when I noticed the loud rattling of the ancient heater had stopped too. The track and running lights were totally out. In the pitch-blackness and without the white noise of the heater, the roaring storm was thunderous and impossible to ignore.

"Owen?" she asked, a tremble in her voice.

Fear lodged itself into my chest. It was like the universe hit me upside the head with a giant bat to remind me to stay focused on the task.

It wasn't ideal to spend the night in this tram, but it was protection from the storm. It was heat and safety. If the power was well and truly out, then the warmth would escape through the cracks. And quickly. There was almost no insulation in The Can. How long until the windows and door iced over? Fear prickled the back of my neck.

I shouldn't have kissed her. I taunted myself by hoping this year might go any differently. Of course, this was a big ole screw you from the karma gods or whoever decided these things. I'd been starting to feel hopeful and excited about the future for once. When she asked me what I wanted and how I might change, I began to hope for the first time in a long time that change was possible.

"It's okay," I said, but I didn't feel that way at all. "Let me just check some stuff. You stay here."

She was silent.

"Okay, Bee?"

"Sorry, yeah. I nodded. Wow, it's so dark. Like *dark* dark. Can't say I love this. Didn't think I was afraid of the dark, but it amplifies every other sense. This tram sure is jerky. Also, it smells like old pennies. I didn't notice that before. Oh God, I hope the spider doesn't come back—"

"It's okay, Bee."

I squeezed her shoulder before I stood, equilibrium shaky. I dug out the radio.

"Hey, Azi?" After a few shaky seconds, the radio crackled with static. I let out a sigh of relief.

"Hey, man. Happy New Year. How're you two holding up?" A slur to his words made my anger rise to the surface. Had he partaken in celebrations even as two people were stuck up in this decrepit tram? What about Bee? What about her safety? My desire to give this job the middle finger and quit was never stronger, but I couldn't risk being totally forgotten about.

"Happy New Year," I said flatly. I had my back to Bee, but there was no privacy, especially now where the silence rang almost as loud as the storm. "The power went out. Is there any way to reboot it or a switch to reset it? Anything on your end?"

"Ah, shit. I was afraid of that," he said. A round of expletives followed. Bee mumbled her displeasure from behind me. "There's nothing to be done until some of the ice melts." I closed my eyes, not that there was much difference, but I needed to center myself before I lost my temper.

I needed to take care of Bee. That was all I could focus on.

"When is help coming?" I asked. My brain raced through the options.

"Nothing's changed. I'm sorry, Soupy."

I slammed the button to shut off the radio.

"Owen? Are you okay?" Bee asked in a small voice behind me.

It would be one thing if I was stuck up here alone, but I had an innocent person to take care of. She didn't even have proper shoes on. I had no idea how long until help would come. Benny Jr. and Azi should have been frantic to get help up here. They should be on the phone with the nearest search and rescue. But I knew the realities—a holiday, this weather, this tiny town. Even if we got outside help, we would be low on the priority list.

We had no source of heat. This was no longer a shitty situation, it was a dangerous predicament, and I had no idea what to do.

"Owen?" Bee's voice was closer. I turned, and she must have been reaching out blindly for me because I caught a finger in the corner of my eye. "Oh, sorry!"

"I'm right here." I grabbed her freezing hands and swore. I shucked my gloves and quickly thrust them toward her. "Put these back on."

"Wh-what's going on?"

"You need to stay warm. Do you have anything else in that bag that might help?"

She was silent for a beat. "No. I didn't think I would be needing anything."

"Shit." I spun in a circle and pulled off my beanie. I realized she should have been wearing that too. Her nose had been icy when we kissed. I tugged it off and found her head, pushed back her hood to slide it on before pulling the hood back up.

"Won't you need that?" she asked.

"No. I'll be fine with my hood." I tugged the hood from my sweatshirt out and covered my head, then zipped up the outer layer as high as it would go. All the heat from moments ago was gone. With every second, the air around us grew colder. I could almost feel the heat waves coming off my head, only to be instantly converted to cold.

This wasn't sustainable.

"Bee, it's going to get really cold now." I rubbed up and down her arms.

"Oh," she said. "Are we going to be okay?"

"Yes," I answered immediately. "We just have to stick it out a few more hours."

I never wished for something to be truer than I did at that moment.

"Okay." Her tone was uncharacteristically tentative.

"We're going to be fine." I grabbed her hand and pulled her back to the seat. I didn't even go through the pretense of asking her and pulled her right onto my lap. I was too scared to speak. I would sue Benny Jr. for every cent if anything happened to her. I rubbed her arms up and down through the heavy material.

When had this switch been flipped? When had she gone from the task I needed to complete to the person whose safety I prioritized over even my own? I'd only really known Bee these last few hours, but I already felt like I needed to protect her no matter what. She had plans and goals and was sweet and funny and a little scary.

"I'm okay," she said softly.

I grunted. She was now.

I pulled her close and had her tuck her legs so that no part of her touched the frigid box. At first, it wasn't too bad. I almost thought we would be okay if it weren't for that damn wind.

But after another silent half hour, my worries became an obsessive loop I couldn't shake. Each worst-case scenario posed was more horrible than the last. The fears were incessant, gnawing. Her body trembled in my lap. What was the right thing to do in this situation? I could give her more of my layers, but if something happened to me, I couldn't help her.

"Owen?"

I couldn't watch Bee succumb to the cold. She had plans;

she didn't deserve this. I should have never listened to Benny Jr. I should have never answered his call.

"Owen?" she said, poking me.

I made another grunt of acknowledgment.

"You're shaking me. With the wind, it's making me feel queasy."

I stopped bouncing my leg. "Sorry."

"Can you answer me a question?"

"I'm not in the mood for any more games," I said.

"I wasn't going to suggest that," she said sharply. "But also, rude."

"Sorry." I squeezed her closer, resting my forehead on her shoulder for a second. "Sorry," I repeated. "I'm just pissed." I didn't want to admit I was scared. "At the situation."

"I know. But this is a serious question," she said.

I had nothing but worry in my brain, so I only grunted again. Anxiety made it nearly impossible to do anything but focus on what was going wrong.

"What would you do? If I weren't here?" she asked.

I wouldn't be here if it wasn't for her. My anger shot out in all directions. It wasn't her fault that Benny Jr. couldn't operate a safe machine. If I left her up there and just lied to my boss, all this would have been avoided and I could have still been paid. Maybe.

"Be honest," she added.

"It would be no different. I would have to wait until morning," I lied.

She shot up off my lap. I couldn't see her but felt the shifting of the thin flooring and heard her footsteps moving back and forth. It was too cold for this. I wished she'd come back.

"You're lying. There were two options when we first got stuck. Staying put was the safer option. It doesn't seem like you feel that way anymore if your worry is any indication."

"Bee."

"Just tell me what you would do. There's that cabin. Not far from here. It's for emergencies. Hunters. Hikers. Uh, whoever might need it. There's food. A wood-burning stove and blankets. We should go there."

I ran a hand over my face. "It's not so easy."

Her voice was right in front of me again. "Neither is this."

"There is a catch. As you can imagine, it's on the ground," I said.

"Right. I figured. I'm clever like that."

"It's risky trying to get down that ladder."

"How risky?" she asked.

I let a long sigh out. "Broken-femur-risky, or worse. I really don't know. It doesn't reach all the way to the ground. We would have to jump."

"Better than freezing to death."

"I'm trying to decide that."

"Owen, we need to get to that cabin. It's colder in here every minute. How many hours until they even get the ball rolling on a rescue attempt?" Her voice came close as she leaned above me, and my hands automatically found her hips. "I'm scratching into frost right now on the glass. If it's only going to get worse, we can't stay up here. We have no idea how long it will be until somebody comes. It's a holiday, and everybody is probably drunk."

I swore under my breath. She wasn't saying anything I hadn't already thought about.

"It's bad out there. You don't even have shoes," I said, though I had no idea why I felt combative. Neither of these options was good.

"I have shoes. And"—there was rustling as she moved about —"I have some plastic bags. I will put them over my shoes to waterproof my feet. It's not that far, right?"

"The visibility is bad. We can't risk getting separated," I said.

"Then we find a rope or something and tie ourselves together."

"Let me think," I growled.

Every option needed to be weighed. Too many things could go wrong. Better the monster you know? I wasn't sure. If there were a clear right and wrong answer, this wouldn't be so hard, but there wasn't. It was just the lesser of two evils. And I didn't know which was which.

"Think of the fire. And the real blankets. Of the bathroom," she added with a whine. "God, there is a bathroom, right?"

I chuckled dryly despite everything. "Yeah." Undoubtedly, we would be better off in the cabin than here. I could all but feel her shivers wracking the whole tram. But that jump, if something bad happened, we couldn't get medical help for hours. I wouldn't be able to live with myself if she got seriously injured. This was beginning to feel like one of those terrible, scary movies where one bad thing happened after another. And just when you thought it couldn't get any worse, the *power goes out*.

"Shit, I don't know," I said, completely torn. "If we jump, there's no coming back. There's no way we'd be able to climb back up," I explained, holding her arm so that even if I wasn't able to hold her gaze, she would feel my sincerity.

She blew air out of her lips, waited a moment, then put her hand on top of mine. "I'll decide for you. We're doing this."

Her determination buoyed me. I chewed my lip. Tugged at my hood. Stood up. Spun in a circle and found her again to grip her shoulders.

"Okay." I swore under my breath. "Okay. But I'll jump first … if it's not survivable, you'll know not to jump."

"Your pep talks could use work, but let's do this," she said with a shaky laugh.

# Chapter 14

Bee

EVERY OUNCE OF BULLHEADED SELF-ASSUREDNESS WENT out the proverbial window the second the literal window opened. Okay, it was the door, but that wasn't clever wordplay.

We spent ten minutes making a plan and gathering supplies. We found headlamps and a few more blankets to wrap around ourselves that would help with the wind. Owen radioed to Azi to inform everyone of our new plan. If I wasn't careful, a sense of guilt gnawed at me.

In hindsight, should I have tried to lock myself in the tourist shop overnight and cut my hair in a fit of desperate inspiration? Probably not, but there was no changing the past and so here we were.

Still, I wished Owen wasn't quite so worried. The fear in his set jaw and pinched brow was bothersome.

Since our kiss—and yes, I was aware that the situation was now dire and my priorities were jacked—I couldn't help but want more of him. It might take some time to get me riled up, but once that motor was revved, it couldn't be stopped. I was aware of every movement he made as I held the flashlight for him. The gentle strength in his massive body. The way he fussed over my clothes, insisting I keep the hat and gloves. His forehead was creased with stress that I wanted to smooth away with kisses. I wanted to be swept up into his lap and let him toss me around in any way he saw fit.

"Okay. We can do this." His shoulders heaved up and down in the beam of the flashlight.

I nodded, shivering from head to toe.

"Just remember to keep a cool head. That's the most important thing," he said.

I clicked my tongue. "You've said that four times now. I'm starting to think you aren't just telling yourself."

He was silent; the light from my headlamp made him squint. "I'm just reminding you."

"I'm great in high-pressure situations," I said.

"Like when you attacked me in the bathroom?"

"Self-defense," I mumbled.

"Or the spider?"

"Are we going or wasting time rehashing the evening's events?"

"Okay," he said and took a bracing breath.

He pulled apart the doors, then used his body to keep them propped.

The breath was stolen from my lungs with the blast of freezing air. With the realities of life outside the tram, I forgot all about the kiss. Or at least moved it down the priority list, just below survival. The snow was no longer friendly fat flakes as it had looked from the top of the mountain. It was sneaky fingers that burrowed into every nook and cranny. The wind sliced icy shards across any and all exposed skin.

Welp. We were screwed.

"Bee?" Owen yelled from where he blocked me from falling out the open door. "Don't look down!"

So, obviously, I did. He should have said "Don't look up" if he was serious.

It was a terrible mistake. Time and space zoomed in and out. My vision narrowed down to a pinpoint at the same time, it shot out infinitely. My knees went watery. My gut churned. There was a deep instinctual voice of survival that yelled, *This is the way to death, turn back!*

This was why it was best to act and not think. Too much planning meant living through scenarios that may never happen. And if they were to happen, why experience them more than once?

I could hardly hear Owen over the screaming weather, but he gave me the play-by-play of how to get to the center pole where the ladder was located so we could climb down and jump.

"Lots of fresh powder. Like a blanket." I nodded, even though only bits and pieces of his words were being processed. "Once I'm down, I'll flash the light three times to let you know when you're clear to follow."

I gnawed at my bottom lip, heart racing. The jump itself was scary enough, but the cabin that seemed so close when traveling on the tram in the past was hardly a pale smear in the pitch-black. How long would the trek in the snow be? God, this was a mistake, and we should stay.

I couldn't change my life if I were dead.

With his body still twisted to block the door, he grabbed my shoulders. "You are right. This is the best plan. The cabin. The fire. It's all good. We got this. Okay?"

I nodded, stomach dangerously close to heaving the Pop-Tarts. "The b-bathroom," I added helpfully.

"Yes. Right. Okay. Come out to the ledge with me. The doors are gonna snap shut without the power on," he said.

Not surprisingly, the tram was not designed to be climbed. However, in the spot where it got stuck, the tower allowed workers to climb to the top and make repairs. That meant we just had to hold on to the exterior rail for a few steps before we reached the relative safety of the tower.

With the supplies on his back, he let me pass. The whole tram rocked more when clinging to its exterior. The air bit through the layers, even with his hat and gloves on. My bag-wrapped shoes had little purchase, so I clung to the handrails that lined the side with my whole body. Every second, I was taunting death.

"We just need to step onto the tower. Then the ladder." He let go of the doors, and they snapped shut, his foot barely getting out of the way in time. The tram swayed dangerously, and I moaned, the bar cutting into my arm. His face was colorless when I checked on him. He blinked back from the beam of the flashlight. "I'm okay. I'm going to go around you," he shouted. "Just follow me as close as possible."

As soon as he passed, I gripped him with one hand and the handrail with the other.

I clung to his middle as best I could as we slowly scooted off the tram onto the massive tower surrounding it. There was more room and more grips to hold on to. My adrenaline was coursing so hard that I couldn't feel the cold anymore.

"I'm going down." Owen descended the ladder, flashlight clenched between his teeth.

Every step away from me, the fears poured in.

*Cold. Loud. Fear. Death. Help.*

This wasn't happening. This couldn't be happening. We were scaling a tower in the middle of a snowstorm because it was the *safe* choice. All because I hadn't been invited to a party. Was I really the world's most self-centered person? Or had my heart been broken so many times that it couldn't find empathy as easily? Either way, Owen didn't deserve any of this. Fear and guilt battered me harder than the wind.

He shouted something, but I couldn't make it out. I could only stare, blinking back freezing tears, as his light grew dimmer and dimmer.

Then gone.

I was meant to follow right behind, but I struggled to get my body moving. This was a first for me. This had been the plan I pushed. I closed my eyes, sucked in a deep, freezing, motivating breath, choked on a snowflake, coughed a few times, then forced myself to move.

I started down the ladder after him, one shaking step at a time. Slowly, and with intent, I moved one foot then the other, arms threaded through the rungs as gravity did its best to help. I started to find a pattern and focused on the rhythm of my body. Just when I thought I might make it, my stupid bagged foot slipped right off the rung. I gasped out and smacked my chin on the step as I flailed to hold on.

There was a shout lost in the wind below.

I squeezed my eyes tight, sweating despite it all. There were no other options. I had to keep moving. I gripped the ladder, pits and hands damp with sweat. I closed my eyes, begging to just hold on a few more feet. Just a few more feet. Just one more jump and the worst was over.

When I reached the point where the rungs ended, I waited for the sign from Owen. The hazy abyss stared back at me, blurred and chaotic. Flakes whizzed past through the beam of light from my flashlight. I squinted my eyes, trying to make him out, trying to see anything.

*Panic.*

*Fear.*

"Owen," I moaned, realizing that my teeth were chattering so hard that the muscles in my jaw ached.

Nothing.

He fell. His legs were broken. I shouldn't have done this. This was all my fault. I was selfish to think I could change my lot in life, any more than a tiger could change its spots. Wait, a lion could change their stripes? Whatever. I wanted to go back to the comfort of my home. I wanted to forget any of this ever happened. Who would feed the cats?

A flash in the darkness.

Then another and a third.

I sobbed out in relief, and the sound was instantly carried away. It wasn't as far as I thought. He was just a few feet below. Fresh snow. Like a bed.

I took a bracing breath. I slid down the remaining rungs so only my hands held me in Owen's too-large gloves. I was slipping with every second; the jump would be made with or without my consent.

"Three ... Two ... One ... Happy New Year!" I screamed as I let go.

The ground came up so much faster than I thought it would. It was both hard and squishy. It moaned with an *oomph*.

That wasn't the ground; that was Owen. His strong arms once again banded around me.

He was shouting questions at me that I could hardly make out through the blood pounding in my ears.

"I did it! I did it! Oh my God, I did it!" I shouted, flailing my arms in victory. I think I hit his face as he continued to brace my hips.

"You did it!" he shouted, a goofy grin on his features as he moved the flashlight to inspect me.

"I feel like a god! I should book a backpacking trip to Europe. I should skydive. I should finally sign up for that fitness class!" Even I could tell that last one was a promise I wouldn't keep outside the heat of the moment.

I spun and realized I was now straddling him where he lay supine on the ground. "Why are you lying down?"

"For the view," he said dryly.

"Not really the time." I scooted off him, slipping as I came to stand. I held out a hand and helped lift him. I was strong.

"Are you okay? Are you hurt?" he asked.

"No, no, I'm fine. Are you?" I patted his face.

"I'm fine. You hit my junk when you landed, but other than that, I'm fine."

"Oops, sorry."

"I'm used to it. I'm gonna tie us together now. Hold the flashlight," he explained.

I couldn't stop whooping as he tied us together. I kept hitting his arms—in a loving way. "I can't believe we did it."

"I'm just relieved to be on the ground." He tugged on the rope, testing the knot, and I fell into his arms. I wrapped my arms around his shoulders and jumped up to kiss his face. I was high on adrenaline and not shattering my bones. He blinked dazedly down at me before a wind pushed me further against him.

"Let's get moving," he said, but not before bending to press one more kiss against my cheek. It thrilled me.

I didn't care if it was motivated by his brush with death. I still liked it.

"Stay as close as possible," he instructed.

"You know where to go?" I tilted to see around him, but as was the theme of the day, I only saw a darkness.

The problem with being on the ground now was that the emergency cabin had completely disappeared. I was completely turned around and discombobulated from the jump and couldn't even tell which way was up. It was still so eerie that anything could be seen at all. Blackness was all around where the flashlight wasn't. In the light, the beam showed drifts of white and never-ending snow falling sideways, like a bad dream impossible to wake from.

He turned in the direction of the supposed cabin, which was, unfortunately, directly into the wind. I had my eyes mostly closed, holding the flashlight, but feeling my way and being mostly pulled along by Owen. His size and strength brought me comfort. It was unimaginably loud. I hadn't expected that. Only the comforting crunch of his boots could be heard, in addition to the screaming wind battering at my face and neck.

The bags on my feet were a terrible idea. Sure, they were dry, but I had no traction. I gave up trying to stomp through the shin-deep snow after only a few yards. Instead, I attempted to glide, being carried along as I was.

By the third fall, Owen stopped and turned.

"Maybe the bags weren't such a good idea," I shouted.

He looked down at me and then behind him. "It's okay. We aren't that far." He bent and scooped me up.

"Owen! You can't carry the bag and me!" I tried to grab the straps of the bag. "At least let me carry the bag."

He looked at me, waiting.

"Okay, I see." Making the connection with a palm to my forehead. "You'd still be carrying us both. All right, well, carry on, then."

He shifted me, and I tucked my face into his neck. He smelled so good, even with the added cold and wet smell. My whole body trembled uncontrollably. His features were twisted with worry, and I smiled in return, wrapping my arms around his neck and squeezing.

"I've got you," he said simply.

And I believed him. I was completely safe with this man. He wouldn't let anything happen to me, and it was as if the weight of the world melted off me.

Right after I'd fallen on top of Owen Campbell was the moment I fell hard *for* him.

# Chapter 15

Owen

IF THE SNOW WASN'T UP TO MY KNEES, I WOULD HAVE fallen to earth to kiss the ground the moment I made it out of the tram and down that ladder. I had never been so damn happy to be stuck in a snowstorm. Anything was better than another moment swaying in the wind. As it turned out, having Bee knock me down and then straddle me was just as welcome.

Everything else felt manageable now, including caring for Bee, which was my priority. Holding her in my arms steadied me. I imagined this was how monks felt in deep meditation. Only her. Only the task at hand. She went so quiet. This scared me more than anything. She tucked her face into me. Her shivers were nonstop.

With every step, her body shook in mine. Over and over, my mind repeated a mantra.

*One more step. One more step.*

I didn't even feel the cold or the weight of her or her thirty pounds of sugary snacks. Just focused on getting her to the cabin.

Any second, the light would have come into view. I was headed in the right direction. I had to be. It was dark. The scariest sort of dark imaginable. It was hard to keep my bearings and sense of direction as the wind messed with my equilibrium. Every footstep, every huff of breath, was the same, seeming to go nowhere. The treadmill steps of a bad dream. Bee burrowed tight into my chest, me trudging forward slowly but surely, the wind screaming in our ears, the darkness all around except the beam of my headlamp and the streaks of white through it.

We would not die out here.

"Well, that's g-g-good," she stuttered through a shiver.

I was distantly aware of the cold wetness seeping into my boots, up to my knees. Every step was careful. A quarter mile at this rate could take an hour. Would she survive? Would I drop her? Or worse.

If I could just see the cabin. If I could just know this had been the right choice to make.

"There!" she screamed in my ear. I jerked my head but saw the light at the same time. Thank every god that ever existed.

I fought the urge to run and risk an avoidable injury, like a car accident close to home.

"Thank you, Owen. Oh God, thank you, thank you," Bee repeated over and over.

I wanted to tell her to stop thanking me that this was just as much my fault as it was Benny's. I had the choice to leave her up there, and I hadn't taken it. Even though the money motivator was not for me, it seemed like such a small thing now.

We made it to the door, and I set her down and punched in the code Azi provided us when I radioed him to let him know we were going for it. My hands were almost frozen without gloves, and I fumbled the numbers.

"Let me do it," Bee said, shoving the gloves at me. "You

should have been wearing these," she grumbled as she got the door open and dragged me inside the threshold.

We stumbled through the door, pushing back to slam it shut against the wind that fought us tooth and nail every step. It wasn't warm by any means, but with the sturdy insulation, it was already light-years better.

We both sagged against the wall and sighed. My ears rang without the roaring of the storm.

I had never been so happy to see a crappy sex hut in all my life.

Inside was a single-room cabin with a door leading to the restroom in the back—a glorified attached port-o-potty, from what I'd been told. The main room had a small kitchen table with two chairs next to a kitchenette area, a wood-burning stove with stacks of wood, and, of course, a large bed stacked with thick comforters smack dab in the middle. Some cheeky previous occupants even left battery votives all around to really set the ambiance. Other than that, it was a basic undecorated mountain cabin space.

We both dropped the multiple layers of foil blankets wrapped around us in a pile by the door. Bee shucked off her hat—*my* hat—and tossed it near where the fire would be before shaking off all the snow from her like a dog fresh out of a lake.

I followed suit, peeling off my soaking boots and heavy wet coat. Bee kept her snowsuit on. Thankfully, it was still mostly dry from the blankets.

"It's beautiful," Bee said, stepping forward to fall face-first onto the bed. "Holy crap, we're alive." Her voice was mumbled from the bed. She lifted her head, arms still at her side like a sea lion, and looked down with a grimace. "I hope whoever was here last changed the sheets."

"We'll change them just in case," I said.

We shared a brief look and quickly glanced away. No need

to discuss sleeping arrangements yet. That may not even be necessary. The adrenaline was quickly crashing, and the exhaustion from this very long day was setting in as the image of bikini-clad Bee wrapped in my arms under all those blankets dominated my thoughts.

"Come here," I said to Bee, even as my voice came out rougher than intended.

She hefted herself off the bed to come over without a single complaint. Her features were neutral and hard to read, if not slightly skeptical. I turned Bee in a slow circle to examine every inch of her. I held her face in my hands and peered over her. Her cheeks and nose were bright red. Bits of her hair stuck out in wild directions or were plastered to her face. There was a small cut on her chin, and the skin around it was already bruising slightly.

"What happened here?" I asked with a frown.

"The ladder jumped out at me."

I huffed an unsmiling laugh.

"I'll clean it after I get the room warmed up. Anything else hurting?" I asked. I soothed and petted her, unable to keep my hands off her. I rubbed up and down her arms, brushing away any excess moisture still clinging to her. Whatever this feeling was that had come over me, it wasn't familiar. I just knew that I had to keep her safe. The urge to protect her, care for her wounds, and get her warm was deep and instinctual.

"Wait? Did I die? This would make sense," she mumbled.

"Take off those bags, and let me look at your feet."

"It's so hot when you talk dirty to me." She shucked off the bags, almost falling over in the process as her eyes moved over the small one-room cabin. "It ain't much, but it sure is beautiful. Oh my God, the bathroom. Bye!" She ran off as soon as the bags and shoes were off, to the small door in the corner of the cabin. "Ah! The toilet seat is freezing," she yelled. "I'm remembering the kid from *Christmas Story* and am terrified my butt cheeks will get stuck ... nope, I'm good. Phew."

"I'll get the fire started," I called back, chuckling as she over-shared. Maybe with anybody else it would feel like TMI, but with Bee, every unfiltered thought was like a yummy bit of candy, snatched up and to be savored.

It was still very cold in the cabin, but it was small, and it wouldn't be long until the space warmed up. I radioed to Azi and let him know we made it safe. He said he would tell Benny Jr., which was good because if I talked to my boss, I wasn't sure what I'd say to him. Nothing suitable for keeping my job at this point.

A minute later, she sauntered out with a sigh. "It wasn't what I expected, but I'm so glad we're here. Since you're taking care of the fire, I'll put the food away." She dumped out the contents of her bag on the small table in the corner. "Okay, done."

I laughed, and the swelling emotion in my chest had doubled at her return. She sauntered around in those ridiculous clothes, peeking through drawers and the single closet.

"Listen, I'm not trying to scare you," Bee started.

I stilled from where the jumping flames started to sting my frozen hands to look at her.

"But I'm ninety percent sure I saw a guinea pig from the little window in the bathroom."

I sucked in a breath. "All the way up here?" I headed to the small kitchen area and rifled through the drawers to see what other supplies were there.

"Yeah, but it didn't look like the ones in town. It had a harder edge. Like it'd *seen* things." I turned to her as she stared into the distance, letting her eyes go unfocused. "They've already formed gangs. What if some have gone completely feral and off-grid?" she asked, horror widening her dark eyes.

"They'd be like the backwoods branch of the ones in town," I riffed back.

"We find them sitting on their tiny porches, plucking at a banjo ... collecting tourists."

"Mm-hmm," I did my best impression of Billy Bob in *Sling Blade.*

"AH!" she yelped and shuddered. "You're too good at that."

I laughed and slid open another drawer to find a sealed bottle of lube and a box of condoms. I slammed it shut and cleared my throat. "Do me a favor and pull up that chair in front of the fire," I said as I kept searching.

"Sure. Are you looking for something?"

"Yep. And I just found it." I grabbed a towel from a small pantry and walked to Bee.

"Sit down," I instructed.

She looked up at me and held my gaze. I thought for sure she was going to argue. Instead, her cheeks went pink, and she obeyed. Why was she suddenly so good at listening when the first part of the evening had been nothing but trouble?

It was a powerful, heady feeling, this commanding her.

"I can't stop thinking about this," I said, standing behind her.

She squeaked. "What?" I laid the towel around her shoulders, and she flinched before relaxing. "What are you doing?"

"I can't let you go back to town looking like this. It would make an impression, but not what you're going for, I don't think." I scratched my nails up her scalp and tugged on all the various lengths of roughly cut hair, trying to see what I was working with.

She shivered but didn't comment. Goose bumps prickled up the back of her exposed neck. "Is it that bad?"

"It's not great. Unless you're feeling the mullet look."

She snorted. "I could rock it."

"Can I give you a little trim?" I asked her. "Not that you haven't done a great job." I held up two pieces with very different lengths.

She snorted. "In my defense, I only meant to give myself bangs."

My eyebrows raised.

"Things got out of hand quickly. We don't need to talk about it."

Without thinking, I bent and kissed the top of her head. "It's not that bad. I'm just going to even things out."

She nodded, mouth slightly parted, eyes wide as she watched me in the small mirror. I combed through her hair as best I could. The wind and hat had done a number on it. She leaned forward, pulled a brush out of her bag, and handed it to me. Carefully, I ran the brush through her hair. When she moaned and closed her eyes, I ground my molars. I began to section off her hair and twist it out of the way as best as I could.

"Where did you learn to do this?" she asked once it was quiet for too long.

"I cut Ivy's hair sometimes."

"And who is Ivy again?" She tilted her head in confusion, and I almost cut her ear.

"Be still."

"Sorry. That's like telling the wind not to blow."

"Ivy is my friend at Golden Sunset," I explained. "She used to be my teacher."

"Oh, Mrs. Flores!" She turned to look at me.

"Bee," I growled. "You're two seconds from losing more than hair."

"Sorry. I usually just cut my own ends at home. When your hair is that long, it's less noticeable if you have no idea what you're doing. And less risk of serious bodily harm."

"This is a big change for you." Bee had always had hair

down to her lower back as long as I'd known her. "All this because of a statue?"

"Yep. That and the realization that nobody in this town knows I exist," she said in that same joking manner that didn't feel like a joke at all. Hurt was hidden in her self-effacing jokes all night. "Like sixty-forty. Do you often cut Mrs. Flores's hair?"

"Just when she asks." I wasn't thrilled the focus was back on me.

"You've kept in touch since school?"

"Yeah."

"You're going to make me drag this out of you, aren't you?" When I didn't answer, she sighed and went on. "Tell me about how you got to cutting Mrs. Flores's hair. Seems like a big change from student-teacher."

The scissors from the cabin weren't meant for cutting hair, but they were much better than the pair she'd been using when I found her. I focused on cutting as I shared without giving too much away.

"She was my favorite teacher. She was there for me a lot in school, and we kept in contact. I like being around her. She sees me." I cleared my throat. Bee was so open it was hard to guard against that. "I like being around there too. Older people have great stories and advice to share. When they're behaving themselves, at least. Ned Fled is awfully surly."

"At that age, can you blame him?" she asked.

"I guess not."

"Does her family think it's weird that you two hang out?"

I snorted. Not one to mince words, that Bee. "She doesn't have much family. Her son isn't in the picture unless he needs something." I refrained from sharing that he'd already taken every penny from her, so he wouldn't be back to visit any time soon.

"That's nice you still visit with her. I had her too. She was great. I should visit her too." She drummed her hand on her knee and then added, "Do you like working for Benny Jr.?"

"Does anybody like their job? Besides you," I added when I felt her getting ready to counter.

"Probably some people. I just mean, is this the job you envisioned for yourself?"

"I'm not really good at anything else."

"Other than what?"

"Being big and intimidating," I said, staying focused on the task.

"That's incredible that you've tried everything else in the world, to know that is the only thing you're good at." Her voice was heavy with sarcasm.

"Don't be snarky to the person holding the scissors."

"I'm serious. You don't know what you're good at yet," she said.

"I don't have a degree or anything. After I lost my football scholarship, college wasn't an option."

She waited a beat, and I thought she would ask about football again. Instead, she said, "You can go back to school. Or get certifications."

"It's not that easy." My voice came out too sharp. This conversation made me uncomfortable. I focused instead on the hair.

My back began to twinge at the bend I needed to reach her head. Dropping to my knees, I knelt in front of her, grabbing the pieces framing her face and bringing them forward.

Her mouth was pursed in a soft O shape as her wide eyes flicked between mine. Her cheeks still rosy from the rapid changes in temperature.

"It wouldn't be easy. But neither is doing a job that you hate that goes against your own personal code of ethics," she said softly.

I frowned, wondering how I'd given so much away. Maybe because Bee seemed to go so unnoticed by the rest of town, she was able to observe others easily.

"I never said—"

"I can just tell you hate it." She lifted a hand to my cheek, causing my heart to hammer hard. I was exposed and anxious under her stare. She bit her lip as she brushed her thumb over my cheek. "You're so thoughtful and gentle, Owen. You got me here safe. Thank you."

I swallowed and gave a nod of acknowledgment. It didn't feel like I had done it all alone. Despite our start, it had felt like we were quickly becoming a team. I balanced on my knees in front of her and felt myself coming undone. In such a short time, all my lines were becoming blurred.

"Maybe that's your calling," she said after the silence went too long for her liking.

"Uh, I'd wait until I finished your hair before you said that." I tried her joking tactic.

"I meant working at the retirement village. You'd be great there," she said, not being distracted.

I was ready to argue against and get defensive like I always did when I felt insecure, but I couldn't help myself. The way she held my face in her small hands made my defenses wobble.

"Why do you think that?" I asked.

"You already know you enjoy being around older folks. And clearly, they like you, or they wouldn't keep letting you hang out there. Sure, you're also big and strong, which would come in handy. But you're also ridiculously patient." She huffed a laugh. "Look at how you've put up with me all night." A frown flashed over her features before she quickly brushed it away. It hadn't felt like I was putting up with her, it had felt like I was falling into her. A blush burned up the back of my neck at her praise.

"All of that could make you really great at working there,"

she went on. "You could get a nursing degree or a certification or maybe even a master's eventually in physical therapy if you really wanted. I could totally see it."

"People cross the street to avoid me," I said, too close to admitting how that fact hurt me.

I leaned back on my heels, and she dropped her hands back into her lap.

"If you let people see this side of you, I bet they would quickly change their opinion." Her hands drifted to the ends of the hair I'd finished cutting.

"I've never been accused of helping people feel safe."

"Yeah, this town isn't really known for being observant. At least not in my case." There was that laugh again she made when she was trying to downplay her own hurt. "Everyone's got you all wrong, haven't they? You're just a big old teddy bear." Her mouth quirked in a smile that made me want to kiss her.

I made a sound of acknowledgment but couldn't look directly at her anymore. My heart and soul were longing for things they couldn't have. I pictured a life where I went to work at a job that made me feel fulfilled and came home to a spunky brunette who kept me on my toes …

I collected the towel and went to shake it in the trash. Bee didn't know the truth about my violent past. If she did, she would understand why none of her ideas were possible.

# Chapter 16

Bee

My feelings for Owen were full-blown. He was so smart and handsome and kind and safe and protective, and so many feelings rushed through me as he knelt in front of me that I couldn't find the words. I felt restless and anxious. We were here safe and it felt like a clock started ticking. I wanted to kiss him again now that the extremely real threat of death was gone. I didn't want this precious time together to end.

I looked in the small round mirror above the table to study his work.

"Whoa. Owen ..." I turned side to side, examining. "I look quite pret-tay," I said in my best Keira Knightly impression, wondering if he understood the *Love, Actually* reference.

Owen cleared his throat. He did that a lot in lieu of speaking whatever first popped into his head. What that must be like—thinking before speaking.

"It suits you," he said.

"I know. I look so chic." I turned to him. "You are a man of many hidden talents, Mr. Campbell."

He made another uncomfortable sound.

I looked back at myself one more time and didn't even recognize the woman looking back. In a good way. A rush of confidence surged through me. The chin-length bob matured me in a way I didn't even realize I was so desperate for. The natural free-spiritedness that represented me was still there in the rough cut and the disheveled waves. More than that, I felt powerful and sexy. That feeling of optimism that could only come with a major life change straightened my shoulders and lifted my chin. Like Mary Poppins, my reflection gave me a saucy wink.

NYNB was back on track.

I spun in a circle, examining the Hookup Hut, with its big lumpy bed and cozy cottage *soft*core vibes, I couldn't help but feel a wave of ... something. Almost like a sentimentality for this moment, even though I was still in it. It made the tightening in my chest worsen.

*Time was running out.*

Owen's large arms and gentle hands stole my focus. His massive frame moved with a grace born of confidence that was irresistible. The way he continued to protect me, and his surprisingly deep well of sensitivity and thoughtfulness infiltrated my brain. My palms longed to run over his muscles and learn his body. I wanted to feel his weight until I almost couldn't breathe. I wanted Owen to be so close to me, in me, that my existence relied on his physical touch.

I wanted to lick that man like the Pop-Tarts filling.

The fire blazed in the stove now, and with the vents wide open, the small space was already warm. Owen built me a fire like nobody's business. Another stamp in his Irresistible Man Passport. His kiss had been wonderful, but he held himself back. I never understood that. What was he holding back for? What was he waiting for? There would never be another night like this. Another opportunity so perfect for us to come together. Maybe he just needed a little push. Owen was a catch, but how did one go about seducing a catch like him? Maybe another treat to set the mood? But not everybody was complex carb motivated.

"So ... what to do, what to do?" I strolled back and forth in front of the bed, gently brushing my fingertips along the quilt, sashaying my hips with emphasis as I bit my lip and fluttered my eyelashes at him. The loud fabric of my snowsuit ruined the effect, but I pretended not to notice. Maybe there were condoms hidden up in this joint I could discreetly toss at him.

Owen stood back from me, hands loosely clasped, color high on his cheeks. He looked like he was running security for a concert. Maybe this was his natural state of being. His thighs tested the seams of his jeans, and his biceps, traps, and all those fancy arm muscles were on full display now under a dark flannel. His eye tracked my every movement, but his features remained hard and unreadable.

"Phew, that fire sure warmed it up in here quickly." I brought my hands to the zipper. "I should take off some layers," I said in a deep, sultry voice.

It must be that my feminine wiles were too much for him. At this rate, he might be seconds from dropping to his knees and crawling toward me.

"What's wrong with you?" he said with a head tilt of confusion.

Or not.

"Ugh." I flung my hands out to the side.

Stupid men. Stupid snowsuits. Stupid forced proximity that should guarantee a hookup, but alas ...

"Bee, are you trying to—Are you okay?" he asked cautiously.

"No. It's a million degrees in this thing. I want to take it off." This wasn't a seduction attempt anymore. This was me roasting alive in these ancient clothes from the humiliation of being rejected in a situation that should have been a guaranteed slam dunk ... home run ... whatever. I never did get sports metaphors.

I tugged at the zipper on the snowsuit in earnest. The fabric was a sensory nightmare as my skin grew damp, and the highly flammable poly-whatever-blend clung to me.

"This frickin' zipper—" With each movement, I tugged at the zipper, but a piece of fabric had gotten stuck in the teeth, and I couldn't even see what I was doing because it was so big my face disappeared into it every time I looked down. My muffled voice held a whine. "Is ... stuck."

I pulled my arms in to try to get out another way, but all that did was turn me into a giant sausage. With my head stuck in a prison of my own making, I could only hear Owen's soft chuckles.

"You look like one of those inflatable things at car lots."

"It's not funny," I said, still muffled.

"It's a little funny. You'll think so later."

"Ugh." I flailed one last time but had only succeeded in getting myself hotter. And accidentally smacking him.

"Ow," he said.

"Help me." I sniffled. So much for my debut seduction.

"Oh, Bee," he said closer now. "I've got you." He'd said the same thing when he scooped me up and carried me through a horrifying snowstorm.

I believed him. I felt so safe with him. I stopped my struggle when the floor creaked with his arrival to stand in front of me. I slowed my breathing, my stifling breath filling the hot space.

My body was pulled to and fro as he tugged. The beautiful sound of a zipper releasing ... and then, ah, sweet, fresh, cool air and light. I took a deep breath in and smiled up at him. He didn't smile back. He looked at me with pupils blown out in his light eyes. He used his two capable hands to push the sweaty strands off my face. My smile relaxed, and I licked my lips; he tracked the movement.

"Thank you," I whispered.

"You're your own worst enemy sometimes," he said softly.

"You have no idea."

Only a few inches were separating us; his chest rose and fell though nothing compared to my own. I was aware of every molecule of air brushing against my skin. The air held enough electricity to power this whole city. So maybe not a seduction fail?

Without breaking eye contact, I pushed the suit down all the way off my body.

Owen swallowed audibly. The hallows of his cheeks deepened as the muscles of his jaw flexed.

His eyes never moved an inch from holding on to my own. I stepped back so that he could take in the whole view without needing to move them.

"Bee," he sighed my name, frustrated. I lifted one foot out and then the other.

When I reached up for the strings of my bikini, his hand shot out to stop me.

"Wait," he said.

My arms dropped to my sides. His own hands went to the buttons of his flannel.

"Now we're talking," I said.

He huffed, trying so hard not to smile. The tendons in his hands popped as his fingers worked with confident dexterity. His fingers were so thick and long, yet they took such care with their actions. Soon, his white undershirt revealed hard planes of muscles that I had only felt but never got to touch or see. His clean, masculine scent made my mouth water as he closed the distance between us again, shrugging out of the flannel. My heart was pumping blood so hard that I felt a little tremor with every beat. The heat. This moment. The way he *looked* at me, directly at me, with such soft fondness.

It meant so much to me. I was having a hard time slowing the growing realization in my chest. This wasn't just about the hookup, and I wasn't ready to examine that just yet.

This was how it could be. This was how people felt when they were really seen.

He looped his shirt over my shoulders. "Here. You can wear this for now."

Break squealing sounds screamed through my head.

"What?" I asked, softly. Stunned.

This was not where I thought we were going, not with that look in his eyes. Not with that earlier kiss in the tram. I knew he was too good to be true.

It didn't take long for my anger to burn away the embarrassment. It was a sinking sensation in my stomach, the utter humiliation of straight-up rejection.

"Bee," he growled my name this time.

"Seriously?" I asked. Fuse lit, rage burning bright, I went off. "Am I in a different room right now? Don't tell me that I'm imagining things with those looks you're giving me."

"That's not what I'm saying." He stepped back, hands up, and eyes looking anywhere else but my body on full display once again.

"What is it, huh? Seduce me to get me onto the tram? I knew nobody would be interested in me. I knew that you were just doing your job." I paced in a circle, grabbing my sides with my arms wrapped tight around my middle. Humiliation churned through me as I let my temper flare. It felt safer.

"Whoa, wait." He held up his hands. "Seduce you? I had to physically carry you—"

"I know I'm weird, okay? I know that despite not fitting in anywhere, I'm still totally invisible to anybody. I was somehow sheltered *too* much and left alone to my devices. I don't act like a normal woman, but I thought—" I flailed my arm to gesture to the bed.

"You're not weird—"

"I knew that I was developing a crush, only to be disappointed." I wasn't familiar with this feeling ripping through my chest. It hurt. It was like all the years of my life had caught up and it was all too much.

"Bee, why are you so angry? I'm being a gentleman," he said, teeth grinding.

"Why?" I asked. "Why don't you—shouldn't you want to—" My eyes were welling with hot tears when I glanced to the bed again.

He stepped closer. "My job is to bring you down the mountain to Benny Jr. What sort of person would I be if I-I crossed any lines?"

"Like when we kissed on the tram?"

"That was—" He scrubbed at his short hair. "I didn't mean to send mixed signals."

I huffed. "Too late. And I already told you that I'm not going to Benny Jr. That isn't happening. I'm going back up there, and you and your stupid Greek god body can't do anything to stop me. I'm going to that mountain, I'm completing my plan. And this town will not forget who I am, even if you do."

I stared to the side, I couldn't look at him. A single tear rolled down my cheek, and I hated that I looked pitiful when I was really angry.

"It's not like that," he said.

"I'm ignoring you." I went to the bed and sat with a harrumph, arms crossed. Feeling unbelievably childish but having no idea how to handle more rejection. This hurt far worse than the town's had.

I felt the bed shift as he sat down next to me, but I refused to look at him. I refused to be pitied. That panicked ache in my chest worsened like it was filling with a big wet paper towel that made a full breath impossible.

I thought Owen might have been a person who would want to be around me. I thought that I had found somebody who saw me when they looked at me ...

I shook my head; nails dug into my palms.

"Bee, please look at me. Let yourself hear what I'm saying."

But I didn't want to listen. It felt like it would cost something to turn and meet his eyes, and I'd already lost so much. I'd already played the foolish, naive woman all night. The price was too high to meet his gaze now, it would hurt too bad.

"Really look at me." He lifted my quivering chin, until our eyes were lined up, or at least I thought. I squeezed my eyes tighter, my heart racing. Why did this feel so scary? "Open your eyes." He chuckled with endearing frustration.

I couldn't help myself. I wanted to look at him; I wanted another moment of falling into his gaze, even if this was going to end and it was futile. Even if it hurt, even if the cost was the fragments of whatever remaining pride I never seemed to be good at collecting.

I wanted to look at him. I wanted to see and be seen, and I couldn't help myself.

I opened my eyes and met his gaze. He smiled softly, and I felt the final shred of dignity burn under his hot gaze.

Oh well. I would never be known for my decorum anyway.

My shoulders slumped, and I let him hold the weight of my head with his finger as I studied his blue eyes, strong jaw, and nose with a tiny little scar at the top, and his full bottom lip and thin top one.

"You keep talking about being overlooked," he said, waking me from my memorization. "But nothing about you and this night has been forgettable, Bee. You're the most interesting person I have ever met. These last few hours have changed me ir-irrecoverably," he said softly and carefully.

All my injustice and hurt evaporated like the superficial thing it always had been. Looking at the raw honesty pouring from him, it became clear that of the two of us, despite my bold claims to the opposite, only one of us here was truthful tonight.

I understood now that any attempt to seduce him was the growing understanding that this night would end, and I would lose a chance at closeness to him.

The desperation to hold him was only to *be* held for a little while longer.

But now it didn't feel so important, *this* felt important. This breathing of each other's air, this learning of how to talk to each other. Maybe that mattered more than any physical connections ever would.

"Trust me, I'm not forgetting about this night or you anytime soon." His hand moved from supporting me to wrapping around my neck, his thumb brushing along my jawline to send tremors throughout me. "But what sort of person would I be if I took advantage of this situation? How would you feel about yourself later? How would I feel about myself later?"

I let his words sink in and truly listened to him like I wanted to be heard.

And I understood then. Owen was a *good* man trying to do the right thing in a bonkers situation. A situation I had caused.

More than that, he was somebody I wanted in my life for more than a night, longer than the objective of a bored, rich man. I wasn't ready for this night to end. Every hour that ticked by meant going back to a life I never felt a part of. I would never be okay without him now, and that realization terrified me. It made me lash out in a ridiculous manner.

I had been lying to myself. I'd been watching and studying how "normal" humans operated from a dusty shelf on the edge of rooms my whole life. And I didn't want that anymore. Hadn't that been what NYNB was truly about? Changing how the world saw me?

I had to come clean about this night and what it meant if I wanted to change.

"It's not just about the statue, Owen," I started slowly, wrapping myself farther into his flannel.

"I'm listening," he said, and the relief was tangible in my neck and shoulders.

"I can't explain to you how it feels to be overlooked and forgotten time and time again. It changes a person's psyche. It makes me feel like I have no value. Tonight, I was meant to take the reins of my life back. I'd heard everybody talking about their big plans for the new year and I started thinking that I wanted that too. I thought getting that story published would help the statue, but it would also help me. And now, after these hours with you, I understand something else."

He held my hands, and I took a deep breaking breath in.

"I don't want this night to end and go back to normal," I started hesitantly, voice wobbling on its way out. "I think that if, in the future, your eyes move over me without stopping or seeing me like everybody else in this town, I-I think that I might just shatter into a million pieces," I said, my entire heart and soul on display for him to see.

And all I could hope was that he continued to handle me as gently as he had been.

# Chapter 17

Owen

BEE'S RAW HONESTY WAS A NEW LEVEL OF AUTHENTICITY that ripped through the last bits of chivalry that held me together. I scooped her fully to me. I held her trembling frame as close as I could without crushing her.

Go back to normal? I'd already forgotten what "normal" life was. Looking back was like Dorothy looking back to Kansas after the Technicolor experience of Oz. I'd been in a world of sepia tone until Bee splashed every color in the rainbow over everything.

I kissed her forehead as I found my words.

"Absurd," I said as I kissed her temple. "Silly." I kissed her other temple. "Maddening." I rubbed my nose along hers. "Woman." My lips brushed along hers.

She gasped, and her arms gripped me tighter.

"There is no going back to before. I just don't want to scare you." She spoke of her heart shattering, and it was how mine felt if she were to look at me the way the rest of the town did. If she saw me as a big dumb brute, but she hadn't yet and probably she never had.

"We only really met a few hours ago," I said.

It was a rationalization, a reminder to slow things down. We couldn't be behaving like this with just a few hours between us.

But did that matter? I said it but I hardly believed it. It felt like my soul had always known hers; I felt that I knew her and her needs instinctually. Poets talked of this connection, and I thought they all were just fools in love, but maybe there was something to finding a person who was genuinely meant to be in my life. A genetic design to it all. How had we been this close for all these years only to see how well we fit now?

It felt so easy with Bee, even when things were decidedly difficult.

Maybe this is what Ivy spoke of when she meant for me to put myself out there more because nothing ever felt like it could go back to how it was before.

"Trauma hours," Bee mumbled.

I pulled her back to study her and make sense of what she said. Her eyes were still closed, her lips swollen, her mouth slightly parted, her cheeks pink, her short hair framing her perfectly.

Gorgeous.

Breathtaking.

"What?" I asked.

Her eyes fluttered open, and it seemed to take her a second to remember what she said. "Trauma hours. It's like dog years. Time is subjective in crisis."

I chuckled as I kissed her lips because I had no idea what she was talking about. To be fair, only half the blood in my body was going to my brain at this point. "What does that mean?"

"We're trauma-bonded. It might have only been a few hours, but they were pretty critical hours. We had to get to know each other quickly and trust each other even faster than that." Her hands cupped my face, and she seemed to peer deeper into my eyes. "But it feels like more than that, doesn't it?"

I wanted to pretend I didn't know what she meant in a last-ditch effort to keep distance between us, but of course, I knew what she meant. It might have been the circumstances, but it was so much more too. It had to be Bee.

"Yeah, it feels like a lot more than that," I admitted, and my heart raced.

"And just in case I haven't made this clear, I'm not afraid of you, Owen." She brushed her fingertips along my cheeks. "If any of us should be scared, it's you. I've lost track of the times I've accidentally poked or hit you." She brought my knuckles to her lips and kissed them. "Why do I have to keep reminding you of that?"

I looked up to meet her eyes and swallowed thickly. I wanted her. She had no idea how bad.

"Being stuck here, I would never want you to think—" These hands were capable of violence. She couldn't understand.

"I don't—"

"But you don't have the whole picture."

"Then tell me." She shrugged and patted the bed next to us. "I'm not going anywhere."

"It's a long story," I said.

She scooted out of my lap and up to the headboard. She leaned back, and I knew what the next words would be out of her mouth before she even said them. "Lucky for us, we have nothing but time."

"I really set myself up for that one," I said and sighed.

"Yep."

As she settled in, I grew more uncomfortable. I wanted to come lie next to her, cuddle in the safety of her small frame, and scoop her up to me again. I wanted to touch her all the time, and she didn't seem to mind. But I saw what it took for her to confess her fears of tomorrow, and I owed her some truths of my own.

I stood to pace, checked the fire, and organized her numerous snacks; anything to avoid looking at her.

"I'm going to say this quickly because I hate talking about it," I said after a few minutes of awkward silence that Bee somehow managed to withstand.

She sat forward, a gentle frown tugging at her features. "Owen, if you don't want to, I understand. There's no pressure to—"

"No. I don't want to, but you need to know the sort of man I am."

She watched me for a moment, mouth open, poised to argue some point. Then she closed it without a sound. She swallowed and gave me one small nod, the familiar look of determination creasing her brows. A few hours and I could read her better than anybody and knew her thoughts and needs. It was insanity to think that. I mocked those who felt instant connections with people as hormones and horniness. I never thought it could be real, but nothing else explained this wild need to tell her the truth about these hands and this body before I touched her.

"Talk to me," she said, and it was permission and comfort. My confessional.

"In high school, my senior year, at the homecoming game, I tackled a linebacker from the visiting team. He ended up in the hospital in a coma for two days and never played football again," I said, like ripping off a Band-Aid. I gripped the basin of the sink, the muscles of my neck feeling like knots on knots. I hated talking about it, thinking about it. Not that it ever stopped. The crunch of his body when I impacted him and we fell to the ground was burned into my mind forever. "I hadn't meant to hit him so hard. I didn't know how strong I was."

A split second of violence made by my body, despite my unwilling mind, forever changed the course of my life.

She gasped and brought her hand to her mouth.

"I-I couldn't handle the guilt. I'd not gotten used to my body yet, before high school it started growing and never seemed to stop. I felt like Mr. Hyde but never got back to Dr. Jekyll. Not a single part of me felt comfortable. And then the one area where I felt like I at least served a purpose was the place where I ended up almost killing someone. It made me sick. It ate me alive. I didn't even like football. I was just good at it."

"I'm so sorry, Owen." Her hands reached for me but then dropped back into her lap when she saw I wasn't done with my pacing.

And now that I started sharing, I couldn't stop. I tossed my arms out as I walked a few feet in front of the bed.

"And the worst part was that nobody even seemed to be mad at me or tell me to back off on the field. If anything, people just confirmed that I was in the right position and pushed me harder. My dad made a joke about it and said it was all part of the sport. Nobody cared that I could have killed somebody."

I hadn't ever talked about this, and saying it out loud made it seem so much smaller. In my head, it was a dark shadow that loomed over every choice I made or decision that came without thinking. But once I spoke, it diminished in size—the opposite of saying the name of a boogeyman. Freedom shrunk its form.

"That's so awful," Bee said. "You were both just children. They should have protected you both."

I swallowed down the gulp of pain at those words. We were children. I could see that now, now that the shadow was out of my head. I was a child, and so was the boy that I'd hurt. But looking back, I'd never felt that way. People saw me as an adult because of my size. I had always been a weapon to be wielded.

I still was.

"I was all set to ride that sports scholarship to college, but I couldn't play after that. I couldn't even put my pads on without throwing up." I glanced at her, desperate to see what she thought of that, but all I found was a patient nod of understanding. "Back then, nobody understood. Except Ivy. She was there. She let me come to her class during lunch. I didn't hang out with the team after I stopped playing. I was exiled. Those first few days, when I wasn't sure if the kid was going to live or die, I had nobody except her. She would let me come to her classroom and let me cry silently in the corner—" I gasped a shaking breath in and out, thinking of that tormented version of myself. "She never shamed me or even tried to force me to talk. She'd just pat my shoulder or give me a book to read and let me be sad. It became a routine after that. To hide in her room and she let me mourn. I will never forget what that meant to me."

I clenched my jaw so hard, and my nostrils flared. My vision blurred, but I wouldn't cry anymore. I just needed to get it out.

"I will do whatever it takes to protect Ivy. When I dropped out of football, I lost my chance at any sort of real education. But I just couldn't play that sport anymore. I couldn't sleep without hearing the snap, that crunch. I hate feeling like I can't control this body—"

She got up and came to me then, a blanket draped over her shoulders. She wrapped her arms around my middle from behind and put her head on my back. I was thankful for her comfort but found I couldn't meet her gaze yet. She'd probably expected some big, strong man who never cried over something over ten years ago.

"After that ... violence was all I represented but never wanted. It's like I have this mark on me that everybody else can see that just says, 'Beware, capable of pain.' That's why I needed to tell you. What I'm capable of. The man I am."

She let out a breath, and I felt it through the fabric of my shirt.

"I know the sort of man you are." She squeezed my sides. "Turn around." I did, and she stood on her toes to cup my face. I could melt into her soothing caress. "You are strong when you need to be, but not violent. You apologized before when I made doing your job extremely difficult. A man who, even when picking me up mostly against my will, managed to do so gently." She took a breath, her gaze flicking back and forth between mine with ferocity. "And you even got me extra clothes and those cute chile socks so I wouldn't be cold. You sacrificed your own comfort to warm me up. You continue to be a wall of patient strength even as I berate and attack and annoy you without so much as lifting a finger in retaliation."

"I sort of like it," I admitted with a shrug.

Something dark flashed behind her already dark eyes. "And if you wanted to scare me or hurt me, you could have done so a hundred times over, but not once have I ever thought of you as violent. You are beautiful and gentle."

Embarrassment and flattery burned the tips of my ears.

"I know you've been told of all the horrible things you're capable of," she said and ran her fingertips from my hand and up my arm. "And I know other people's perception of us can shape us more than we want or know or wish, so, if that's the case, if you need a set of eyes to see yourself through, then you can borrow mine for a while. Because I think you are wonderful. Let yourself see you the way *I* see you." And the look she gave me caused everything I ever thought I knew to fall to the ground, and in the ruined ashes of my mind, there was only Bee and her outstretched arms.

I let out a sigh so long it felt like the first time I'd really breathed in a decade. "Bee." I bent and pulled her into my arms.

"So few have shown you love and gentleness throughout

your life, yet you seem to display it so fully for others like me and Ivy while not thinking yourself capable," she said. "Imagine the sort of love you'd bring people if you believed you could. Imagine the pleasure to be shared if you were simply instructed how." Her blacked-out gaze met mine, and desire flared in me.

A deep, unidentifiable, guttural sound of need came out of me.

"Prove everybody else wrong," she said, stepping closer; her sweet smell filled my senses and shot awareness through my whole body. "Let me be right."

"What do you mean?" I asked her.

"Show me how gentle you can be." She stepped back, and my eyes roamed over every inch of her as my flannel fell from her shoulders.

She stood before me, fearless and breathtaking. Her eyes were dark and patient, her lips freshly licked. She was a temptation like nothing else. Her breasts, her hips, the angle of her neck into her shoulder. Every inch of her was a feast for my eyes, and I couldn't stop looking.

*Show me they're wrong. Show me how gentle you can be.*

I couldn't make any promises, but I could try. I felt safe to go slow and be what she needed.

I stepped forward and wrapped my whole hand around her supple neck, pulling her up to me as I bent to her. Strong and soft.

She moaned before our lips met in the middle. I brought my other hand to her hip at a respectful height on her waist. I wanted her to know that she had the power here, that she could stop anytime. I was nothing to fear. My fingers tightened as her hips collided with mine. But I also wanted her to know that I needed her.

I never wanted anybody as I wanted her right now at this

moment. It was an all-consuming heat. The lightness of a man unburdened. She knew the truth, and she trusted me.

If perception made reality, then I was ready to be the man reflected in her eyes when she looked at me like this.

I needed her. It became evident that everything I'd kept buried, a long-harbored crush on the woman I thought was too good for me, came exploding to the surface with a pressure that could only come from long suppression.

I was vaguely aware of the person I thought Bee was before this night, but I couldn't remember any of that. That illusion was a projected idea formed from a small town's opinion and glimpses caught through a storefront window. Now, there was only this woman here. This beauty who'd revealed herself to me in these short hours of my longest night. Fiery and fierce, gentle and fragile. Forgiving. I wanted all her multiple facets like a gem that only got more beautiful the more the flaws were studied and its brilliance brought out by contrast and light.

I lowered my mouth to kiss her as she came to meet me. A tender and tentative brush of lips like in the tram. Only this time, Bee wasn't having it. She pushed up on her toes to deepen the kiss, pressing her mouth harder against mine, opening her mouth to let my tongue in. Her hand rested on my chest, and my heartbeat slammed against her palm.

Our mouths explored each other, and it was delicious and perfect. We broke the short kiss, and I blinked at her, my own shock reflected in her look. Should kisses feel that good? Should it feel that right?

"My neck hurts," she whispered.

Maybe not.

"Oh. We can stop—"

"No, you're just tall, and I'm not a giraffe. Let's move to the bed." She grabbed my wrist, and I let myself be yanked.

We landed on our sides in a tangle of limbs, though I was

careful not to crush anything in the process—including my heavy erection. Our heads met on the pillows, equal playing field now. And we kissed more. Her taste was incredible. The sounds she made drove me wild. My hands fought to stay respectful, but there was so much exposed skin they couldn't find one area to settle. Our bodies rocked closer and closer with the passion of our kissing until I was aware I'd pushed one of my thighs between her legs, and she was rubbing herself against it.

"Can I touch you?" I asked.

She sucked in a shaking breath. "God, please."

I smoothed my hand over her waist, stomach, and hip. I ran my fingertips up and down her legs, enthralled by the goose bumps that followed my touch.

"You're so beautiful, Bee," I said. "I've thought so for a very long time."

Maybe I'd expected a quip in return, but when she looked at me, lips swollen, color high on her cheeks, there was only raw honesty.

"I wish you had told me sooner," she said with soft vulnerability.

"I do too," I said.

"I didn't think anybody—" She cut herself off, deciding against something. "Thank you for telling me now."

"I should have told you that any time I see you in town, my mouth goes dry, and I cross the street so that I don't risk sounding stupid in front of you, but I think you're the most beautiful woman in town, and more than that, the most interesting. If I'm being honest, I don't actually notice any other women." As I spoke, my hand continued to explore her hot, smooth skin. Her face was torn between focusing on my words and enjoying my caresses. My middle finger dipped low into her bottoms, and the muscles of her abdomen contracted.

She sucked in a breath.

"I should have told you that day I passed your shop that I dreamed about you," I whispered. I watched her face closely as my middle finger brushed slowly down her pelvis until I reached her seam. I released a shaking breath when I was met with slick moisture. "Fuck," I said, feeling my control start to fray.

*Be gentle, stay calm.*

"I-I thought of you too," she said on a hitched breath when I barely dipped one finger into her center. Color rushed to her cheeks, and I leaned forward to kiss her again briefly.

"Is that okay? Does that feel good?" I asked.

"Yes. Go over to—yes, there, and then use your middle finger to—oh." Her head went back, and her mouth parted on a sharp gasp in. "Yes."

"Yeah?" Her words sank in as I used her wet to slick up and down and all around her. Petting her, teasing her, studying every twitch of her mouth and intake of breath. I hadn't learned these new expressions of hers yet and would need to translate them.

"And this?" I brushed my thumb over her swollen clit as my fingers crooked inside her.

"Ah! Wait, lighter, yes. Okay." She panted and squirmed. It was intoxicating to watch. I did this. I made her writhe in pleasure.

"You did?" I stilled, thrown off, losing focus in the heat of the moment, but not wanting to lose that thread of her confession that she dreamed of me too.

"Well, not a dream. A fantasy," she admitted. More heat flushed up her chest, and I lowered my mouth to suck lightly at her collarbone. She groaned. "That day you rescued Binxy Boo," she said, breaths coming faster as I kept my strokes long and luxurious, occasionally passing her core to dip back into her, spreading more of her moisture around.

It was a claim for the state of me that I didn't even blink at the name she listed.

"That beast had it out for me. I just wanted to do something for you. I had no idea what I was doing." I kissed her neck and inhaled her, memorizing her. Her breasts and body were pressed hard against my arms, the muscles aching from the angle and the hard work, but not even close to stopping. "I just want to make you so happy."

"You did save the cat. You really seem to know your way around a pus—"

I pushed my finger deep into her and hooked it, searching for ... She cried out. There it was.

"Tsk, tsk," I said, but she wasn't listening. Her hips were rocking as she fucked herself on my hand. "Focus, Bee."

"Ugh," she said. "What was I saying?"

"The day that cat almost killed me," I supplied.

"Oh. Right." She continued to grind against me, and I watched her, eyes closed, mouth parted. Absolutely beautiful as she sought her pleasure with my fingers. I could do that for her. I could prove that I was more than brute violence. "That night, I thought about you when I used my toy. I imagined you coming back to the cat café to kiss me and some variation of this."

"You naughty thing." My chest burned with pride. God, I hoped it was true and not the heat of the moment. I would have never imagined that I could do that to somebody.

"I know. I'm so ashamed." She did not look ashamed.

"No, you're not."

She bit her lip and grinned. "That was before I knew about your allergies. Guess I can't use that fantasy anymore."

*Anymore.* Just how many times had she thought of me?

She moaned, head thrown back, flush spread over her chest and shoulders now. Her hard little nipples pushed up against the neon green material of her bikini. A moment of weakness. A distraction. A desperation I couldn't ignore.

"I can help with that. Give you some new memories," I said.

Leaning up onto my elbow, free hand occupied, I pushed up the loose strands of her bikini with my nose. I found her nipple with my mouth and tongued it, all the while, she continued to ride me. I loved this. I loved my body being used for pure pleasure.

"Oh my God," she called out, arching her back, pressing her nipples more fully into my mouth.

"Yes," I said, popping off her as she started to unravel.

I was losing control alongside her. My cock was pressed painfully against my zipper, but all I could focus on was her pleasure.

"You're so wet, Bee." Her moisture dripped down my fingers, cupped in my palm as I worked it against her. My body burned, every inch coiled up, hotter and more desperate than it had ever been. I was a ball of tension, incoherent, not sure if I was talking a lot or listing my desires in my head. I wouldn't stop until I tasted how fucking sweet she was. How my tongue would slide so deep into her.

"Yes, yes. Oh, don't stop."

I had been saying my dirtiest thoughts out loud.

"I want to hear you cry out my name, Bee. I want to make you come so hard." I brushed my thumb over her clit as she said she liked, fingers still working as I sucked her nipple into my mouth.

She threw back her head and, in fact, did scream my name as she came.

# Chapter 18



Owen watched me as we lay face-to-face, and I came back to my body, still panting. I tingled with sensations I'd never felt. I had to be glowing like a beacon from the intensity of it all. He studied me in a way that had my heart pounding even harder, my body wanting more. As intense and truly once-in-a-lifetime as that orgasm was, I needed more closeness, more intimacy. Any space between us felt like too much.

"I want to squish myself so hard against you that we become one big blob." I settled for biting his shoulder to get out the surprising aggression.

I needed him in me and over me and pressing me down into the mattress until I forgot my own name. Until I forgot a world existed outside this cabin.

He chuckled, breathless, tense.

"I'm still in you, technically." His voice was gravelly deep.

"Not enough." I wrapped my arms around his sturdy middle and squeezed. He slowly removed his fingers from me.

Still holding my gaze, he brought them to his mouth and sucked. His eyes rolled back, and he moaned.

"You're right. Not enough," he said.

He sat back, half sitting up to look down at me. I must have made quite the sight. Bikini top pushed up, bottoms pushed down, sweaty skin, and goofy satisfied grin. I tugged at him, trying to move the heft of him over me, my hands futilely grasping and releasing as he remained unmoving.

He chuckled again, and I growled.

"I'll crush you," he said, laughing as he brushed kisses up and down my neck, gently toying with my nipples.

"And it'll be the best way to go." I sprawled out my arms and legs. "I'm ready. Flatten me."

He laughed harder, mirth in his eyes as he looked down at me. Maybe I didn't make a huge impact in town, but I made Owen Campbell laugh freely, and that was starting to hold more value than anything else.

With a few quick movements, he divested me of the rest of my string bikini.

"You know, I bet if we looked, there might be condoms in here," I said, biting my lip. "Not to assume." I rocked my hips until I brushed against his solid iron erection, currently bruising my thigh.

He held my gaze for a searching beat.

"I want to. Do you?" I asked breathlessly, scared.

It was one thing to get off on his hand, but my insecurities mounted a defense the longer he didn't ask for anything in return. Was this just another way of him assuaging his guilt by always taking care of me, or ...

He pushed up onto his knees and did that incredibly sexy thing men do where they grabbed the hem of their shirt and lifted it over their head from the back. Seriously, was that taught in some sexy man class? Did he practice in the mirror so that every muscle in his chiseled chest and abdomen flexed just the right way? He tossed his shirt to the side and looked at me.

His gaze went darker, yet he licked his lips. He undid his jeans and pushed them just low enough to pull out his sizable—

"Whoa," I said, forcing myself to meet his gaze but only having luck fifty percent of the time.

Thirty—seventy.

"I want to," he growled.

He was gorgeous and thick. As he palmed himself, a slow stroke up and down, a little bead of moisture danced on his tip. I watched it, my mouth actually watering as he ran his thumb over it to smooth it all around. I tightened where I had only just found relief. Now, my body felt achingly empty, clenching to be filled.

"Fuck, Bee, you gotta stop looking at me like that, or I'm going to come already," he swore.

With a smooth motion, he managed to get off the bed without tripping on his jeans, even though they were only hanging on by the perfect roundness of his booty. I would have fallen three times already, no doubt.

I felt my breasts jiggle with the shaking of the mattress. He noticed too, because his eyes fixated on them before he shook his head, seemingly forcing himself to stay on task. He went to the drawers in the kitchen, shuffled things around, and came back with an unopened condom. He presented it to me like a magic trick revealed.

"I really love this place," I said. I threw back my head and kicked my feet with glee.

He grinned, teeth gripping the edge of the foil as he tore it open, his other hand still working himself. God bless a man who can multitask. He got distracted momentarily when the shaking of the bed once again caused my breasts to jiggle.

Had I known that I had this much power with these two

little ladies, we probably could have avoided this whole mess, to begin with. I could have simply flashed him, stunning him, then shoved him back into the tram and on his merry way.

And the feelings that fake scenario caused in me almost derailed everything. I wanted to be here, right here, right now. I didn't even think about NYNB. I didn't know when it happened, but I was so incredibly thankful for every moment that led to this. I was fearful for this to end instead of just existing in it.

Owen hovered above me on his elbows, inches from my face. A look of worry furrowed his brow. "Hey, are you okay?"

I leaned up to kiss him and ran my hands along his broad back to bring him closer. "Yes. I was just thinking about how glad I am that the tram got stuck," I admitted.

His worry melted into something gentle. He swallowed. "Me too. Who would have thought one of the worst nights of my life would lead to one of the best?"

I sighed contentedly even as my body thrummed with new building tension. I scratched my fingernails down his incredible back to find his perfectly sculpted backside. "Aw, when did you take off your pants? I missed it. Boo."

He nuzzled his nose up my neck and inhaled into my hair. "Maybe you should have stayed focused."

"Shame on me." I let out a shaky breath as I reached lower to find him sheathed.

His eyes rolled back as I carefully stroked him, squeezing his base, trying to get a sense of how this would work. He was so big and thick.

"We'll go slow," he said, his Adam's apple bobbing.

I nodded as he hovered above me. I spread my legs wide to accommodate him. I would need to start yoga after all if this became a regular occurrence.

*Please* let this become a regular occurrence.

"Bee," he said, gently prodding at my entrance, his body trembling with self-control. "You're thinking again."

"Ugh. Can't have that." Since when was I such a thinker? Not when I was in this glorious moment.

I closed my eyes, inhaled his clean, masculine scent, and ran my fingertips along his shoulders and quivering arm muscles. I replayed his words, his sentiments that he wanted me in his life. This wouldn't be just one night.

I had to trust his words at face value. I had no reason not to when he'd only been truthful and gentle with me.

I rocked my hips up and let my thoughts go.

Then there were only sensations. Hot breaths panted. Cautious, slow increments spread me, filling me to a point I'd never been so full before.

Then.

Deep thrusts. Grinding hips. Creaking wooden joints of the bed. The crackling of the fire. Heat dampening skin. Gasps and pants, moans and caresses. A rough, deep voice encouraging.

"Yeah. Good. You're doing so good."

Hands tugging at my hair. Hard muscles pressed against my breasts. Thighs spread wider by strong hands. Everything in glimpses, all elements of a greater machine guiding me to another precipice.

I pushed back and up, gripped and scratched, hot and sticky. Body tightening, needing, needing more than it's ever needed. Shaking. Trembling.

"Need a minute," he said, his forehead dropping to my shoulder. "Just need to be still. You're so hot and tight. And I— just be still."

I clenched and pulled him deeper.

He growled my name in warning. I never was good at listening. I wanted him completely undone, unrestrained.

*Mine.*

"Take what you need, Owen." I brushed my thumb along his temple. Kissed his damp skin. Gave him my body and heart on a golden platter, along with my snacks. "I trust you."

He dropped his head to kiss me, and his hips started back up. He took exactly what he needed.

Eyes hooded with blissed-out pleasure, muscles firing and contracting. He pumped into me carefully but with less obvious restraint. He made me feel powerful and beautiful. I braced my arms above my head, holding myself from being pounded into the headboard. I took it all as he rocked over and over. He was so big, and I was so full and stretched, and my body was used, and ... it was *everything*.

The muscles in his neck and shoulders were red and tensed. He groaned with much gusto as he came.

He shuddered when it was all over, a blissed-out grin blurring his usual hard features. I couldn't help myself, I giggled.

He panted, looking down at me when he collapsed onto his side. "Are you laughing at me?"

"No." I covered my mouth. Giddy and laughing.

"It really feels like you are."

"I'm laughing *with* you," I explained.

When I turned to read him, his mouth flattened into a line, but his eyes had a mischievous gleam. Nobody could actually be cranky after what we just experienced.

"You'll laugh about this later," I quoted him mockingly, as he had told me when I made myself into a giant corndog in the snowsuit.

"Why are you laughing?" he asked, breathless.

"Post-orgasm adrenaline. I dunno. Also, your coming sounds were unexpected."

"I would never mock your orgasm sounds." He carefully removed the condom and tied it off before tossing it into the wastebasket. Another man skill that impressed me maybe more than it should.

"I don't make sounds." He scooted so we were both propped on our elbows, face-to-face and smiling. "I'm like a quiet little church mouse."

He made a series of high-pitched moans until I covered his mouth with both hands.

"Okay, so we are both incredibly sexy when we are lost in the moment, and we can't even help it," I said.

He grabbed my hands to pull off his mouth and kissed my palms. "You *are* incredibly sexy," he said seriously.

"You have no idea," I said back, no longer teasing.

"I really meant to make you come again before I did." He rubbed up my arm softly.

"Oh no, you only made me come once. Poor me," I said sarcastically.

"I guess we'll just have to go again."

"We've got nothing but time." I grinned and leaned forward to kiss him.

"And that box of condoms I found was unopened."

"Good thing I packed all those panties."

"And still no pants ..."

# Chapter 19

Owen

Bee dropped a piece of candy into my mouth, and I chewed it contentedly, leaning back against a stack of pillows like a king being cooled with palm fronds. We had moved to sit on a soft blanket in front of the fire, cuddled close under the comforter, sharing food and stories. Bee made me laugh more than I thought possible. Even when she wasn't trying, she was funny. I never knew what she was going to say, yet I felt like I understood her inherently.

I discovered she was one of the most ticklish people on the planet, and she flailed violently when tickled.

I also discovered her elbows were sharp enough to temporarily knock the wind out of me.

"Serves you right," she said when she could breathe again.

I rubbed at my chest as I eyed her smooth shoulder where the blanket fell down, insatiable and already wanting her again. She threatened to throw a candy at me. "Don't even think about it. I need to hydrate."

"You can't control what I'm thinking. I'm thinking so hard

right now," I said as she had earlier but in a deep voice and far more innuendo.

She licked her lips, grinned, and reached for me until I held her on my lap. We hadn't stopped touching each other in hours. We were desperate for each other, as though we were making up for something. It wasn't only the incredible lovemaking either. I couldn't stop inhaling her neck and hair, kissing any bit of exposed skin, rubbing my hands along her hips and curves. She, too, always found ways to grip my shoulders, scratch her nails through my hair, or lean into me. We were two magnets that always needed to find at least one area to touch.

"You aren't mocking the junk food now, are you?" she said.

"Certified genius," I said.

For all the rigorous activities we'd partaken in the past few hours, we needed all the instant sugary energy we could get. This was as close to bliss as I'd ever been.

She went to drop another candy in my mouth, but I shook my head, lips zipped. She twisted up the rest and set it on the nightstand before burrowing back into my lap. I crossed my arms around her and held her close.

I kissed her head.

"This has been a really great time," she said.

"Yeah," I said. "This must have been your plan all along."

She made a soft sound and rested her head back on my chest. "I have a confession," she said.

I stiffened. "Okay," I said cautiously. This would be a really bad time to learn that she was married. Or a convicted organ harvester, and maybe this was her plan all along. The sad thing was, I was in too deep to say for certain that it would matter. I hadn't been lying when I told Bee there was never going back to the life I had before. There had always been something between us, but I was too damn scared to act on it. It took an actual catastrophe to get me to talk to her.

"I'm not as strong as I've been letting on," she said in a rush.

I blinked but didn't speak, thankful she couldn't see the confusion on my face.

"I know I come off as this super confident, successful, sexy woman, and maybe a little scary and elegant person who knows what they want and who they are," she said.

An image of her stuck in the snowsuit popped into my head, arms up and flailing like those inflatables. Or when her hair stuck up all around her, the first time I found her in the bathroom ...

I opened my mouth and closed it.

"But that's all a front. Especially lately. I am intimidating. True. And incredibly good-looking. Obviously. Especially now. With this hair." She sighed and twirled her finger around my nipple, shooting electricity down my spine. "But the truth is, I'm not doing well. I've been struggling."

I let out a breath and pulled her closer. I was tempted to mention that I could tell she wasn't doing well when I caught her cutting her own hair in the bathroom of a tourist shop at the top of an abandoned mountain on a holiday when people usually celebrated with their loved ones, but she was sharing, and I wouldn't derail her.

"Struggling with what?" I asked.

"Loneliness," she said simply. Her raw honesty twisted the knife in my chest that she'd lodged there the first moment I held her. "I want to be okay with being single and quirky, but isolation can be so suffocating," she said. "I'm in my head so much. My parents are living their best-retired life. Deckard is a good friend but has his own stuff going on. And as close as we are, we were never each other's person. You know?" She turned to face me, still resting on my chest. Her features were so beautiful and expressive. My heart hammered loudly as the feeling of being on a precipice tingled my toes. This was all so unexpected and maybe too fast, but looking down in those dark, vivacious eyes, I had already fallen. I was in a free fall now.

I nodded, tucking her short hair behind her ear. "I'm lonely too," I admitted, not knowing just how true it was until I said it out loud.

"I'm sorry, Owen," she said. She trailed her fingers over the back of my hands. "I talk big about living in the moment. And I do. But it used to be easier. Nothing changes. No matter how I act or dress, I'm still invisible. I want to live a life that is mine, but at the end of the day, I want to be able to tell somebody about it."

I leaned down to kiss her forehead. "I understand."

She held my gaze, searching. Had I said the wrong thing? Was I meant to say more? Loneliness was a universal epidemic but so rarely talked about. Ivy. Myself. Most of the people at Golden Sunset. Probably half this town. We were all these solo-manned vessels orbiting around each other, so rarely connecting, desperate for a real moment to tie us to this time on Earth. I'd felt a connection with her tonight. I felt the universe shifting around me.

"I'm so sorry I got you mixed up in my turning thirty crisis," she said, her voice cracking when I was silent too long.

"I'm not sorry. There is no other place I'd rather be."

She sucked in a ragged breath. "Really? Even with all the stupid things I've done because I'm scared of fading into oblivion?"

"Really. You're just trying to change your life, and I admire that," I said, understanding that so much of Bee's persona was protection. The faux confidence, quick temper, and tempestuous decision-making were all the masks of a little girl screaming out for attention or love.

"I'm scared," she said with a shaky voice. "I feel myself fading away, and I'm already a wisp of a person in this town.

Nobody sees me. Nobody cares about me. And soon, I'll just be a ghost. I'll be worse than the abandoned statue—" Her breaths came faster, her eyes welled.

I pulled her up my body to cup her face gently.

"That's simply not true. I see you, Bee." I poured everything into my words. "You are the most vivid thing in every room, and it's everybody else's loss that they can't see what's right in front of them."

She closed her eyes in pain and nuzzled into my hand. When she opened them again, she said, "And after tonight? This morning." We both turned to the window where, outside, the storm had moved on to reveal the gentle hues of pink and dark purple, signaling the sun's imminent arrival. Thereby ending this bubble of seclusion that led to this most wonderful turn of events. "What happens when you aren't forced to be with me? Are you going to remember me?"

"Of course," I said without hesitation. Would she want to see me when I was walking around town and she saw how people responded to me?

"You're just saying that because you just rocked my world."

I blushed. "I was always aware of you but chickened out every time I tried to talk to you. I'm drawn to you. Before ... now... tomorrow," I said, watching her face closely. "We will figure out what comes next since it's new for us both," I answered honestly.

What was after today? What did she want? What would she think of me when I had to complete my contract with Benny Jr.? *Could* I complete my contract after all this? The thought suddenly made me feel very sick.

"I've been waiting for you for so long," she said on a sharp exhale like she'd been holding her breath too long.

"Me too," I admitted.

An emotion so strong swelled in my chest that my palms

went icy. This didn't feel like a crush. It didn't feel like a pressure or a weight to bear at all. It felt like the opposite. It was taking off a heavy mask that had been weighing me down. It was being able to take a full breath in.

It was the relief of meeting a person who inherently seemed to understand me and knowing that I was meant to have her in my life. It was knowing we'd never be the same again.

*There you are.*

"I'm glad you shared your past with me, Owen. Now you don't have to carry it anymore. You aren't that boy who didn't know his own strength. You are the man who saved a kitten while being attacked. Who saved my life probably a few times tonight. Who made me come several times with his gentle touch." I flushed. "You are so much more than that story in your head."

"Bee ..." I closed my eyes and held her.

Soon, she turned to me, and we were kissing again. I had to show her how much I needed her.

I kissed her hard, and we fell back. I cherished her, held her, and reached for her time and time again.

She was worried that the light of day would change everything, and though I assured her, I couldn't know for sure.

I would never be the same after tonight. Bee *had* changed me. But Ivy had given me a life, and I couldn't betray her just because I met a person who made me want to live it.

The morning would bring an end to this perfect bubble, and only time would tell where we went next. I already felt my heart being torn in two directions. I wasn't sure there was a right choice where someone I cared about didn't get hurt.

# Chapter 20

Bee

"Go away!" I yelled at the rude person banging on the door.

I pulled the blankets over my head. The room was now so cold the tips of my ears hurt. The fire must have gone out during the night, unbeknownst to us with all our vigorous activity. It was warm under this blanket and smelled yummy, like Owen's body, and I just wanted to bite this big muscle I laid on.

"Ouch. Bee. No biting," Owen slurred, half asleep.

"Now you don't like it."

I rolled onto my back and stretched with a big yawn, arms over my head, gently brushing Owen's chin.

"Control your body," he said, removing my fist from his face.

"You control my body," I said, not fully awake.

*Bang! Bang! Bang!*

I was flung almost off the edge of the bed as Owen shot up.

"Coming! Hang on!" Owen yelled.

"Rude." I pulled the comforter back over me and burrowed under a pillow to block out the sun and noise.

"Bee, you gotta get up. They're here." Owen sounded frantic.

I peeked out to glare, but it went unnoticed. He was too busy scrambling into jeans, hobbling and hopping as he balanced. I didn't miss appreciating the strong muscles in his legs even though I was cranky.

I rapidly blinked away the burning sunlight from my eyes. "What? Who's there?"

"They're here to get us out," he said. "The storm must have passed."

"Yeah. I got that from the bright white light burning holes into my corneas."

"It's Azi and Mateo. We have brought the snowmobiles to save you!" Azi shouted and banged again.

"I'm going to murder him." I launched myself in the direction of the door. Owen grabbed me by the middle to stop me.

"Easy there. Might want to get some clothes on first," he rumbled from behind, his hot chest hard against my bare back.

My mind flashed to last night, on our second or third round, when he had me pressed into the mattress, face down, grinding into me from behind, while he teased me with his hand. I felt myself melting back against him now at the memory. His large hand sprawled and cupped both my breasts and squeezed to emphasize my nakedness. My head lulled back, and I was seconds from purring and rubbing myself all over him. It was like he found my reset button, and I immediately lost control of my body.

He groaned.

"Fine. I'll get dressed. But then somebody is getting punched in the gut," I said, letting him release me. I found my dried-out snowsuit and tugged it on, though I had absolutely no desire to. My options were limited.

"I thought you'd be a morning person," he said.

I looked over at the loose smile on Owen's face and the gleam in his eyes.

"Ew. You're a morning person, aren't you?" I made a disgusted face.

"You are adorable." He kissed my head, and I swatted at him as he ducked out of the way.

"Pretty cold out here," Azi called with another knock.

"Just give us a minute," Owen said.

The two low voices outside exchanged laughter after a mumbled comment. So much for subtlety. Owen's face turned bright red as he busied himself gathering our meager supplies. Was he embarrassed by me? Or was he worried about the sort of assumptions they'd make about his character? He wouldn't meet my gaze as we rushed to open the door, and my first knot of worry formed. We hadn't discussed what came next for us ... other than each other. That took most of the night, and we fell asleep before logistics. I wanted to know where we stood.

After our clothes were situated, I quickly packed my bag—emergency or not, the rest of these snacks would not go to waste. Owen let the guys in. I recognized Azi from the shift the day before. He had short curls currently hidden under a winter hat and dark eyelashed-lined eyes that had the tourists all over him. He was with Mateo, an EMT for the local rescue crew, but he also worked on The Slope as needed. He had lighter hair and was a little taller, but both men seemed short compared to Owen. They unabashedly eyed up the place, including the rumpled sheets. No doubt they were fully aware of the amenities here. Owen blushed harder. The arrival of the new people had completely popped our perfect bubble.

Azi's eyes moved up and down me. "Nice hair, Perkins."

I blinked, shocked that he acknowledged me and knew my name.

Was he being sincere about my new cut, or did I have messy

sex hair? I tried to subtly check my reflection, but when I looked over my shoulder, Owen was right behind me, an arm protectively wrapping around me and glaring daggers at Azi before I could answer. Which ended up being for the best because I was tongue-tied and indecisive. I felt like the person I'd been yesterday, and I hated that. This wasn't the side of me Owen had seen. He'd seen NYNB Bee, not this shy-side character Bee.

"Let's get going," Owen said.

I had questions about how the sheets would get washed and who would replenish the firewood, but I recognized that this was not the time.

"I'll take Bee if you wanna ride down with Mateo," Azi said.

Azi looked me up and down again, and my indignation rose. He hadn't noticed me yesterday, even when he'd looked directly at me. Now, because he assumed a new fact about me, I became worth his notice. I was about to say something when Owen spoke up.

"No. Bee is coming with me," Owen said, a warning low and deep.

"Do you know how to drive the snowmobile? I don't know if Benny Jr. would be okay with that," Azi argued, looking at me again as if he could X-ray vision through the snowsuit.

"He's down there with Officer Martinez," Mateo said.

"I was told to bring her to Benny Jr., so that's what I'm doing," Owen said.

My heart sank, and an icy chill ran down the back of my neck.

"Wait—" I started, but the boys all began to talk over each other, not a single person looking at me anymore. I faded into the background once again.

My heart thrashed against my chest. This wasn't the plan. This wasn't NYNB. This was all sliding immediately back to the way it used to be. But it was the new year, and I had changed. Owen had changed me when he saw me and when he reassured me that he wouldn't forget me. That I wasn't forgettable, but now he thought the plan would be the same? That he could just take me to Benny Jr.? Not a chance.

I wasn't going back.

All the warmth and bliss from minutes ago burned away in a flash. My temper drove the show now.

"I'm not going down there," I said, but nobody heard me over their bickering. Louder, I stepped forward. "I'm not going to Benny. I'm not," I raised my voice. They all stopped, finally remembering I was there as my voice rang through the air.

Owen nervously flicked his gaze around. "Bee," he said, putting his palms out to calm me, "I'll take you and—"

"No!" This time I shouted it. I was so tired of not being heard. Not being seen. I wasn't going down this way. I thought Owen was better than the rest. That I was more ... just that I was different. "And stop talking about me like I'm not here. Like I'm just some sort of statue!"

Owen winced and looked down.

The other two exchanged a confused look. "We'll give you two another minute," Azi said and then stepped back into the bright, cold day, letting in a pocket of cold air that reminded me too much of reality.

"I'm not going down, Owen. I told you that a hundred times." A violent shiver shook me.

Owen tugged at his hat to scratch at his short hair. "Nothing's changed. I still have to get you to Benny Jr."

"Are you kidding me?"

"Are you kidding me, Bee? I told you from the beginning that I needed this job."

"Did I hallucinate the past few hours?" I said it out loud, but I was mostly talking to myself because nothing else could explain the shift in Owen.

"No. And it was incredible, but I still have responsibilities and people counting on me." At least he seemed earnest.

"You're really gonna ship me off to him and whatever bologna he plans for me? How can you be so calloused? You do have a choice here."

Several looks passed over his features: pain, then sadness, then determination. "It's not that simple. I need to stay in good standing with him. I need the money."

"You can get another job, good gravy. You act like being a professional bully is the only option you have. We talked about that. You don't have to be that person." I stood to him, chest almost to chest. Well, chest to upper stomach. He had a distinct advantage, but that didn't slow my temper.

"It's not so simple for me to change my whole life on a whim," he said, nostrils flaring as his gaze moved over my features.

"Don't mock me because you're too scared to change."

Owen's jaw flexed, and he put his hands on my shoulders. He glanced to the door and then back to me, voice lowering.

"I am scared, Bee. But not for me. For right now, for today. I have two rents to pay and no way to pay them if I don't get this money from Benny Jr. I don't want to have to do this, but I don't know what else to do. I really don't—I can't have Ivy—"

I frowned. The wheels turned. "Why are you paying Ivy's rent?"

"I-I didn't mean to—Pretend I didn't say that. I didn't want to burden you with any of this."

"Tell me now." I crossed my arms.

Owen glanced to make sure the others weren't listening. "Her son took off with her savings last summer. I've been paying for her stay at Golden Sunset. But please don't share that information. Nobody knows except a few people at the home. It's just temporary until I can get a little saved up and figure out what comes next, but for today, I can't change the plan. I can't rock the boat. I need the money he offered for you." He'd gone almost frantic as he spoke, real fear in his wild eyes.

He looked down, and as the truth settled into me, so did the cold.

"I never meant for things to go so far. I wouldn't ever want you to think that I was using you or—"

"I know you didn't, Owen," I said softly, voice cracking.

Poor Owen. He had done everything for Ivy. I understood that now. All the little pieces of the night lined up and made more sense. How he would go on the tram when it clearly terrified him. Why he continued to try to get me back down the mountain when all I did was fight him at every turn. It wasn't about his wants, it was about Ivy's this whole time.

And I'd been so selfish.

I understood then. NYNB was out the window. This whole time, throughout the freezing cold and the jump from the tram, I still thought that I would change my role in life to be somebody else. Maybe some people are destined to play the filler for the main characters.

After all, even those who manage to make significant changes still get lost in time. Maybe it was all pointless. It was all temporary. It was that same cold, dark feeling that had been consuming me the past few months slowly seeped into the edges of my vision. That feeling that there really is no point to any of this.

"Bee, I'm sorry." He looked wrecked.

I wrapped my arms around his middle and squeezed until my arms shook. I couldn't do my plan but we could still get Owen the money he was owed and help Ivy.

"Okay." I nodded once, voice loud and clear. "Take me to Benny Jr. The little jerk. You get your money, and then I will figure out what needs to be done."

"Bee. I'm sorry. I hate this. If I had another option ... if I thought." He tugged off his winter hat to put it on me. "I'll talk him out of pressing charges. I'll make sure you're okay."

"Don't apologize. I'm aware of my privilege and that this was all a half-baked idea to begin with." My voice sounded flat. "I'll just figure out something else. There's always next year. But this is in no way your fault." I made him meet my gaze. "You've done nothing wrong."

"You aren't alone in this. I promise," Owen said.

I tried so hard to believe him, but in my experience, out of sight, out of mind. But that wasn't fair to Owen. I could see the torment in his features, and I knew that he didn't want to be doing this. It wasn't like we'd made plans to go get croissants and throw them to (at) the guinea pigs in the park. He didn't owe me anything. I was insecure and sad that none of my plans came to fruition, but I still cared about Owen and wanted to help him.

"Let's go get your money," I said, determined.

But crap, was I really about to get arrested?

# Chapter 21

Owen

Guilt churned in my gut as we rode down the hill, following Azi and Mateo toward Benny. The storm left a foot of fresh powder, but the sky was bright and blue. The top halves of the pine trees were weighted down by snow and looked as mournful and burdened as I felt. Bee was silent as she clung to my back, head resting against me, presumably to block the worst of the cold. They'd given her a helmet, but she was still bound to be cold this icy morning.

I'd hated how her normally bright, sturdy countenance melted out of her voice, leaving a shell of the woman I'd grown to know when she agreed to go down the mountain with me. I hated to share Ivy's business at the risk of emotionally manipulating Bee, but I didn't know how else to prove to Bee that I didn't have any other options. If there was any other way.

I had thought of Ivy moving in with me into my tiny apartment above the cannabis dispensary, High Altitude, on Main Street. But I couldn't take care of her as I worked strange, long hours. She needed things the medical staff provided that I didn't know about. She didn't deserve that life. She deserved to be in a safe place like Golden Sunset. Not to even mention the practical issues like getting her up and down all those narrow wooden stairs that led up to my apartment or if she even wanted to live in a space that would always sort of smell skunky. It wouldn't be fair to her.

But Bee didn't deserve this either. I had been honest from the beginning. I never meant to hurt her.

How could I not be hurting her? I had just slept with her, and now I was delivering her to a man with an ego trip. Benny Jr. was out to send a message to those in town who thought his father did a better job. What sort of person was I? There had to be a better way.

Snow stung my cheeks as I squinted ahead, a growing awareness that no matter what, I was going to hurt someone I cared about. It might not be physical pain this time, but I still could only manage to hurt.

We went over a hill and then dipped low, coming down the final stretch to the base building. There, two black dots on the horizon waited—Benny Jr. and Officer Martinez.

Azi and Mateo zipped down and away as our snowmobile rolled to a stop. I cut the engine and sat still. I shook my head, the sudden cessation of the engine causing a ringing in my ears.

"No." I got up and out of the seat to kneel before Bee. My helmet reflected back as she stared down at me. Presumably.

I tugged mine off and she matched me; her revealed face twisted in confusion, head bowed to meet my gaze.

"I can't do this. I'm sorry I even got this far, Bee. Let's turn around and I'll take you to the top of the mountain. You should still have time for your New Year, New *You* plan." I stumbled over the words as I rushed to get them out. "I'm sorry."

A flash of her usual ferocity blinked in her eyes, quickly replaced with a sad acceptance.

"I can't let a woman lose her home just so I can show off my tatas to Slippery Slopes."

"Wait, what—"

"Well, it's not like I *intend* to show them," she explained with a flick of her wrist. "But you've met them. I mean, they really have trouble staying in that bikini top."

I stared at her covered chest and remembered all the times I'd licked and played with her breasts just a few hours ago. Even before she graciously gave me access to them, they did seem to crave freedom.

"Owen?" She clapped gloved hands in front of my face. I shook my head and focused on her here and now. "It's too late. You don't get to be the stoic, self-sacrificing one this time. I'm choosing to do that. I'll be the hero," she said teasingly but determined. It was the same look she'd had when she didn't want to get on the tram last night.

I dropped my head. All this really had been my fault.

"And stop blaming yourself!" She shook my shoulders roughly. "Seriously, there are at least five people before you to take responsibility, and I'm pretty sure I'm four of them."

I shook my head, grabbing her hands. "I'll figure something else out."

"Not a chance." She slid them away and roughly patted my cheek. "We're getting you that money. Honestly, what sort of person would I be if I let Ivy get kicked out?" She sighed dramatically and shook out her hair. "No. No. I'll go down there and see what Benny Jr. thinks he can do. I'm not scared of him."

I scrubbed at my face. "I hate this. I'll come find you as soon as I pay her rent, okay? We will make a new plan for you and your boobs."

She leaned forward to kiss my nose, and I was tempted to kiss her deeply there and then, but I wasn't sure where we stood now if she could still trust me.

"Okay," she said, and I let her pull me up to stand.

I looked down at her one last time, cupped her cheek, and kissed her forehead.

Back on the snowmobile, we made it the rest of the way down, coming to a stop in front of the others waiting.

"Looks like you're not a total idiot," Benny Jr. said. "For a second there, I thought you were about to do something stupid." He spoke to me, but he glared at Bee.

I felt her tense at my side. I slipped an arm through hers.

"Come on, really?" I gestured to Office Martinez. "This isn't necessary. Bee didn't do any damage to your shop."

"I bet we can clear all this up without any arrests. She's just a passing tourist who got confused, no doubt," Officer Martinez said, looking like he'd rather be anywhere else on New Year's Day, barely glancing at Bee.

My head dropped back to glare at the bright sky. This was not happening again.

"I just made him his double espresso yesterday morning," Bee said to me, put out but not surprised.

"I looked up Ms. Perkins, and she doesn't have a record," the officer explained.

"Shoplifting!" Benny jabbed a finger in the direction of Bee's snowsuit.

"Hey, now wait. You made me drag her out in the weather. She needed clothes." I spoke without thinking, only realizing too late how it sounded.

"Why didn't she have any clothes?" My boss eyed her suspiciously. "What sort of deviant am I dealing with here?"

Azi and Mateo shared a look before Azi's gaze lingered on Bee. A protective instinct had me stepping closer to her.

Even the cop looked more interested in being here. His gaze flicked up and down Bee, like Azi's had. All of a sudden, these men in town took notice of her, and that wasn't fair, not when she'd been here all along. But something about the jump and the stay in the cabin changed her, and she seemed to exude this pheromone that had all the men sniffing around.

I hated it. I ground my jaw and balled my fists.

"Indecent exposure, shoplifting, loitering, and ... and breaking and entering!" Benny Jr. listed.

"I didn't break anything!" Bee shouted, then pointed at Azi. "It was your employee who didn't see me when doing closing shift duties. I could sue for neglect."

"She must have been hiding," Azi said, scratching at the back of his neck, fully avoiding her gaze. "It was an honest mistake."

"Yeah, right," Bee mumbled, and I wondered if it would draw too much attention to cover her mouth with my hand. She had confessed to me that, technically, she'd been hiding from Azi in an effort to stay the night.

"See. I'm sure there's no need for this to go any further," the officer said. "Come on, Ben. I'm sure we can just call it a day and celebrate the new year."

"It's Mr. Gauner." Anger spread up Benny Jr.'s cheeks. "I'm pressing charges," he said because he would always do the opposite of any suggestion.

The others rolled their eyes. My own anger pumped blood to my fists that curled for action. I didn't want to be this person, but I could. I stepped forward and used my bulk to make myself as large as possible.

Benny Jr. flinched back, his eyes darting side to side.

"I think we can work something out," I said.

"I don't pay you to think. You take your money and get out of here." He shoved a thick envelope of cash at me. Thicker than I expected. Enough for both rents when I quickly checked. I ground my jaw, unable to move. Shame flashed over me.

Bee patted my back and whispered, "Make sure they're not fake bills."

I glared down at Benny Jr., feeling like the smallest man here, even though I towered over them all. Shame for needing the cash this badly and being unable to provide it any other way. Shame at not being able to defend Bee. Shame that once again, my tongue was tied, and I felt incapable of saying or doing the right thing.

It was as though Benny Jr. could read the thoughts flashing over my face.

"That's what I thought, Big Guy. You get a command, and you follow it like a good boy." His tone dripped with condescension as he pushed my buttons. I wasn't sure why. I blinked down at him. Yes, his words hurt, but I was used to his disdain. I knew that he believed me to be a violent criminal with zero brain cells. I couldn't control what he thought of me. I might not ever be seen any other way, and I had to be okay with that if I continued to want money.

I ground my jaw, but I didn't react.

"Would you just shut up?" Bee said, exasperated. "You're not half the man Owen is, and you never will be. And I'm not just talking physically. Nobody in this town would ever listen to you if you didn't have money."

Benny Jr. went purple with barely suppressed rage.

"Shut that nobody up." Benny Jr. looked at me. "I can tell you had your fun with her, but you're done now."

I shook my head, anger and frustration at being called out. Just like when Azi and Mateo showed up and immediately assumed that we'd had sex. They all made it seem dirty and cheap. It took away the deep connection we'd shared and made it tawdry. It was one thing to make me a kicking post, but it wasn't fair to Bee. She wouldn't be treated like that.

That had been a mistake. I clenched my fist. I could break

him so easily that the heat of it hit me by surprise. I never wanted to hurt anybody.

"Watch your mouth," I growled.

"Or what?" Benny said, his embarrassment making him reckless.

I stepped closer.

Distantly, I heard the cop warning me off and the other guys murmur warnings as I stepped up to Benny Jr., making myself large and imposing. I glared down my nose at him, shoulders tensed.

"Not worth it." Bee's voice cut through the haze of anger controlling me. She rubbed my back soothingly. "You aren't the person they think you are. Their opinion doesn't matter." Bee was whispering, and the edges of my vision returned to normal. It was everything I'd just told myself. I let her pull me back as I locked my eyes on hers. I thought of our connection last night, the secrets shared.

"Just as I thought," Benny said with a huff, like a bully out of a poorly written teen drama. It was one of life's greatest injustices that the content of a person's character never determined their financial security. "You're all talk, Big Guy," Benny spat.

The change in Bee's eyes happened so fast. The soft reassurance burned away to nostril-flared rage in a flash.

"I'm not." Bee swung her fist before she even finished her sentence. There wouldn't have been time to stop her, even if I wanted to.

Benny Jr. collapsed forward with a loud grunt. I knew how sharp those bony little fists of hers could be, and he'd just been nailed in the gut.

The cop sighed and mumbled something about paperwork. "All right. Come on, Perkins. You shouldn't have done that."

"No regrets," she yelled, shaking out her fist.

None of us seemed particularly worried about Benny Jr.'s writhing form on the ground.

I turned to her. "He's right. You shouldn't have done that," I said, unable to hide my amusement.

She shrugged. "What can you do?"

I leaned forward to drop a kiss on her forehead as handcuffs latched her from behind.

"This is giving me an idea for the future," she said as she wiggled her eyebrows.

Despite her attempt to be brave and lighten the mood, my heart sank. Benny Jr. must have wanted to escalate the situation so he could be validated for getting Bee in trouble, and I fell right into his trap.

"I'll come get you as soon as I can," I promised.

She smiled up at me, and for once, I spotted the smallest crack in her facade. This made it all feel much more real. "At least my parents are out of town." Her cheesy smile wavered.

"They'll have quite the story waiting for them."

"All right, come on, Perkins. Really, what were you thinking?" Martinez asked as he led her away.

"That's not really my brand," she said.

Their voices faded away as he led her to his patrol car in handcuffs.

I felt sick.

What had I done? I had to start making things right.

# Chapter 22

Owen

As soon as I finished dealing with the January payment at the home, I headed to Ivy's room to explain why I might be late for dinner. I had no idea how long it would take to bail Bee out of jail or even what that entailed. I had shockingly little experience dealing with the Slippery Slopes Police Department in my life here, most likely contrary to everyone's belief. Depending on how much her bail was, I might have to sell a kidney or beg for another job. After getting punched, Benny Jr. stomped off to lick his wounded pride in privacy. I'd have to beg Benny Jr. to smooth things over, I might have to grovel. I pictured Bee sitting in a jail surrounded by Slippery Slope's roughest characters and ground my jaw. If I had to grovel, I would.

Not to sell Bee short. She could obviously hold her own. There was a fifty-fifty chance that she'd befriended everyone in there or incited a riot that would lead to more serious charges.

Maybe thirty-seventy.

I owed it to her to get her out. No matter what, I'd figure it out.

"What's all this about you being stuck up in that death trap?" Ivy said by way of greeting.

I bent down to kiss the top of her head where she sat in her usual chair, and she cupped the back of my head with her shaky hand to receive me. Instead of stepping away, I held her warm, knobby hand for a moment longer. The relief at knowing she was safe for another month was palpable.

Only worry for Bee knotted my guts now.

She patted our linked hands and gave me a lingering inspection. I cleared my throat and acted naturally.

"News traveled fast." I reluctantly folded myself in the too-small folding chair across from her. I was anxious to get going but could feel her studying me closely after my lingering greeting. "Everything worked out, though."

"Okay. Then why the sourpuss?" she asked, her eyes narrowing.

"I've told you, this is just how my face looks."

She snapped her fingers impatiently at me. "Out with it. Talk to me."

I glanced at the clock on her nightstand, but she wouldn't let me go without more information. And so I unburdened myself. Just as she had since I was fifteen, I let Ivy guide me through my feelings. I explained the traumatic events of the night since I left her side—leaving out the more salacious details, of course— ending with Bee's gut punch.

"I always liked that girl," Ivy said, nodding her approval.

No doubt in my mind that these two would be fast friends. I imagined them, with faces close, whispering back and forth, shooting me glances before they cackled.

On second thought, maybe I wouldn't reintroduce them.

"Sounds like you two had a real connection," she said, breaking through my worry. "Such a rare and beautiful thing."

"I can see myself making plans for a future with her. I've never felt that way about anybody. I don't think I can go back to who I was before. She met me without judgment but also fully as her authentic self, so I felt like I saw her clearly too. Is that normal? It's like I know her so completely but also feel desperate to learn everything about her."

"Oh," Ivy said softly, a smile spreading as her eyes went glassy. "Maybe not typical, but a sort of magic."

"If she's not in prison."

She snorted. "Don't be so dramatic. Javier isn't going to let her get arrested. He just did what he needed to do to appease Benny Jr." She referred to Officer Martinez, who was most likely also her student, at one point.

"I hope so. I shouldn't have let Benny Jr. get under my skin."

"Ah, but he's so good at annoying the shit out of people. Why take away what he's good at?"

I chuckled without real gusto and glanced at the clock.

"Go get her. You don't have to sit around here with me. Go tell Bee how you're feeling before she thinks you aren't coming for her. Do something big and exciting. Hopefully, you used the Hookup Hut to its full capacity, but I never understand the younger generations anymore." She patted my hand. "Oh, don't look so shocked. That cabin has been there as long as the tram, if not longer. Every generation thinks they invented being wild."

"Okay, well, this is getting dangerously close to things I never want to think about, so I will go." I stood, my butt already half asleep.

The intern from last night poked his head in the door, paling slightly when he spotted me. Hard to think that it wasn't even twenty-four hours ago when I had been here. I felt like a totally different person.

"Mr. Campbell, uh, sir. The billing admin has a question. I guess your payment—"

I cut him off before he could say anymore. "I don't know what you're talking about," I spoke with slow emphasis, giving him plenty of time to backtrack and get out.

"They just want to make sure you meant to pay through February." I gave him a look that should have melted his face, but he wasn't the brightest bulb.

I sighed and pinched the area between my brows. "I'll be right there."

I thought maybe she'd let it slide, but just when I crossed the threshold to leave, Ivy said, "I know you aren't thinking about taking another step without explaining what that was about."

*Shit.*

"It's nothing," I said, not meeting her gaze. "Just a clerical mix-up. They must think I'm your son."

"Boy, sit your butt in that chair and tell me why you're paying my rent."

I scrubbed at my short hair, scratching my palms. I went to the chair and sat back down. I would have to tell her sooner or later. Maybe I should have told her a while ago. I held her gaze and explained the horrible truth as I held her hands. "I'm so sorry. He took the money from your account and hasn't been back since. As you know."

"What about the cards he sent?" she asked, her eyes narrowing.

I cleared my throat. "I-I sent those too."

"I thought it was weird that he finally remembered my birthday." She sat back and blew out a low whistle through her crepe-skinned lips. "You know, sometimes I wonder if he resented me because I gave so much to my students. Or maybe he just took the personality of his father. Shame."

"I shouldn't have lied to you. I'm so sorry. I just didn't want him to hurt you anymore," I said, feeling smaller than a GP.

I wasn't prone to violence. That much was obvious at this point.

But I could sic Bee on her son.

"You're telling me you've been paying my rent for over six months?"

"I-I'm sorry. We don't have to make a whole thing out of it. After everything you've done for me."

"Sometimes, I think you are an overlooked secret genius, and then other times, you don't seem to have enough common sense to find your own nose," she said.

"It wasn't that I expected a thank you, but I wasn't expecting to be insulted." I blinked at her.

"You insulted me first."

My jaw dropped.

"You think I'm dumb enough to let that numbnuts of a kid have full access to all my accounts?"

I blinked, slouching back. "What am I missing here?"

"Everything, apparently. The account I gave Jonny access to only had enough to cover my bills here. He's been scamming me since he could walk. I'm not saying it's his father's fault, but ... anyway. I knew he would take advantage of my age the second he thought he could. I would never be stupid enough to give him access to all my money." She rubbed her forehead and blew out a long breath. "No wonder you've seemed so damn stressed lately."

I didn't know what to say, so I just shook my head. I had assumed that her son had taken it all. It hadn't even occurred to me that there was money kept from him.

"I'm sorry," I said.

She waved away my apology. "Here's the deal. There's no reason for you to be paying my rent. I came to Slippery Slopes because I wanted to teach until I could ultimately retire here with the supposed healing waters and all that. I'm a little bit of a woo-woo in that way. You'll see when you read my will in thirty years."

I huffed out a laugh. I could only hope we had that much time.

"Though honestly, if Ned Fled is any indication, I may not be exaggerating that number," she said. The oldest man in town was a modern miracle. "But the point is, I have money. And this isn't your burden anymore. It never was. I appreciate you looking out for me, but you're getting that money back. Trust me."

I tried to argue, but she wasn't having it.

I let the truth settle into me as she explained how much I'd be getting back.

"You really screwed the pooch. That girl is sitting in jail, and you're here. I thought I raised you better than that."

Despite her scolding tone, her words sent a frisson of pleasure into my heart. She *had* raised me, hadn't she? I had parents who I had lived with, but this was the woman I shaped my values after, who took care to nurture me.

"You did raise me," I said, throat wobbling. "And I'm so thankful." I held her gaze and poured my earnestness into it.

This time, she didn't make a joke. She held my gaze with her own watery eyes and gave me a tight-lipped smile. "It was my honor to." She wiped at her face, annoyed at the emotional display. "I hope you see now that I'm not just a lonely old woman. That other people will see you for who you really are if you let them."

I nodded and let out a breath, anxious to get to Bee.

"I hope you have plans to make it up to her," she said.

"I have money to go bail her out," I said, half out the door.

"I know you're not about to spend the money I'm giving you

back on somebody else already. Better plans than that, mister. Money is an easy, empty gesture when it's given out of guilt."

I opened my mouth and closed it, a fresh thought popping up.

"Actually, there is one more thing you might be able to help with."

I explained what I needed quickly so that I could get to Bee. I could only imagine how terrified she was.

# Chapter 23

Bee

I DIDN'T SUPPORT A LIFE OF CRIME, BUT JAIL WAS PRETTY cool. I wasn't a whole new person, but I was edgier now. I might shank somebody. That guy in the corner was giving me funny looks. Oh, wait, that was a recruitment poster.

Never mind.

I understood why so many manifestos were written from jail —loads of thinking time. Not that I was a martyr of caliber like so many, but I had earned some sympathy, no doubt.

"How long has it been?" I asked, voice cracked from dehydration and arms sticking out through the bars of my holding cell. I just needed a metal cup to bang across them.

Was that why it was called a clinker? I bet Owen would know. Sweet Owen. How long until I might see him again?

Officer Martinez sighed loudly. "About two hours, Bee. Five more minutes than when you asked me last time."

"Feels so much longer," I said wistfully.

"Probably because you've talked the whole time. You should probably stop. Conserve your voice."

"So. Thirsty." I smacked dry lips.

"Then get some water. The cooler is over there. You aren't even under arrest. That door isn't even locked."

To be fair, I wasn't in a holding cell like the ones I'd seen in the movies. It was an average conference room inside the police station with the door open, and I had free use of the phone as the officer repeatedly reminded me. And there were no bars, technically.

It was underwhelming. My imagination was much more titillating.

"You are free to leave. In fact, soon, I'm going to have to insist on it." He snapped out the pages of the local paper, *Slippery Slopes Sheets,* with a little extra emphasis. There was a story on the front about something or another involving Deckard's mom, the mayor, and a policy she was trying to pass being blocked by the council. I wondered if our tram troubles would make the news? I wondered if anybody even noticed I was gone.

I snorted audibly, knowing the truth. Not a single person would have noticed. If this garnered any attention, it was in thanks to Owen. Officer Martinez sighed and turned his back to me. Maybe I wasn't as easy to ignore now that I was a hardened criminal.

"I'm waiting on my ride," I lied.

Sort of.

I didn't have a car here as it was still at the base of The Slope. I hadn't technically called anybody for help, and not just because my phone was dead. I could walk the mile home, but Owen had said he was coming. I didn't want to doubt him already. I'd wait here until they made me leave. With each ticking minute, a little voice in my head warned that he'd forgotten about me and was no different from the rest of the town.

I fidgeted with the zipper on the snowsuit I now owned. Regrettably.

He would be coming. I trusted him. I remembered his face last night as he held me. The regret in it this morning as he delivered me to Benny Jr.

The officer looked at my jumping knee, shaking his cup of coffee, and sighed even more loudly. I smiled endearingly. He blinked slowly back.

Officer Martinez was surprised to learn that we'd gone to school around the same time, and I had lived in Slippery Slopes my whole life. I found this out in my nonstop questioning. Sure, he had a job to do, but that didn't mean I wouldn't ensure he remembered me in the future.

Just then, Owen came sliding to a stop in the front entry. "Bee?" he called out. His deep voice rumbled, sending shivers down me.

"Back here!" I called.

I almost collapsed forward in relief. I trusted him, but there had still been worry.

Owen came through the small wooden half door to where Officer Martinez and I were sitting, me in the guest chair and him behind his desk. The officer straightened, wary. I guess I could see how intimidating Owen might look from his point of view—large, balled fists, anger tugging his brow to sharp points. But to me, Owen just looked ... sweaty.

"Slow down, Romeo. She's fine. Please tell me you're here to take her?" he asked Owen.

"I got here as quick as I could. What does she need?" he asked the cop. To me, he said. "Are you okay?"

"I'm a little thirsty," I said softly, voice rough, looking up at him through my lashes. I coughed dryly.

"For crying out loud," Martinez mumbled and shoved a water bottle at me. "Just get her out of here. Please."

I stood and went to Owen. My body trembled with nerves. I had worried some part of me romanticized the evening as I sometimes did. That I had inflated our connection and my feelings to the point of fantasy, but seeing him now, my knees were seconds from giving out, and my arms ached to hold him.

There he was, my big, lovable man with a heart like nobody else. I wasn't sure what I'd done to deserve his attention, but the fear of losing it was palpable.

I kicked his shoe with my own.

"Why are you panting? Did you run all the way here?" I asked.

"Yeah," he said with his hands on his knees, looking up at me.

"From where?" I handed him the water bottle.

"Ivy's." He chugged it.

"That's just behind the park," I teased, but my heart felt like it was growing so big it might burst out of my chest. I imagined him sprinting through town, calling my name—passersby, likely thinking he was being chased by an actual bumble bee.

"I have a lot more weight to carry when I run," he said.

"You should think about adding some cardio to your routine. Clearly, you have weightlifting covered."

"Bee." He straightened and pulled off his winter hat. He huffed a frustrated laugh as he shook his head. He smiled down at me. How I loved making him smile. "Are you okay?" he asked.

He examined my body and ran a thumb over the bruise on my chin from last night. I closed my eyes and leaned into his hand.

"If I say 'no,' will you keep checking me? You haven't checked all areas," I said.

Officer Martinez stood and tossed the paper on the empty front desk. "I'm out of here." He headed toward the back. "She's free to leave," he said to Owen. "Benny Jr. didn't press any charges."

"Oh. Good." Owen seemed surprised, if not a little disappointed.

"Were you planning to come save the day?" I asked him, looking up at him with what I'm sure were hearts in my eyes.

His shoulders slumped. "Yeah."

Once the cop was gone, I said with a shaking voice, "Owen. Thank you."

He stepped closer and cupped my head, gently tilting up my chin to meet his gaze. "I told you I was coming."

"I know. I just—" I shook my head. "I'm just really glad to see you."

The edges of his eyes crinkled with a soft smile. "I'm glad to see you too."

I took a bracing breath and shook out any remnants of fear. I looped my arms through his and smiled brightly. "Take me back to my car at the base of the tram?"

He nodded and bent to kiss my forehead. Just like that. Just like we were a couple for years and this was a normal thing for us.

"Is Ivy okay? Did you get things squared away?" I asked as we went out the front of the police station. Pretty sure I heard Officer Martinez groan *finally* once we were outside.

"You're not going to believe this." He told me about his conversation with Ivy as he walked me the block back to his car. "Turns out she's secretly loaded." Owen shook his head like he was the one who couldn't believe it.

"Ha! Good for her," I said as we came to a stop at the passenger door of his car. I huffed a laugh and toyed with my zipper. "I guess that basically means all the trouble we went through was completely pointless. All that drama and excitement for nothing. Ah, life is funny," I said cheerfully.

Owen did not laugh as he opened the passenger door for me. He just looked above my head at the horizon, deep in thought.

Main Street was quiet this time on New Year's Day. The usual bustle of tourists and locals were likely sleeping off their celebrations. The sun shone bright, but the snow was thick where it wasn't plowed by Pat, our singular snow plow in town, "Snow Business." The mountain slope cast a long shadow on these short days. The cables of the tram could just barely be seen.

"Not for nothing," Owen eventually said, lowering his head to kiss me on the mouth briefly. I bit my lip and tucked my chin as pure joy bubbled through me. I hadn't been forgotten or left behind.

He hesitated to start the drive, so we stood there, and after a minute, he said, "She always talked about her having these Swiss bank accounts. I thought that was one of her jokes. Like how she jokes about blowing up the tram."

We shared a concerned look. Then we glanced in the direction of the tram. Then back at each other. We shared a nervous laugh.

"Nah, she wouldn't," Owen said.

"Boom!" I yelled as he jumped about a foot in the air. "Just kidding. But that would have been great timing, you have to admit."

Owen let out a shaking breath. "Why do I have a feeling you're always going to keep me on my toes?"

I shrugged, tucking my short hair behind my ear, hiding my smile as he discussed a future *us*.

"Wait, how did you get out of charges? Not that I'm complaining, I just didn't think Benny Jr. would ever let things go. And I guess I wanted to come rescue you a little."

"You're so dang sweet. But it's all good." I finally got in the car, but not before patting him on the cheek. "Benny realized I hadn't done anything wrong," I said sweetly.

He shot me a look as he walked around to the driver's side. Once inside, he asked cajolingly, "What did you do, Bee?"

"Nothing, we just had a little chat. He apologized for almost getting us killed. I made it clear it was all a misunderstanding. Maybe he just had a visit from the ghosts of New Year's Past, Present, and Future. But mostly past. Maybe he remembered all the shady stuff he's ever done. Maybe he feels a little repentant about it." I tossed my arms out with a shrug.

I called Benny Jr. and laid it all out on the table the second I got to jail. I told him about lawsuits from shoddy safety checks and how the *Slippery Slopes Sheets* might be interested in hearing about some of his business dealings. Long story short, I threatened to expose him for the crook he was if he didn't let me be and guarantee Owen work as long as he needed it. I probably could have gotten him to agree to bring the tram up to date, but I didn't want to push it. Benny Jr. was just a scared little kid in a grown man's body.

Owen looked over at me, eyebrow raised skeptically. "Yeah. Maybe." He shook his head as he pulled into the direction of The Slope. "You're full of surprises," he said.

"Never underestimate quiet people. We're the ones to fear."

"Quiet?" He snorted.

We were back at my car too quickly. I felt a welling of sadness mixed with that fuzzy post-adrenaline feeling of exhaustion, but too wired to rest filled me. Neither of us slept much last night due to all the naughty noodling. Any rush I got from being locked up had long crashed. Also, Owen had done all that running to save me.

"What are you smiling about?" he asked once he parked next to my car.

"Nothing."

"Huh. The tram must still be frozen. There are no cars here."

"Yeah," I said.

"We can still get you up there." Owen turned toward me and grabbed my hands. "Let me make this happen for you. I still want to help you make your dreams come true."

"I think you did, Owen," I said, holding his gaze, feeling my throat lock up. I wanted to confess something to him, something I'd been thinking since last night, but what would happen next? I was still so scared to be forgotten, or maybe if I came on too strong, he'd get freaked out and run. I just didn't know how to function normally around people.

Instead, I swallowed my confession and added, "I spent the day in jail. Old Bee would never!" I risked a glance up to Owen with a forced laugh. He watched me carefully.

"What about the journalist?" he asked. "The statue?"

At the thought of Jane Smith, my heart clenched in pain. I had wanted to make things better for her. I wanted to guarantee a spot in history, but that wasn't something I had any control over.

"They had to head back. They couldn't get back up the mountain and had to go home." I saw the text when I had reception and before my phone died. "But it's okay. Honestly. The shine of the idea has sort of worn off."

"This sucks," he said.

"I'm a new me. Trust me, I'm changed." I kissed his knuckles. "It wasn't about notoriety. I mean, it was, but maybe I just needed to prove I could do something different. I think I understand that now." I looked out the window for a long, dramatic beat. "My time in jail put things in perspective for me."

He chuckled.

"Honestly, Owen. I'm basically a felon—"

"Technically, you were only being held—"

"But the point is, I am so cool now. Major street cred." I lifted my chin. "I just hope you're not embarrassed to be seen with such a troubled young woman."

His eyes bounced with light as he held mine. "I guess we will have to see how it goes. On our next date? A real date."

"A real date?" I smiled with my whole body. I could float in the air.

"Maybe we could find an old elevator to get trapped in?" he suggested with a grin.

"Maybe we could go explore some strictly off-limit caves with very small openings?" I added,

"Or we could do that workout class you're so eager to try."

I shuddered. "Okay, too far." He put the car in park but left the heat running as he turned to me with another smile that I snatched up and stored away. I turned to him, pulling up my left leg to tuck under my chin. It slipped back down because of this stupid snowsuit, so I settled with leaning against the headrest. "I look forward to hearing what you come up with," I said.

He had to want to go home and rest and change after the last twenty-four hours. I couldn't wait to set this outfit on fire. But so long as he sat here looking at me like that, the windows slowly fogging, I wasn't about to send him on his way.

He prodded for more information about Benny Jr. and hinted at maybe going back to school. (Thanks to my suggestion, no doubt.) I asked him more about Ivy and the home and things we might be able to do to help make it better around there. We shared stories about New Year's gone by. We talked about lonely nights and cold beds.

He said s'mores Pop-Tarts were the best flavor, and I ignored his absurd joke.

We just talked. Even after all the talking last night, I couldn't get enough of him. I didn't want to let him go. My heart ached with desperation to keep him near.

But it was too soon, and I was too much. I had to let him breathe.

Eventually, he glanced at his watch. "I have to head back to Ivy's. I promised her dinner."

*Don't go. Invite me. Let's stay together.*

"Okay." I sighed. "I have to find a metal trash can to burn this in," I said with a smile and a forced laugh.

"You want to—"

"I should let you—"

We both started and stopped at the same time.

"You go ahead and head out," I said and tentatively leaned forward until we hovered with our faces just a breath apart. "Tell Ivy I'll help her blow up the tram any time."

His low laugh rumbled through the warm comfort of the car.

"Happy New Year, Bee," he said.

"The best start to a new year ever," I said.

He kissed me softly on the lips, and I squeezed my eyes shut tight.

I ran up to my door before I could do or say anything I couldn't take back. I lay in bed too long, staring at the dark ceiling, a hand on my racing heart, willing myself to believe that I would hear from him soon.

# Chapter 24

Bee

"I STILL CAN'T BELIEVE YOU GOT STUCK IN THE TRAM. Everybody is talking about you going to the police station, but I feel like not nearly enough people are focused on the bigger issue," Deckard said as he followed me, bundled in his winter coat.

"Wait, who's talking?" I asked, pulling out my keys to Grizabella's.

"How is that even allowed?" He went on, looking a little ill. "How many people ride The Can every day? There has to be safety protocol." Deckard's mismatched eyes looked hazily into the distance, his shaggy brown hair mussed.

"You'd think," I said, remembering Benny Jr.'s stuttering apology when I'd brought that up.

Deckard continued his anxiety spiral as he followed me into Grizabella's back entrance for employees. He always kept me company in the café the few minutes before opening on the days he went to work. My phone remained text- and call-free from Owen. And every time I checked, the old insecurities crept to the surface.

When I turned on the main lights, I was met with a chorus of meows. The cats were never really alone, but you wouldn't think that with how they reacted to my arrival.

"You're not starving," I said to the closest few as they rubbed against my ankles and hopped onto nearby shelves to get my attention. "I missed you too."

It was nice to be back, nice to have the familiar routine, but a little black cloud hung over my head that I couldn't outpace. I tugged down a black-and-silver streamer that had been missed by whoever cleaned up from the party. When I'd left here on New Year's Eve, I'd been so down but so determined to change. I had imagined that when I returned in the new year, I would be a new person. But I still felt like me, just with a new haircut. I checked my phone again, and my heart twisted in disappointment. I shoved it to the back of my bag so I wouldn't keep looking at it.

"What a wild ride, literally." Deckard bent to pet Godzilla. "I'm glad you're back safe. You must have been so scared."

"For some parts, yeah. It was pretty bananas, but Owen made sure I was okay," I said.

I felt his stare on the side of my face. "Is that right? I heard they found you two at the Hookup Hut."

"From who?" I asked, but then added, "A lady never makes out all night, comes a bunch of times through several rounds of very active and enthusiastic lovemaking, and then talks about it," I said coyly. No reason to be gauche.

Deckard tilted his head, squirming slightly. "Good for you both, I guess?" He picked up one of the cats, Maximus, and scratched behind his ear. "You really like him? I only ever knew him as the scary muscle that worked for Benny Jr. But he's good to you?" Deckard watched me.

I nodded eagerly, hands clasped under my chin. "He took really good care of me even though I was—well, you know how I can be."

He nodded too enthusiastically for my liking.

"Also, all the aforementioned orgasms," I added just because of the enthusiastic nodding.

Deckard held up his hand. "Yep, okay, got it."

I counted the till, started brewing a carafe of coffee, and put out the pastries from Trailside Treats next door. *Seriously*, what was with this town and alliteration? Lazy wordplay, really. Very little creativity. "He even busted me out of the clink." More or less. Or he had tried.

"I had heard that." Deckard came to the counter as I prepared his usual order before he went to work.

"Seriously, from who? How have you talked to so many people already?"

He shrugged and waved off my question. It wouldn't be unusual for him to talk to so many people in such a short time. "I guess." He hesitated. "I don't understand why you didn't tell me about your big New Year's plans? I could have helped you."

I slid his muffin over with his Americano. "Exactly." I patted his hand when he looked crestfallen. "I needed to do it on my own."

He nodded. "So, now what? Do you feel changed?"

I shrugged. "I don't know. I guess I don't feel the need to prove myself to Slippery Slopes anymore."

"You never did need to."

"I'm starting to understand that, but it's easy for you. The whole town knows and loves you," I said.

"I'm one of six siblings, and my mom is the town mayor; I understand a little bit about wanting to make my own path," he said with tension gathering around his eyes.

"I know you do. But you're still seen. You have to be aware

of how the rest of the town never notices me. At most, I was Deckard Sparks' weird little friend." A dark thought occurred to me then. Would I only be Owen's weird little girlfriend now? Had I only succeeded in attaching myself to another man? Not that it mattered what they thought. I just wanted to make a name for myself.

"You are a wonderful person, Bee Perkins, and plenty of people see it," Deckard said, meeting my eyes.

"Thank you. Ditto." I gave him a half smile. "But now I feel all these insecurities popping up. Maybe he's already forgotten about me. Maybe without the extremely real threat of frostbite, he's not as willing to snuggle. Because he said he'd call, me but—"

"Maybe he just—"

"And then that night was just so wonderful. I can't explain the instant connection that we had. It was a sort of magic." I sighed.

"That sounds really great, Bee. I'm actually envious, but—"

"And then he's so deep and thoughtful. People can't see him as he is at all. I'm trying so hard to think that he isn't ignoring me because if you were there, if you felt ... I mean, it *felt* so real." I raised my eyebrows meaningfully.

"Bee, please."

"And that connection was so *deep*, if you catch my drift."

"Dear God, make it stop."

"We had such an amazing night, and now he's gone. I just don't know where he could be," I said with a sigh and went to the front door.

"Bee!" Deckard shouted, coming to stand in front of me, arms flailing.

"What? Yeesh, no need to yell."

I flipped the sign to open quickly and turned to him, my back to the door.

"It's not even been a day," Deckard said.

"I know. I never thought he'd be one to play hard to get."

"Yeah." Deckard looked to the side and made that face like I wasn't thinking clearly. I'd show *him* not thinking clearly. He must have seen something in my features because he held up his hands and patted my shoulders. "I'm just saying he may have needed a minute. Had to get some ducks in a row."

"What ducks? What's with all the bird metaphors?" I groaned.

"It's not even been twenty-four hours since you two left each other," he said.

"Yet more than twice the duration of our relationship," I mumbled.

"Give him a chance to prove himself." His gaze moved back over my shoulder and snagged. "Whoa. Looks like a morning rush."

I spun to see a line already formed up front, large for the small town. They looked at the door, little puffs of breath coming out as they chatted eagerly with one another. "Maybe because we were closed yesterday? Aw, everybody missed the cats."

Deckard laughed at that for some reason. Deckard moved to his usual table to do his job as I started helping the stream of nonstop customers.

The first order was with the town's biggest gossip and local hairdresser, Tess. She gasped when she saw my hair. "Oh my God, you look so chic."

"I know, thanks." I touched the tips of my hair and thought of Owen's quiet focus as he cut my hair. How gentle and kind he'd been.

I glared at where my phone sat in my bag.

I didn't think Tess would have been able to pick me out of a lineup yesterday. She dove into questions right away. She said that she heard from Deb at Deb's Diner (of course) that Samuel Clemens saw me taken to the police station in handcuffs.

I glanced up to share a look with Deckard. He shook his head with a silent laugh.

"See. Not a ghost," he mouthed. He'd been right. Slippery Slopes was *buzzing* with Bee gossip. This was my time to shine.

"Yeah. I spent time locked up." I sucked in my lips and looked to some distant horizon. "I can't really talk about it."

I didn't need to look to know that snort was Deckard.

After that, the next few customers asked similar thinly veiled questions about why I was in jail. *Wait a dang minute ...* People weren't here for the cats at all and, in fact, were only here to learn some gossip about my time in jail or what was going on with Owen and me.

"You've really made a name for yourself, Bee Perkins," Maybel said when she came for pastries and coffee for her B and B.

"Really buzzworthy," I said.

She threw her head back and laughed. "Also, loving the new look." She patted her own hair where my hair ended. "You had that long hair forever, this suits you."

"I'm just winging it," I said.

"Oh, because bees." She blinked. The joke sank in, and she started laughing.

Maybel remembered my long hair. And in fact, the more people who came through, the more I understood that I wasn't a total apparition.

Hour after hour, the customers kept coming. It seemed the whole of Slippery Slopes had not only heard about Owen and me getting stuck in the tram but that alone was not nearly shocking enough. But the mystery of why I ended up being in jail the following morning really ramped up the rumor mill. Someone even asked if I had taken Owen "out." And they didn't mean as a date, they meant, like, murdered him. So silly.

At one point, Natalie, a pretty woman our age who worked for the mayor's office, walked in with her shoulders set with her typical determination. I'd thought she'd come pick up her usual order for Mayor Sparks and herself, but the second she headed toward Deckard, about two feet behind his back, she stopped, went sort of pale, and left. I glanced to Deckard to see if he'd clocked her odd behavior, but he was lost to his work, as always. It was strange, but there wasn't time to dwell because more customers kept coming.

The more I told the truth in bits and pieces (it really wasn't their business), the more I got into this role as being the subject of the town's attention, at least until the next gossip stormed through town.

And in this town, there was always some fresh drama.

I may have embellished some parts the more times I told the story.

"And so I said to Benny Jr., you can take me to jail, but you'll never take my freedom!" I held my balled fists in the sky, completing my story, this time to Azi (who came with flowers to apologize and see what happened after I was taken away). Deckard met my eyes where he sat by the door, his blue and green eyes rolling hard at me. I shrugged.

"Wow. You are really something, Perkins." He leaned in, and the smell of his cologne tickled my nose. "I was thinking, maybe sometime I could take you out?" Azi asked.

Deckard's eyebrows shot up, matching my own.

"Aren't you like nineteen?" I asked Azi.

"Twenty-one in April. Aries, baby."

"Um, flattered but no—"

"Azi." A deep voice growled from behind him.

Azi's eyes widened, and he spun around quickly.

"Never mind. Gotta get back to it." Azi left so fast that there was practically a cloud in the shape of him. I fought not to fling myself over the counter and into Owen's arms.

"I thought you didn't want people to be scared of you?" I teased, even as my heart leaped, and I held the counter with a white-knuckled grip.

"He should be scared," Owen said. Here, in the light of day and standing in Grizabella's, I saw a flash of the man he projected around town, a brief glimpse of his intimidation tactics.

He was as cute as a button.

"Green doesn't suit you," I said and grinned.

Owen looked into my eyes, and the whole rest of the world faded away. I leaned forward. He leaned forward. Our lips hovered inches away over the counter that separated us. Owen's eyes went soft as the smile spread over his lips. I missed him so much. The relief of having him here relaxed muscles throughout my whole body.

Even after just one night, it was such a relief to see him. It didn't make any sense, but I wasn't going to question it.

"Hi, I'm Deckard." Deckard stepped in front of me, blocking my view of Owen.

I was about to throw a croissant at my best friend's head.

"Owen." The two men shook hands. Standing next to Deckard, who was pretty tall in his own right, Owen's massive build was all the more pronounced.

Deckard smiled between the two of us. I hinted for him to leave with a subtle tilt of my head and lifting of my eyebrows, but he wouldn't look at me.

He was looking down on Owen in what might be an attempt at intimidation.

It quickly melted away, and Deckard stuck to the easy affability that trademarked his personality. "Well, anyway, I just wanted to meet the man who saved my friend."

"First, he kidnapped me," I said.

"Wait, what?" Deckard asked.

At the same time, Owen said, "No, I didn't. She attacked me."

Deckard's head tilted from side to side. "No offense, Bee, but that does seem pretty in line with your MO."

I clicked my tongue but didn't argue.

"I'm sorry it took so long to get to you," Owen said, and I gave Deckard a pointed look that conveyed *see I was right about the long passage of time.* "I had to get some ducks in a row," Owen finished.

Deckard returned a similar, *and I was right too* face. Freaking bird metaphors.

"Well." Deckard cleared his throat. "I better get back to my work business. You two carry on."

Owen's eyes briefly left my face, where they'd been since he arrived, I would like to point out, to glance around the café. As if just the awareness of his surroundings brought on symptoms, his eyes started to water.

His head tilted when he spotted François the pug. "That is a dog."

"Shh. Don't you dare. He's a cat," I whispered.

He brought his focus back to me, eyes narrowing seductively, sending little tingles up my legs. That or he was about to sneeze.

"Bless you," I said.

"Thank you. Do you have a minute? I'd like to show you something."

Mel had come in for the closing shift, and things had slowed way down. "You two kids go for it. I'll woman the shop," she said with a wink.

Owen sneezed. "I'll bring her back soon," Owen said.

Then he sneezed again.

She waved us off without worry as I got on my hat and coat. I was so happy to see Owen, I didn't even take the usual twenty minutes to say goodbye to each cat. (I'd be back and would rectify that before I went home for the night.) He raised an eyebrow at the bright green poof on my winter hat.

"Don't judge the hat."

"I'm not. I'm just happy to see you do own outerwear." He flicked the ball on the top. "It's the same color as your bikini." His voice was low and gravelly as heat flooded me.

He grabbed my hand to loop through his arm, and I smiled big up at him. We strolled across the street into the town square, where the large gazebo was still decorated from Christmas. Families were out rolling giant balls for snow people and throwing snowballs at each other in the grass town square. Owen and I walked hand in hand, my chin held high, knowing without a doubt that this town wasn't going to forget about me anytime soon.

# Chapter 25

Owen

"Where are we going?" Bee asked after two and a half minutes of silent walking. Longer than I thought she'd manage to be quiet.

"Almost there." Unexpected nerves had my palms sweating under these gloves. I'd spent the past day working on this surprise for her, but what if she didn't like it?

"Guess what?" she said, her joy effusive.

"You found out there is a special edition Pop-Tarts flavor?" I teased.

"Har har. No." She stopped, eyes widening. "Wait, is there?"

I shrugged. "Probably."

"Not something to joke about," she mumbled under her breath. "What I was going to say was that I'm famous!" She wiggled her shoulders, unable to contain her excitement. "Well, for Slippery Slopes. At least for today."

"Is that right?" I glanced at her and almost tripped on a guinea pig when I forgot to look away. She looked beautiful with rosy cheeks and the tip of her nose red, alit from within with whatever magic made her. Probably the same magic that made Keebler elves.

I couldn't believe how much I'd missed her, though we'd only been a part for a little while. These feelings had grown so fast it had to be part of that same magic.

"Yes! So many people came into the café to see me and talk to me and ask me about my time in jail or about getting stuck in the tram or about the jump to the cabin."

The side of my mouth pulled into a smile.

"Not to let this life of crime go to my head, but I'm sort of a big deal around here." She nodded like she accepted her newfound burden of popularity.

"As you should be," I said. I squeezed her to me.

We'd made it to the bench I wanted to bring her to. Despite the cold and snow, it couldn't wait. The town of Slippery Slopes was tucked in the valley between mountain peaks, somewhat protected from last night's storm, but a fresh layer of snow blanketed everything, like a clean, fresh start to the year.

The snow was already cleaned off the bench and the thick wool blanket sat waiting for her. She pushed them out of the way and sat.

"That was for—" I started. Her wide brown eyes blinked at me. "Never mind." I sat next to her, the cold bench seeping through instantly. This could be my life. A joy like I never imagined warmed me from within. Sharing cold benches and making sure Bee was comfortable for decades to come made me feel excited.

If I was lucky. I unfurled the blanket and wrapped it around us. "Are you happy now?" I asked.

She shrugged. "I don't love wool. It's pretty itchy."

I couldn't help myself. I bent and kissed her cold, rosy cheek. "I meant with all your newfound notoriety."

"Oh. Yes!" Her head tilted. "Well, I mean. Sure." She slouched back. "I think so?" She shook her head. "I don't think so."

"What's going through that mind of yours?" I asked, accountably nervous.

I knew what I wanted. I understood that Bee was it for me. But I also understood that she'd spent her life being overlooked, and we just got close in the past couple of days. I wouldn't want to scare her or make things happen too fast.

"I guess I thought it would make me feel different. I was surprised at how many people came in today to talk to me. How many people commented on my change, implying that they had seen me before? I guess I thought I would feel a sense of relief, a sort of validation?" She shook her head once. "Really, it just made me realize I didn't need the whole town to see me." As she spoke, her shoulders went to her ears. Finally, she took a deep breath, dropping them. She turned to me and said, "I just needed one person to really see me."

My heart beat a heavy, hard thump once in hope. "I see you," I said softly.

"I know. You always have. I don't know why—" She cut herself off and leaned forward and kissed my cheek. "Thank you, Owen." She pulled herself closer, and I could see her thoughts gathering. "I thought people knowing my name, wanting to talk to me might make me feel ... Well, as silly as it sounds, I thought it might make me feel important. Loved. I don't know. It wasn't a conscious desire, in hindsight. Not any more than you actively seek food or rest, just something you long for on an instinctual level. I never thought that I would be worthy of a romantic sort of love." She blushed furiously and met my gaze. "I thought that I was too forgettable or different, too whatever, to have anybody really notice me that way. Not that I should have derived my value from that either. I just ..."

She sighed and stretched out her fingers, seeming to collect herself.

"I spent a lot of time in jail thinking, you know. And I think that the thing that I really wanted was to feel that I had something to offer the world, and maybe I found that just by existing. Because all the attention that I got from town today was nice, but it was like eating cotton candy when you're really hungry, when you really need a good meal of steak and potatoes. And trust me, I have had many meals that consisted only of cotton candy." I wasn't surprised at all. "I thought that would change me. But I understand that none of those people really saw me today. It was nice, sure, I think because I might just be chatty by nature, but I didn't really feel like anybody cared. Not like when I talk to you. When I talk to you, I feel like I don't have to try, that bits of myself just pour out, and you are waiting there with a little butterfly net to catch them all."

I swallowed, my throat too tight to talk. But I nodded to show I understood.

"I'm sorry about the tram. I'm sorry you had to come get me and all the dumb stuff I did because I thought I needed some sort of validation," she finished, fully depleted of her thoughts and feelings.

How she'd come to trust me in such a short amount of time was truly a gift.

I grabbed her hands, and emotion swelled in my chest. "Do you remember how you told me to look through your eyes if I needed to see a better version of myself?" I asked her.

"I'm so wise," she said with quiet awe.

I laughed softly. Her features lit up as her gaze moved from my mouth to my eyes and around my face. "You are wise, Bee. And I want you to know that it's the same for me." I lowered my forehead to hers. "If you need somebody to see you, to hear you, to listen to you, let it be me. Tell me your stories and your bad jokes. I would love to share your food and lint roll your cat hair."

"It's a real problem." She flicked off a stray hair.

"Let me be that person," I said, but the wobble of my voice made it a question. "I want to be the person who shares the load with you."

Her large eyes welled with tears, expressive eyebrows contorted with joy. "Only if you let me give you all the love that you needed in the past," she said, voice tight.

"I'd like that very much." I kissed her freezing knuckles before I pulled her sleeves down to cover them.

We held each other, and I kissed her face and cheeks and neck. "You're so cold."

"I have lost a lot of insulating hair." She leaned back and sniffled. "No offense, because I'm loving this, but why are we out here in the freezing cold? I thought we'd had our fill of that."

I kissed her one more time and turned to gesture to the side. I didn't follow her gaze because I knew what she would see. I only watched her reaction as her eyes took in the scene, and she gasped. "Oh my God, you cleaned up Jane Smith."

She shot up, elbowing me in the chin in the process, and went to the larger-than-life bronze statue.

"We got a few volunteers to trim the vines and cut back the weeds. I owe some people for working out in the snow," I explained.

"It looks so good! She's so shiny," she said. "Wow, are those lights new?"

"Yep. Little spotlights so she'll even be seen at night." I grabbed her hand and brought her closer. "But this is really what I wanted to show you." I pointed at a small, printed sign. "I was just going to clean Jane up, but as I was doing it, I saw a name I recognized engraved on the side. Fled."

"As in Ned Fled? Resident centenarian?" She gasped.

I nodded. "Who just happens to live down the hall from Ivy, as you may recall. His great-great-grandfather was one of the gold rushers who came to settle Slippery Slopes back in the day. It was his father who erected the statue in the thirties on the centennial anniversary of Slippery Slopes. He had a lot more to say and would love to talk to you. He said he was sorry that your meeting slipped his mind, but that happens sometimes."

Her chin quivered as she nodded. "I would love that. I already plan to make more visits to Golden Sunset. Oh, maybe I could bring the cats." She waved a hand like putting a pin in the thought for another time. "How did you find all this out in such a short time?" she asked. "Seriously, I'm like ten percent frustrated because I really did look."

"I asked Ivy, and she had some ideas. Ned had old articles in his room, and a story passed down in the family. Someone at the Santa Fe clerk's office confirmed some details, and here we are."

Bee went quiet, her hand covering her mouth as her other gently pressed her fingertips against the words. She gasped and snorted. "No way," she said.

I knew what she had just read and chuckled. "Yep. That's her actual name. Or at least the one she provided when she moved here to Slippery Slopes."

"Jane Smith." Bee laughed as her eyes softened, and she looked into the distance. "I really am psychic." She brought her focus back to the statue and started to read the paragraph that would be the future plaque that would mark the woman.

"We don't have the full story yet, but we have narrowed it down. Some speculate that she made her name up when she moved here because she was hiding from her abusive husband or ex-lover. I've heard two versions of her story. One's a love story, and the other was a tragedy."

Bee stared up at her face and smiled, her eyes gleaming. "It was definitely a love story."

"I even heard that there's a legend that says she hid some treasure in Looters Lake."

"Alliterations," we said at the same time and then smiled widely at each other.

"Now we will have to learn how to scuba dive," Bee said seriously.

My heart swelled. This was everything I had hoped it would be for her. It wasn't perfect, and it wasn't complete, but she seemed so happy. I felt so much relief at her joy.

"Like I said, this sign is just temporary. Once the earth defrosts in spring, we'll put the real one in. With some funds Benny Jr. has generously decided to donate."

"This is ... I'm crying. Thank you so much for this, Owen. I can't tell you what this means." She squeezed me until I grunted and then turned back to Jane. She placed her hand on the foot to the statue. "You won't be forgotten," she whispered to her.

"She'll never be forgotten ... and neither will you." I pointed at one last thing.

"'Generously donated by local legend Bee Perkins.'"

"But I didn't ..."

"Benny Jr. did. In your honor. We came to an arrangement. That's part of the reason I hadn't called you yet. Sorry I took so long."

She blushed, went up on her toes, and kissed my cheek. "You better be careful, Owen 'The Soupman' Campbell. I am dangerously close to falling for you." We kissed deeper, arms interlocked, there in the middle of town. She paused to pull back and study me. "You know, I'm not as scared now. I'm not afraid of fading away. I think because if I have you to share the day-to-day with, I won't feel like I'm a ghost. As long as I'm here making memories with you, I think that's more than enough. More than I thought possible."

My throat tightened, and I nodded. "I'd love the chance to get to know our story together."

She looked back at the statue and shook her head. "I can't believe you did this. Most people would think this is so silly, that *I'm* so silly for caring."

"You're not silly, Bee. You are fierce and brave and hilarious and beautiful, and I can't wait to get to know you more," I said, tucking her under my chin so she could admire her statue.

"I'm so glad I got us trapped in the tram with my hare-brained idea," she said.

"I didn't realize how stuck I was. You've shaken me up and turned my whole world upside down. I thought I was only capable of violence. I thought there was no coming back from my mistakes, but nothing feels like a mistake anymore. How could it be when it all led me to you?"

"Even getting stuck in the tram?" she asked, voice shaking.

"Especially that. That night meant so much to me. You mean so much to me. You are extraordinary. You make me excited about life again; you are exceptional. I'll remember you forever. You aren't a forgotten statue, Bee. You are a marker in time. There was after I met you and everything before. I will never be the same again. And I wanted you to know that, no matter how many years pass, I will never forget you."

She turned into my arms and stepped up on the low wall until we were face-to-face.

"I know it would be crazy to say I'm falling in love with you after just one night on a tram—"

"Don't say crazy, it's not nice."

She grinned at my mirrored words. "But also crazier things have happened in this town."

My throat bobbed at her confession. She grinned so wide.

"I feel the same way," I said.

I leaned forward, and we kissed. The future lay ahead of us, and I couldn't wait to see what it brought.

# Chapter 26



"Aw, come on. Why would he do it that way?" I threw a hand up at the screen of the new fancy TV in Ivy's room. A comedian was attempting to transfer spaghetti sauce from one container to the other using a teaspoon and failing epically.

"They're idiots," Ivy said with a shake of her head.

"Idiots," I repeated.

Ivy detailed how she would have done the task presented, and I agreed. Though truthfully, under pressure, I probably would have done way worse, but it was fun to feel superior.

Ivy's room was decorated from Christmas still, but she wore a pointed tinsel New Year's hat and held on to a noisemaker for when we had our New Year's countdown.

Ivy and I had become fast friends in the last year, sometimes to the chagrin of Owen. We shared a love of sweets and the darling man who brought us together. I genuinely enjoyed spending time with her and the other residents of Golden Sunsets.

"How much longer until lover boy is off?" Ivy asked, straining to turn in her chair and look toward the hall.

"Lover boy is off," Owen said as he walked into the room.

He looked happy but tired at the end of his shift.

"Yay!" I jumped out of the chair and into his arms, giving him just enough time to drop his jacket to the bed and catch me.

"Ouch," he said, but smiled down and kissed me.

I wasn't even sure where I hit him that time.

"Did I ever tell you how hot you look in those scrubs?" I whispered, tugging at the powder-blue material that made his eyes pop.

"Once or twice." His gravelly voice sent shivers through me.

"Children, please. I just ate," Ivy said.

"Haters gonna hate," I said, but wiggled out of Owen's arms. "Plus, you've said way more inappropriate things, lady."

"Now that he's in school again, I've slipped back into his teacher role." She sniffed haughtily.

"I don't think it works that way when I'm going to the local nursing school and you aren't teaching," Owen said, stretching his back. He'd started working here in the spring when the Head Nurse, Laura, offered him a position as he worked on his nursing degree. It was a no-brainer to quit working as muscle for Benny Jr.

He slid off his name badge and put on one of the party hats I handed to him. "How long until midnight?" he asked.

It was 6:03 p.m., according to the large print alarm clock on Ivy's side table.

"I just have to open the app on the streaming service, and it starts a twenty-minute countdown."

"Start it!" Ivy said, giving Owen a kiss as he bent to greet her. "I've been dying for a glass of bubbly, but Bee said we had to wait."

I clicked my tongue. "See what I get for being responsible?"

"In her defense, you two were wasted by the time I got off on Thanksgiving," Owen said.

Ivy and I shared a smile. "That was a fun night," I said.

"That poor intern got an eyeful." Ivy cackled.

"He should be so lucky."

After the sparkling wine was poured, the three of us held up our glasses in our little trio of love. "Anybody have any resolutions?" I asked.

"I guess since blowing up the tram is off the table," Ivy grumbled.

"We let you hit it with a sledgehammer," Owen said smoothly. "We weren't even technically allowed to do that." I scooted closer to him on the comfortable loveseat that sat across from Ivy's upgraded auto-reclining chair with all the fancy bells and whistles.

Over the summer, the town petitioned to have the old tram knocked down and rebuilt with modern technology with the help of Mayor Sparks. The demolition process was very satisfying, and we all saw a darker side to Ivy that day. I liked it.

The older woman sighed wistfully. "That was great. If it couldn't be Benny Jr., at least it was his tin can."

Benny Jr., for all his oozing charm, had a change of heart and let Owen quit without fuss when he realized he wasn't as all-powerful as he thought. Neither of us was aware of how much the coward had been hiding behind empty threats made, unbeknownst to Owen. It explained why so much of the town had feared him. I set Benny Jr. straight after a few guinea pigs and I cornered him behind The Tipsy one night. He has stopped hiding behind my boyfriend's size and stopped spreading untrue rumors about his violence.

Rumors of my violence had increased tenfold, according to Deckard.

"I just want to spend the new year with the people I love," Ivy said.

"Cheers to that," I said.

Owen snuggled me closer. "Really? No big plans to change?" he asked.

"Nah. Why mess with perfection?" I said. "Though I might organize more classes."

The cat visit days had been a huge success at the home, and soon, Whisker Wonderland, the local no-kill animal shelter, had volunteered a worker to come once a week to visit with a different little pet for adoption. (Though the guinea pig population remained unchecked and hardy as ever.) Because I had started a sign-up sheet for all of Ivy's alum to regularly visit the home, which was most of the town, there were always people coming through, and pets were constantly being adopted. The home had been through many improvements and renovations, thanks to a rise in donations. Ivy and the other residents had a steady stream of visitors and activities to partake in, and I was happier than ever. I didn't need to do some grand gesture to be seen. I just had to be me. And being involved in the local community outside the cats in the café had been infinitely rewarding.

Owen bent to kiss my forehead. "No resolutions here either. Just finish my degree and continue working here. Other than that, my life is perfect."

"You are very lucky," I said.

"I love you," Owen whispered, sending shivers down my back.

"I love you too."

We stared at each other until Ivy threw a decorative pillow at us, and the countdown began in earnest.

Owen told me he loved me on our second official date, which was great because I had been attempting to get the words out, and he did it for me. We'd spent pretty much every night together since that first night on the tram. I kept waiting for him to get sick of me or to want some space, but all he did was ask to move in after his lease was up in March. He was already over all the time anyway, so it was a smooth transition. Occasionally, an old fear would creep in, but then he would look at me with sincerity to tell me he loved me, and every fear melted from my shoulders.

We'd also come up with a system where I changed out of my work clothes the second I got home and dropped them into the washer, so the cat hair never became an issue.

The silver lining was that it was an excuse to get naked for him every day. Between his classes and the work at the home, he was busy a lot, but I'd taken the time to hang out with Ivy and the other residents and make little upgrades to Golden Sunsets. Turned out, I had a knack for mural painting and interior design —so long as they liked their murals Jackson Pollock-esque and their room design "cozy eclectic chic."

"Three ... two ... one. Happy New Year!"

The three of us clinked our glasses and sang a terrible rendition of "Auld Lang Syne." By the time we left, Ivy was falling asleep into her glass of champagne.

Owen and I had a full night of plans ahead of us.

* * *

*Later...*

The Hookup Hut had gone through some renovations of its own. Most notably, an online sign-up sheet for a more organized usage allotment. Owen and I claimed New Year's Eve in perpetuity. Why mess with tradition?

We used a snowmobile to get here and planned to snowmobile up to the peak for the second half of our plans in the morning. But for now, we had a night of reminiscing and sweet, sweet lovemaking ahead of us.

"I've missed this place," I said as I threw my overnight bag in the corner.

"I'll get the sheets out and change them," he said.

"I'll unload the snacks." I hid an extra pack of Pop-Tarts for the special occasion. If Owen played his cards right, I might be inclined to share.

Owen always played his cards right.

And by that, I meant he was very good in bed.

"I never thought I'd choose to come back here," he said. "Let alone actually really want to."

He still hadn't ridden the new tram. I couldn't say I blamed him.

"Happiest memories," I said and then noticed a small sign above a drawer in the kitchen. "'Take a condom/leave a condom, bro,'" I read out loud.

"That's probably our fault." A flush went to the tips of Owen's ears. "We burned through half a box last year."

"Go us."

When Owen had finished starting the fire and making the bed, and I'd laid out an assortment of snacks, I walked to the room and waited for him to look at me.

"You look like you're up to something," he said.

I dramatically shrugged out of my winter parka. "Tada!" I yelled.

Owen's mouth dropped open. At least four emotions passed over his features, ending on confusion. "I thought you burned that."

He reached out to run a hand up the sleeve of my faded multicolor snowsuit from the nineties that he'd stolen for me last year. "I tried to but alas. Too much sentimental value." I pointed at a melted part near the cuff. "Also, strangely inflammable. Wait. Flammable?" I tilted my head. "Contranym?"

He shook his head. "Non-flammable is the opposite. Inflammable and flammable mean the same thing."

"That makes zero sense." I shook my head.

He chuckled and came over to me. "Are you wearing the bikini underneath too?" He tugged at the collar, trying to peek down the neck.

"No. No," I said, and he frowned. "I'm not wearing anything," I clarified.

He grinned and started to tug down the zipper. I giggled as we fell into the bed and quickly stripped each other of our clothing.

We had a condom record to beat.

As we waited for official midnight, we alternated between laughing and talking and great orgasms, obviously.

As the clock turned over into the new year, we kissed passionately as I was lying in his arms by the fire in a burrow of blankets and pillows. The snow fell softly outside, but nothing compared to last year. I hummed contentedly, twirling my fingers along his chest and listening to the hard rhythm of his heart beating.

"Happy New Year, Bee." Actually, his heart was thumping so loud I was about to tell him to turn it down, so I could hear him properly.

"Happy New Year," I said again as I kissed his chest, feeling the hard beat bouncing against my lips.

We had finished our last round of horizontal hustle ten minutes ago. It shouldn't be hammering so loudly. I was about to tell him to see the local GP (general practitioner, *not* guinea pig in this case) when he cleared his throat.

"I was lying when I said that I didn't have any resolutions at Ivy's earlier," he said with a shaky voice.

"Oh?" I propped my chin onto my fists so I could meet his gaze.

"I'd really like to plan a wedding. Even if it's just a small ceremony. Or maybe an elopement." His eyes watched me carefully as he spoke, a careful flatness of features.

I sat up quickly, feeling the blood rush out of my face and my fingertips tingle.

"What are you ..." I started.

The blanket had fallen down, and my breasts were on full display, and Owen stared slack-jawed.

"Does this mean ..." My own heartbeat now rushed through my ears, my mind zoomed around my head, throwing her hands up in the air and screaming, *This is not a drill!*

Owen didn't respond. I snapped my fingers in front of his face. He cleared his throat. "Sorry. Those things really are troublemakers."

I looked down at my breasts, trying to steal the moment, and crossed my arms over them to keep him on task. He rolled to the side and grabbed a small velvet box from his pants, divested earlier on the chair next to us.

"Oh, this is happening." I turned back around to face him fully, my whole body vibrating. I'd been hoping and thinking, pretty much since our second date, that we would make a life together officially, but I never thought he'd make me wait a full year. "Should I put on a shirt?"

"I will never say yes to that question," he answered dryly. He scooted until he knelt in front of me.

"Owen. This is important." I knelt too. My whole body trembled in anticipation.

"It's just me," he said, meeting my gaze with earnestness. He extended the box and opened it to reveal a beautiful engagement ring.

I'd been wrapping the blanket around me like a towel after the shower when I stilled, and I felt my eyes bulging.

"Bee," he said, his throat bobbing, "This whole last year—"

"Yes! I will marry you!" I threw myself at him and started crying.

He kissed the top of my head and then pulled me away to pepper my face and neck with kisses. "I had a whole speech."

"I want to hear it. I do. Sorry." I looked up at him through blurred vision as he spoke, but I couldn't retain or process anything. I was too happy. I was screaming too loud on the inside.

Plus, I was sure I'd have him tell it to me at least four more times tonight.

"Will you marry me?" he finished.

"Took you long enough." My voice came out wobbly. "Yes."

* * *

*The following afternoon, New Year's Day*

It seemed the whole town was at the top of The Slope and decked out in their finest swim gear for the first inaugural Whisker Wonderland Charity Ski Event. I'd spent half the year planning this event, the proceeds which would be going to, of course, the animal shelter.

"Such a turnout," I said, surprised, looking at what had to be half the town coming to join us at the top of The Slope. "All thanks to you," Owen said, shifting from foot to foot on skis next to me.

"I am awesome," I said.

In the periphery, Benny Jr. handed out hot chocolates from Peaked Interests and wasn't too miserable looking. He'd graciously agreed to volunteer his time and money for the event. I waved to Deckard, shivering in his skivvies, and the brunette I didn't recognize on his arm.

"I hadn't thought of the logistics of seeing all my friends and neighbors scantily clad when organizing this event." I crinkled my nose and turned back to Owen.

The sun shone brightly, and the mountain had been dumped with fresh powder the week before. The conditions were perfect to ski down a mountain in a bathing suit.

"Maybe next year, we push for parkas," Owen agreed.

I shuddered after seeing Mateo, the EMT, in a bright red banana hammock.

"Remind me to research how to burn images from your retinas," Owen mumbled.

"I'm way ahead of you."

"Are you okay? Too cold?" Owen leaned into me, and warmth instantly spread over my side.

"I'm perfect. I can't believe so many people came out for this."

"I can't believe how much back hair Samuel Clemens has. Don't look," he said.

"Well, of course, I looked. You can't tell someone not to look and expect them not to look."

Owen grinned down at me. He smiled so much these days, and I swore every smile added a year to my life. At this rate, we'd be giving Ned Fled a run for his money.

"Oh my God, Connor Finkle has a full-back tattoo." I gasped.

"Who's that?" Owen bent toward me to whisper. His eyes followed my gaze and widened slightly. "Wait, the librarian guy? Whoa, sick dragon. It is always the quiet ones," Owen muttered and straightened. "The list of things I didn't need to know about my neighbors grows ever longer."

I shifted on my skis, my body shivering as the initial adrenaline of getting up here and seeing everybody started to wear off. "Good news is, if you ever have to deliver a speech to the town, you won't even have to use any imagination to picture them in their underwear."

"God, that's a scary thought." It was his turn to shimmy in disgust.

"Holy freezing snowballs." I laced my cold fingers through his warm ones.

"It's so much colder than I thought."

"You've handled worse," I said. I gave him a long, suggestive look, pointedly looking at his swim trunks. "Also, you don't seem cold."

"Bee. Please don't look at me like that. There are things I don't want our mailman to see."

Azi snowboarded by with two tourists, giggling delightedly. "Soupman and Bee, what is up? Gorgeous day to tread some pow pow." He fist-bumped Owen as they glided by.

I waved as Owen mumbled, "I have no idea what he said."

"He seems happy, at least." I stomped my skis to get blood flowing just as Mayor Sparks got her megaphone. She made an announcement about the town and the charity and all that, but I was too busy looking at Owen and thinking about how much our lives had changed in the past year. Owen gently prodded me when the crowd whooped and called my name.

"Thank you, Bee Perkins, for all that you have done to organize this event, the proceeds of which will be donated to the local animal rescue shelter."

I waved to the crowd before extending a low curtsy. My neon green bikini barely contained the ladies trying to spill out.

Owen moved to block the view.

Then we all made our way to the starting line, Owen and I leading the pack.

"Ready?" He squeezed my hand. We pushed our goggles down our faces.

"Ready." I nodded.

"I love you, Bee Perkins."

"And I love you, Soupman." I cheesed a grin. He shook his head with a laugh as we pushed forward with the crowd. "Let's do this!" I yelled, and the town roared behind me just as Mayor Sparks blared the air horn.

I skied into the new year with the love of my life and a town who knew my name.

"Happy New Year!"

*Want more Owen and Bee? Check out a bonus scene for* All Downhill From Here *when you sign up for Piper's newsletter!* **CLICK HERE**

**If you are interested in more Slippery Slopes Shenanigans, you can preorder ALL JOKING ASIDE, a workplace rivals, romcom coming May 23, 2025!

*** *But wait, there's more! If you enjoyed ALL DOWNHILL FROM HERE and want more by Piper Sheldon, read on for the first chapter of Book 1 in the Unlucky in Love trilogy, "Stranger Than Fan Fiction." An epistolary, friends-to-lovers, Romcom about a former child star with a major glow-up who starts an online friendship with his fan fiction writer across the sea. Little does she know her online pen pal is actually her celebrity crush.*

# Stranger Than Fan Fiction

Two Years Ago
Charlie

I gestured to let my new housekeeper lead the way out of the dining room. Not *just* out of a sense of chivalry, but because I didn't trust her behind my back.

"The kitchen is right through here," I explained.

The older woman's sensible trainers hardly made a sound on the worn hall carpeting. *The better for sneaking around ...*

Agata had been so quiet since she arrived. Normally, I relished silence, but this felt like a form of torture. Did she have misgivings about my scandalous past? Or was she simply wondering how I'd managed this long alone?

Based on how she eyed the stack of dishes near the sink, I suspected the latter.

It had been years since I had people working for me, and as it turned out, I still found the whole experience of managing people when I couldn't manage myself incredibly uncomfortable, if not hypocritical. If Emma hadn't insisted that I hire someone to keep the ancient estate from crumbling, I might have just gone on alone forever. After all, the whole point of disappearing from a life of celebrity and into the English countryside was to avoid uncomfortable interactions at all costs.

"No dishwasher?" She sniffed, looking down her nose even though she barely reached my chest.

Did she scare me? Absolutely. I didn't like it, but dammit, I respected it.

An inoffensive light lemon smell clung to her gray frock. Her blond hair was tight in a low bun, and she had a tiny, pinched mouth.

"I plan on doing some renovations and additions over time. But for now, it's a bit rustic," I said.

I glanced away when she scrutinized me. The thing with sobriety was, as fast as everything goes to shite, it takes a hell of a lot longer to work back up to any sense of normalcy. I had intended on updating the Vicarage ages ago, but some days simply existing was chore enough.

She nodded; hands clasped in front of her. "Okay," she settled on.

The small reassurance unclenched my jaw.

"The Vicarage is a bit of a drive from the nearest town. But you can have groceries delivered. I'm assuming the agency told you about ..." I scratched the back of my neck.

"No booze," she said in her soft Polish accent.

"Right. Except in your cottage, of course. I just ask not in the main house."

She nodded firmly. "I don't drink. It's no problem."

Straight to the point and no nonsense, Agata was beginning to grow on me. Emma likely had these traits in mind when she set up this appointment with the agency's recommendation.

"I guess that's everything. Do you have any questions?" I asked.

She looked me up and down. "What you want for lunch?"

"You just got here. You don't have to—"

A hand snaked out and pinched my abdomen sharply. "Too skinny."

I flinched. That's something I'd never been accused of. "I just—"

"You don't pick. You have sausage soup." Her mouth hardly moved when she spoke, but the words felt as threatening as a yell.

Feeling more than a little frightened, I acquiesced. "Ah, that's good. Thank you."

She turned her back to me and got to moving in the small kitchen.

I looked around, feeling useless. I'd already brought her single worn suitcase to the small guest house. I knocked once on the counter. "Welp, I'll let you get settled. It's been nice meeting you. Welcome to the Vicarage, Agata."

I moved to walk away.

"It smells like boy feets in here," she said as she set a large pot on the hob.

"Ah. Right." Honesty was an admirable quality in a home-maker. "I suppose you got here in the nick of time."

She sniffed again. "My children watched you when they grow up. That space show." She looked me up and down. "You were chubby funny one."

Her kids must be grown now too. Probably close to my age. That space show she referred to was *TerraFormative*, part of a multi-billion-dollar franchise based on the science fiction books written by G.S. Sedar. The series followed three children through adolescence upon a spaceship adrift in space, looking for a new Earth. Eight solid years of my adolescence I was Freddy Finks, chubby comic relief of the Intrepid Trio. My real-life best friends Emma Flynn and Harrison Evans played my two closest comrades in trouble, Lucy Lennon and Adam Abbott, respectively.

Almost twenty years ago, over in the blink of an eye to most, and yet the thing that would always define me. I was used to these types of conversations. I kept my face blank.

"Freddy." I dropped my arm before I could scratch the back of my neck again. "Yep. That was me."

"Skinny Charlie is not so funny. You eat more. You be funny. Funny man gets wife. Or husband," she added. "I'm modern woman. I understand."

"Good. Right. I'll keep that in mind." I was hardly skinny. As I'd aged, my notable baby fat had melted off my face, but I would always be described as sturdily built—now with defined cheekbones.

Her gaze narrowed on me. "Soup will be ready in one hour. Come back. Have bread too."

"I try not to eat carbs—"

"You eat the bread."

I swallowed before I nodded, afraid to do anything but agree.

"Well, I better get back to my office to ..."

*To pretend to work.* I finished in my head.

She paused from taking inventory of my cabinets to give me another sharp nod.

I slunk off to my unused office. I didn't really work. Hadn't really needed to in the ten years since the show wrapped. I'd been sober three of those years thanks to therapy and rehab. My only job now was to ensure I stayed on track and didn't put the people who cared about me at risk for bystander humiliation. Each day, I spent about an hour responding to fan mail, but even that had dwindled down considerably over the years. That, reading, and working out occupied most of my time.

Maybe it wasn't an exciting existence, but it was a safe one.

It was Emma who insisted I bring in help now that I had gotten most of my life back in order. Emma was all about goals and motivations and life purpose. I didn't have the heart to tell her that simply making it day to day took so much emotional toll, there wasn't much room for anything else. I would get back there eventually, but right now, I lived tucked away safely at my home in Devon.

After rehab, I moved away from the temptations of London and bought a former vicarage. The plan was to eventually modernize the estate, but I hadn't gotten around to it yet. AA didn't recommend too many major life changes once sober, so I'd been waiting until I felt secure. Sobriety had taken more focus than I had anticipated. Employing Agata felt like a step in the right direction, another level of accountability.

It was almost time for my monthly meeting with Emma and Harrison. Their schedules were far more packed than mine, but we at least tried to arrange monthly video chats. I had dubbed those first few meetings as "proof of life," but I think seeing my face reassured Emma as much as it did me.

It was five minutes until our appointed time when they both texted to say they couldn't make the call today. Emma had got caught up in the details of arranging clean water for a town in a developing country and Harrison was working on a film bound to land him another Oscar nod. And here I was, doing absolutely nothing except getting bullied by my new homemaker.

I let out a long sigh. They weren't my keepers; they had busy lives, but this wasn't the first time I felt stuck in limbo because of my actions as the world blurred by.

I opened a tab on the internet when a wave of something crashed over me. Boredom? Listlessness? Loneliness? I fought hard to keep the indescribable emotion from pulling me under. One thing about sobriety that I wasn't prepared for was how both crucial and yet mind-numbingly boring routine would be in my life. It was better than the alternative: waking up without knowing whose bed I was in ... or what country, for that matter. This was a slow and tedious process to feel secure in myself, but how many months of monotony stretched ahead? Every day safe, but uneventful?

Agata hit the mark when she made the comment about my getting a wife. At least, she recognized my restlessness. I was lonely, but that was a whole other aspect of moderation I wasn't ready to tackle yet. Without my two best friends, who I was lucky to still have, I didn't really have anybody else to talk to. I could call my sponsor, but I didn't want a drink. I just wanted ... I didn't know, someone to talk to.

*God, how pathetic.*

Poor rich child star, all alone in his big country house with all his money.

I sighed again loudly and did the thing I told myself I wouldn't do any more. *One* of the things. Because what else does a retired child star do when amid a pity party? They googled themselves.

The articles about me had slowed down in the years since rehab. My publicity team had done a great job of keeping press to a minimum. The top results were old articles about England's biggest "glow up," whatever that meant. All the links led to "articles" that included countless GIFs and JPEGs of shirtless photos taken in the past few years, side by side with chubby Freddy bulging out of his *TerraFormative* flight suit.

I rested my chin in my palm as I lazily scrolled. Bored. This was pathetic. I should just close out the browser to go workout or something.

A clickbait article at the bottom of the screen caught my eye. "Top Ten Freddy Fanfics—Can't get enough of the UK's hottest former child star Charles Downing? Check out these Freddy fan favorites that take this heavenly body out of this world."

"Oh lord," I said out loud to the pun-tastic title even as I clicked the link.

I'd heard about all the fanfic that *TerraFormative* had manifested over the years. Emma, Harrison, and I had been paired in every possible combination. It was an unavoidable product of being part of one of the world's largest franchises. I'd always stayed away, feeling a new level of skeezy hearing about the various scenarios people had placed my character in. Especially with Harrison and Emma. We'd grown up together and were closer than siblings. Anything romantic was ... icky.

The headline took me to a website called FanFavz. The interface was not terribly user-friendly, but after clicking around a bit, I got the gist. You could search by franchise, author, story popularity, etc. I sorted by author popularity within the *TerraFormative* world since I'd already committed to spending time in the gutter. The very first result was the story that had been mentioned in the article. In fact, the author had a few dozen "fics" under their name. The article dubbed this particular story, "Fresh Stars," "the top Freddy post-grad fantasy." It had been favorited an astounding forty *thousand* times, and comments were a never-ending gushfest, consisting mostly of emojis and lines of repeated vowels. Post-grad referred to the time after the show ended, when Freddy had graduated from the flight academy.

"Bloody hell," I mumbled. So many people out there reading a version of myself far more interesting than the one that existed. The top author on each list was someone called FreddyStan4Life.

"Regrettable username." My face contorted, leaning closer to the screen. "Who the bloody hell is Stan?"

I read the first sentence.

Then the next.

Then several chapters. The story focused on my—er, Freddy's post-flight academy life, as he worked up the ranks to become a captain of his own vessel and featured a particularly strong romance with a cyborg named Nix, who had been in the show but only briefly in season four. I'd loved that subplot when it had debuted in the show. I had approached the writers about stretching out their love story over a few more episodes but had been shot down. The writers had reminded me that Freddy's character only existed to relieve the tension when things got too heavy. But this "Fresh Stars" I read now was … *good*. Really good.

I also couldn't help but notice that FreddyStan4Life's description of Freddy resembled me as I looked now, instead of the child I was in the series. Interesting.

It felt like only a minute had passed when a loud rap on the closed door caused me to jump in my seat.

"You come eat, Mr. Downing." Agata's soft voice was a deceptive ruse, like calling the shake of a rattlesnake as soothing as a child's rattle.

"You can call me Charlie," I shouted through the door.

"Mister Charlie, come eat."

"Can you bring me a bowl in here?" I asked.

"No. Break from computer better for your eyes." Her footsteps retreated back to the kitchen.

I sighed loudly but pushed away from my desk.

At the kitchen island, Agata shoved two warm crusty rolls on my plate and wouldn't stop staring at me until I ate them along with the soup.

The whole meal was delicious, but she side-eyed me as I shoveled bites into my mouth. I couldn't focus on anything but getting back to my computer.

"Thank you. It was fantastic," I said.

She nodded knowingly as I rushed out of the room.

I thought I knew what fan fiction was—admittedly, I

thought it was primarily an excuse to make characters have sex —but this was unlike anything I expected. The writing was compelling and thought-provoking from the first line. The world was as familiar as sliding into a worn jumper, but the new scenarios were intriguing and the additional settings captivating. It felt so familiar and yet unlike anything I'd ever read. My eyes couldn't read fast enough. My heart raced, desperate to get back to it. I missed feeling ... *excited*. About anything.

I would just read a few more chapters, just to see what happened next, and then I'd stop.

Continue reading *Stranger Than Fan Fiction...*

# Acknowledgments

Hello readers! Thank you so much for being here. This was a super fun, albeit slightly zany story that I wanted to write as a fun distraction from the realities of life. I hope you enjoyed Bee and Owen and will join me as the rest of the series continues with more roaming guinea pigs, wild shenanigans, and spicy tension.

I don't know how many little easter eggs you were able to catch from my other books but they were there! If you were like, what is this show *Terraformative*? Don't worry, it's not technically real (much to my dismay). It's a fictional show I created in my Unlucky in Love Trilogy in which three former childhood actors and best friends navigate life and love as adults after starring in one of TV's biggest franchises of all time. So if you like my writing style, definitely check it out.

Follow me on any of my socials (you'll see those linked on the next page) and shoot me a message or email me directly at pipersheldonauthor@gmail.com. I absolutely love hearing from readers. Leaving a review is hugely helpful to indie authors like myself. THANK YOU SO MUCH FOR READING <3

Special shout out to my reader group Pipe's Peeps (Piper Sheldon Reader Group) . Thank you for being the OGs. I love you all. Thank you for helping me name all the cats. I wish I could have used all your suggestions!

To all my friends and family who continue to support me on this journey. I really am incredibly lucky/thankful/supported.

And once again, to you reading this now. I am not kidding when I tell you that I would not be able to do this without you. THANK YOU!

# About the Author

Piper Sheldon writes Contemporary Romance and Paranormal Romance. Her books are a little funny, a lotta romantic, and with just a little twist of something more. She lives with her husband, daughter, and elderly dog at home in the desert Southwest. She finds writing about herself in the third person an extreme sport in awkwardness.

Sign up for her newsletter here!
http://pipersheldon.com/newsletter

If you are a Piper Sheldon fan, join her Facebook reader group to get all this insider info!
Pipe's Peeps (Piper Sheldon Reader Group)

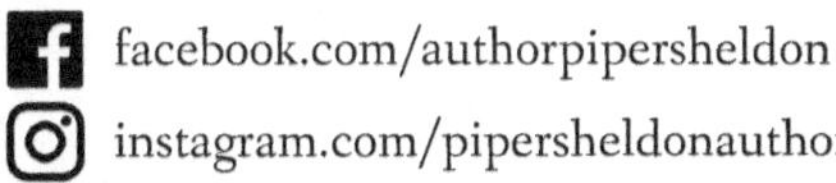

facebook.com/authorpipersheldon
instagram.com/pipersheldonauthor

# Also by Piper Sheldon

**Unlucky in Love Series - Contemporary Celebrity Romance**

Stranger Than Fan Fiction Book 1

Better Date Than Never Book 2

Down For the Word Count Book 3

**Slippery Slopes Series - Small town, Romantic Comedy**

All Downhill From Here Book 1

All Joking Aside Book 2

**The Unseen Series - Paranormal Romance**

The Unseen Book 1

The Untouched Book 2

**Cozy Creek Collection - Small Town Romance, collaborative series**

Fall Shook Up, Book 5

**Smartypants Romance**

## The Scorned Women's Society - Small Town Romance

My Bare Lady Book 1

The Treble With Men Book 2

The One That I Want Book 3

Hopelessly Devoted Book 3.5 - A novella

It Takes a Woman Book 4

## The Teacher's Lounge - Small Town Romance, collaborative series

Band Together, Book 2

You can find all of Piper's books at pipersheldon.com or on her author page on Amazon.

* 9 7 9 8 9 9 1 0 7 5 5 2 7 *